HOW TO KILL KINDLY

"No, no," Mula-*ay* shook his head. "The very thought of a human winning any physical fair fight between himself and a Dilbian is unthinkable to the point of ridiculousness. But don't worry, little Pick-and-Shovel. I'm going to save you from your cruel and heartless superiors, as well as from Bone Breaker."

Bill stared at him.

"You?" he began, and then remembered to hide his emotions just in time.

"To be sure," said Mula-*ay*, rising softly to his feet and cocking his ear toward the noises of the forest behind him. "Reassure yourself, Bone Breaker won't kill you. No, indeed," said Mula-*ay*, "you will lose your duel and your life, instead, to the most feeble and decrepit Dilbian that the local area provides."

GORDON R. DICKSON
SPACEPAW

A BERKLEY MEDALLION BOOK
published by
BERKLEY PUBLISHING CORPORATION

BERKLEY MEDALLION BOOKS are published by
Berkley Publishing Corporation
200 Madison Avenue
New York, N.Y. 10016

BERKLEY MEDALLION BOOKS ® TM 757,375

Printed in the United States of America

Berkley Medallion Edition, MARCH 1976

Chapter 1

Spiraling down toward the large, blue world below, in the shuttle boat from the spaceship which had delivered him here to Dilbia. Bill Waltham reflected dismally upon his situation. Most of the five-day trip he had spent wearing a hypnohelmet. But in spite of the fact that his head was now a-throb with a small encyclopedia of information about the world below and its oversize inhabitants—their language, customs, and psychology—he felt that he knew less than nothing about this job into which he had been drafted.

The shuttle boat would land him near the Lowland village of Muddy Nose. There, presumably, he would be met on disembarking by Lafe Greentree, the human Agricultural Resident here, and by Greentree's other trainee-assistant—an Earth girl named Anita Lyme who had, incredible as it seemed, volunteered for her pre-college field training here, just as Bill had originally volunteered himself for the Deneb-Seventeen terraforming project. These two would introduce Bill to his native associate—an Upland Dilbian named the Hill Bluffer. The Hill Bluffer would in turn introduce him to the local Lowland farmers who had their homes in Muddy Nose, and Bill could get down to the apparently vital job for which he had been drafted here. He could hear himself now
. . .

". . . This is a spade. You hold it by this end. You stick the other end in the earth. Yes, deep in the earth. Then you tilt it,

5

like this. Then you lift it up with the dirt still on it and put the dirt aside. Fine. You are now digging a hole in the ground. . . ."

He checked the current of his thoughts sharply. There was no point, he told himself grimly, in being bitter about it. He was here now, and he would have to make the best of it. But in spite of himself, his mind's eye persisted in dwelling on the succession of days stretching ahead through two years of unutterable dullness and boredom. He thought again of the great symphony of engineering and development that was a terraforming project—changing the surface and weather of a whole world to make it humanly habitable; and he compared that with this small, drab job to which he was now headed. There seemed no comparison between the two occupations— no comparison at all.

But once more he took a close rein on his thoughts and emotions. Some day he could be a part of a terraforming project. Meanwhile, it would be well to remember that he would be given an efficiency rating for his work on Dilbia, just as if it was the job he had originally intended to do. That efficiency rating could not be high if he started out hating everything about the huge, bearlike natives and everything connected with them. At least, he thought, the Dilbians had a sense of humor—judging by the names they gave each other.

This last thought was not as cheering as it might have been, however. It reminded Bill of something the reassignment officer had said at the space terminal on Arcturus Three, where his original travel orders had been lifted and new ones issued. The officer had been a tall, lath-thin, long-nosed man, who had taken Bill's being drafted away from the Deneb-Seventeen Project much more calmly than had Bill.

". . . Oh, and of course," the reassignment officer had said cheerfully, "you'll find you've been given a Dilbian name yourself, by the time you get there. . . ."

Bill scowled, remembering. His only experience previously with a nickname had not been a happy one. On the swimming team at pre-engineering school, he had failed to rejoice in the given name of "Ape"—not so much because of anything apelike about either his open and rather ordinary face under its cap of black hair, or his flat-muscled, square-boned body. The name had arisen because he was the only member of the team with anything resembling hair on his chest. Bill made a mental note to keep his shirt on when Dilbians were about, during the next two years—just in case. Of course he reflected now, they had hair all over their own bodies. . . .

The chime of the landing signal rang through the shuttle boat. Bill looked out of the window beside his seat behind the pilot and saw they were drifting down into a fair-sized meadow, perhaps half a mile away across plowed fields alternating with stands of trees from a cluster of buildings that would probably be the village of Muddy Nose. He looked down below him, searching for a glimpse of Greenleaf or his assistant—but he saw no human figures waiting there. In fact, he saw no figures there at all. Where was his welcoming committee?

He was still wondering that, five minutes later, as he stood in the clearing alone, with his luggage case at his feet and the shuttle boat falling rapidly skyward above his head. The shuttle-boat pilot had not been helpful. He knew nothing about who was to meet Bill, he had said. Furthermore, he was due back at the ship as soon as possible. He had handed Bill's luggage case out the hatch to him, closed the hatch, and taken off.

Bill looked up at the rich yellow of the local sun, standing in the midafternoon quarter of the sky. It was a beautiful, near-cloudless day. The air was warm, and from the stand of trees surrounding him a little distance, some species of local bird or animal was singing in high liquid chirpings. Well, thought Bill, at least one good thing was the fact that Dilbia's gravity was a little lighter than Earth's. That would make carrying his luggage case up to the Residency a little easier. He might as well get started. He picked up the luggage case and headed off in the general direction of the village as he remembered seeing it from the air.

He trudged out of the clearing, through the trees, and had just emerged into a second clearing when he heard a shouting directly ahead of him through the farther stand of trees. He stopped abruptly.

The shouting came again, in a chorus of incredibly deep bass voices, deeper than any human voice Bill had ever heard, and, it seemed to him in that first moment, more threatening.

He was about to change course so as to detour prudently around the noisy area, when his hypnoed information of the Dilbian language somewhat belatedly rendered the shouts into recognizable words and the words into parts of a song. Only "song" was not exactly the word for it, Dilbian singing being a sort of atonal chanting. Very crudely translated into English, the so-called singing he heard was going something like this:

> *Drink it down, old friend Tin Ear,*
> *Drink it down!*
> *Drink it down, old friend Tin Ear,*
> *Drink it down!*
> *Here's to you and your sweet wife,*
> *May you have her all your life!*
> *Better you than one of us.*
> *Drink it down!*

> *Drink it down ... etc.*
> *Here's to you and your new plow!*
> *Does it make your back to bow?*
> *Well, better you than one of us.*
> *Drink etc. ...*

Bill abruptly changed his mind. If the song was any indication, a happy gathering of some sort was in progress on the other side of the trees. All the hypnoed information he had absorbed on the way to Dilbia had indicated that the Dilbians were normally good-humored and generally friendly enough— if somewhat boisterous and inclined to take pride in observing the letter of the law, while carefully avoiding the spirit of it. Besides, Muddy Nose Village had a treaty agreement with the human members of the Agricultural Assistance Program, and that officially put him under the protection of any member of that local community.

So there should be no reason not to join the gathering and at least get directions to the Residency, if not some help as well in carrying his luggage to the village. The situation would also give him a chance to size up the natives before Greenleaf gathered him in and gave him Greenleaf's own, possibly biased, point of view about them. Bill was still not clear why a pre-engineering student with a prospective major in mechanical engineering should be needed to explain simple things like hoes and rakes to the Dilbians.

Accordingly, he picked up his traveling case from where he had put it down, and tramped ahead in under the trees before him. The grove was not more than fifty to seventy-five feet thick, and he reached the other side shortly, stepping out into what appeared to be the front yard of a log farmhouse.

In the yard a plank table had been set up on trestles, and at that table were half a dozen towering, bearlike individuals, nearly nine feet tall, and covered with brown-black hair plus a few straps, from which each had hung a monstrous sword, as well as various pouches or satchels. The crowd at the table was eating and drinking out of large wooden mugs refilled constantly from a nearby barrel with its top broken in. A dozen feet or so from the table was a pile of what appeared to be sacks of root vegetables, half a carcass resembling a side of beef, and an unopened barrel like the one from which they were drinking—together with some odds and ends, including a three-legged wooden stool. A small piglike animal was tied by a cord to one of the heavy vegetable sacks, and it

9

was grunting and chewing on the cord. It was plain the creature would soon be loose.

But no one in the farmyard was paying any attention to the animal as Bill joined them. They had stopped singing and their attention was all directed to a smaller, more rounded— you might actually say fat—native, a good head shorter than the nine-footers at the table, and with a voice a good octave or two higher than the rest. From which, in addition to the fact that this one wore no sword, Bill concluded that she was a female. She was standing back a dozen feet from the table and shouting at the others—at one in particular who Bill now noticed was also not wearing a sword, but who sat rather more drunkenly than the others, at the head of the table facing down at her.

". . . Look at him!" she was shouting, as Bill stepped into the yard and approached the table without any of them apparently noticing him. "He *likes* it! Isn't it bad enough that we have to live here outside the village because he won't speak up for our right to live at the Inn, when he knows I'm More Jam's dead wife's own blood cousin. No, he's got to sit down and get drunk with rascals and no-goods like the rest of you. Why do you put up with it, Tin Ear? Well, *answer me!*"

"They're making me," muttered the individual at the top of the table who was evidently called Tin Ear. His tongue was a little thick, but his expression, as far as Bill could read it on his furry face, was far from unhappy.

"Well, why do you let them? Why don't you fight them like a man? If I was a man—"

"Impolite not drink guests," protested Tin Ear thickly.

"Impolite! Guests!" shouted the female. "Ex-Upland runagates, reivers, thieves. . . ."

"Hold on, there, Thing-or-Two! No need to get nasty!" rumbled one of the sworded drinkers warningly. "Fair's fair. If there's something in that stack there"—he pointed to the pile to which the animal was tied—"you really can't spare, you're free to trot yourself over and talk to Bone Breaker—"

"Oh yes!" cried Thing-or-Two. "Talk to Bone Breaker, is

10

it? He's no better than the rest of you—letting Sweet Thing stick her nose in the air and treat him the way she does! If there were any real men around here, they'd have settled the hash of men like him and you, long ago! When I was a girl, if a girl didn't want to leave home just yet, much she had to say about it. The man who wanted her just came in one day and swept her off her feet and carried her off—"

"Like Tin Ear, here, did to you? Is that it?" interrupted the male with the sword—and the whole table exploded into gargantuan laughter that made Bill's ears ring. Even Tin Ear choked appreciatively on the contents of the wooden mug from which he was swallowing, in spite of being, as far as Bill could see, in some measure the butt of the joke.

Thing-or-Two shouted back at them, but her words were lost in the laughter, which took a few minutes to die down.

"Why, I heard it was *you*, Thing-or-Two, who broke into Tin Ear's daddy's house one dark night and carried *him* off!" bellowed the speaker at the table, as soon as he could be heard, and the laughter mounted skyward again.

This last sally apparently had the unusual effect of rendering Thing-or-Two momentarily speechless. Taking advantage of this, and the gradual diminishing of the laughter, Bill decided it was time to call the attention of the gathering to himself. He had been standing in plain daylight right beside the table all this time, but for some strange reason no one seemed to have noticed him. Now he stepped up to the side of the Dilbian who had been trading insults with Thing-or-Two and poked him in the ribs.

"Hey!" said Bill.

The head of the Dilbian jerked around. Seated, his hairy face was on a level with Bill's and he stared at Bill now from a distance of less than three feet. His jaw dropped. Behind him, the laughter and other sounds died out, giving way to a stony silence as everyone at the table goggled incredulously at Bill.

"Sorry to bother you," said Bill, stiffly, in his best Dilbian, "but I've just got here, and I'm on my way to the Shorty

Residency building, in Muddy Nose Village. Maybe one of you would be kind enough to point me in the right direction for the village, and maybe even one of you wouldn't mind coming along and giving me a hand with my luggage case?"

He waited, but they only continued to stare at him in fascinated silence. So he added, cautiously, knowing that bargaining was as much a part of Dilbian culture as breathing:

"I could probably scrape up a half-pint of nails for anyone who'd like to help me."

Again he waited. But there was no answer. Amazingly, the silence of the Dilbians persisted. They were still staring at Bill as if he were some strange creature, materialized out of thin air. Bill felt a slight uneasiness stir inside him. It seemed to him they were gaping at him as if they had never seen a human before, which was strange. His hypnoed information plainly informed him that Shorties—as humans were called by the Dilbians—were well known to the Muddy Nosers. Perhaps he had made a mistake in stopping here, after all.

"A Shorty!" gasped the Dilbian he had spoken to, finally breaking the silence. "As I live and breathe! A real, walking, talking, little Shorty! Out here, all by himself!"

He turned about in his seat and slowly reached out a long arm, which Bill avoided by backing away out of reach.

"Come here, Shorty!" said the Dilbian.

"No thanks," said Bill, now fully alerted to the fact that there was something very wrong in the situation. He kept backing away. "Forget I asked." It was high time to remind them of his protected status, he decided. The sworded individual he had been speaking to was already beginning to rise from the table with every obvious intention of laying hands upon him.

"It was just a thought—that I might get one of you to help me," Bill said rapidly. "I'm a member of the Residency, myself, you know."

The Dilbian was now on his feet and others were rising. Alarm rang as clearly in Bill as the clanging of a fire bell.

12

"What's the matter with you?" he shouted at the oncoming Dilbian. "Don't you know we Shorties have a treaty with the Muddy Nosers? According to that treaty, you all owe me protection and assistance!"

The male Dilbians, still rising from the table, froze and stared once again for a long second before suddenly bursting out into wild whoops of laughter, wilder and louder than Bill had yet heard from them.

Bill stared at them, amazed.

"Why, you crazy little Shorty!" cried the voice of Thing-or-Two furiously behind him. "Can't you tell the differences between people, when you see them? These aren't honest folk like us here around the village! They're those thieves and plunderers and no-goods from the Outlaw Valley! They're *outlaws*—and *they* never signed any kind of treaty with *anybody!*"

Chapter 2

Thing-or-Two's shouted warning explained matters, but it came, if anything, a little late. By the time she had finished speaking, the leading outlaw was almost upon Bill, and Bill was already in motion.

He dropped his luggage case and ducked desperately as the big Dilbian hands made a grab for him. They missed, and he spun about only to find himself running in the wrong direction. With whoops and yells the whole crew of outlaws was after him. Every way he turned, he found a towering, nine-foot figure barring his escape.

Not that an immediate attempt to escape would do him

any good at the moment, he realized almost at once. Bill's first reaction had been that of any small animal being chased by larger ones—to duck and dodge and take advantage of his reflexes, which were faster simply because he was smaller. The Dilbian outlaws, being all nearly twice Bill's size and several times his weight, were by that very fact slower and clumsier than he was. In fact, after the first leap to escape, he found himself evading their clutches with relative ease.

But even as he realized he could do this, he saw the spot he was in. At first he had been dodging about only in order to find a clear space in which he could make a run for the forest. Now he realized that simply running away was no solution. The reflexes of the Dilbians might be slower than his, but their huge strides could cover the same amount of ground at double his speed. They could catch him in no time if he simply tried to outrun them in a straight-away chase.

His only hope, he realized now, still dodging desperately about the farmyard, was to keep evading them in this small area until they began to grow winded, and then take his chances on outrunning them. If he could only keep this up, he thought—ducking under a flailing dark-furred arm as thick as a man's thigh—for just a few minutes more ...

"Hold it!" the outlaw leader was shouting. "Don't let him run you ragged. Circle him! Circle him! Herd him into a corner!"

Bill's hopes took a nose dive. He dodged and spun about, but without finding an opening. Already the outlaws were forming a semicircle, long arms extended sideways, that was herding him back against the front wall of the house. They were closing in, now ...

Bill made a feint toward the right end of the semicircle, and then made a dash toward the left end, with the wild thought of diving between the legs of the outlaw leader, standing at the corner of the house. But at the last second the outlaw stepped forward and whooped in the powerful voice Bill had come to recognize.

"Got you, Shorty!"

Bill braked to a frantic halt. Glancing over his shoulder, he saw the rest of the semicircle closing rapidly on him. He looked back at the outlaw leader, standing crouched now and ready by the interlaced butt ends of the logs at the corner of the house. The leader spread his arms and reached forward—

—And went suddenly flat on his face with a furry figure atop him, as a wild war cry split the air.

"*I'm* a Muddy Noser and proud of it!" roared the still-drunken voice of Tin Ear, in triumph. "*Run,* Shorty!"

But there was no place to which Bill could run. Other outlaws had rushed over to bar the escape route opened up by the fallen leader. Glancing wildly about, Bill looked up and saw that where the roof of the house joined the wall there was an opening leading to some dark interior, probably a loft or attic. The alternating ends of the logs in the front and side walls of the house were notched and interlocked together so that they stuck out like the tips of the fingers of two hands, interlaced at right angles to each other. They were as good as a ladder to someone Bill's size. He had not won a climbing medal in Survival School, back on Earth, for nothing. He went up the log ends like a squirrel.

A second later he had dived into the dark, loftlike area to which the opening he had seen gave entrance. For a moment he simply lay there, panting, on what seemed to be a rough bed of poles, which was probably a roof to the room or rooms below. Then, as he began to breathe easily once more, he squirmed about, crawled back to the entrance, and looked down and out.

Tin Ear was slumbering or unconscious on the ground at the spot where he had jumped the outlaw leader. The leader himself was on his feet with the other outlaws clustered around the corner of the house, and one of their number was trying to climb the sixteen or eighteen feet up the same ladder of log ends Bill had used.

However, the log ends were too small for the big feet and hands of the Dilbians. The climber was finding fairly good support for his toes, but he was able to hang on to the log

15

ends higher up only by his fingertips. His attention was all on those fingertips, and Bill had a sudden inspiration. Leaning out and reaching down the short couple of feet that separated the climber's head from the entrance, he put his hand on the top of the hard, furry skull and shoved outward with all his strength.

The head went back, and the climber's fingertips lost their precarious grip. There was a yell and a thud, and the climber landed on his back in the farmyard dirt. Roaring with rage, he scrambled to his feet as if he would climb again, but checked himself at the foot of the log corner, and dropped his upreaching arms.

"It's no use!" he growled, turning away toward the outlaw leader. "There's nothing you can really get a grip on. You see what he did to me?"

"Go get some fire from the stove inside," said the outlaw leader, struck by a happy thought. "We'll burn him out of there!"

"No, you don't!" trumpeted the voice of Thing-or-Two in the background. "Paying outlaw-tax is one thing, but you're not burning down our house! You try it and you'll see how fast I get to Outlaw Valley and tell Bone Breaker on you! You just try!"

Her words stopped a concerted move toward the front door of the house. The outlaws muttered among themselves, occasionally glancing up to the opening from which Bill was looking down. Finally, the leader looked up at Bill's observing face.

"All right, Shorty!" he said, sternly. "You come down out of there!"

Bill laughed grimly.

"What's so funny?" glowered the outlaw leader.

Bill had a sudden, desperate inspiration. His hypnoed information had just reminded him of a double fact. One, that preserving face—in the human, Oriental sense—meant a great deal to the Dilbians, since an individual Dilbian had no more status in the community than his wit or his muscles

16

could earn for him. Two, that in Dilbian conversation the more outrageous statement you could get away with, the more face-destroying points you were able to score on an opponent. Maybe he could bluff his way out of this situation by making it so humiliating for the outlaws that they would go off and leave him alone.

"You are!" he retorted. "Why'd you think I stuck around here instead of running off? Laugh? Why, I could hardly keep from splitting my sides, watching all of you falling all over yourselves trying to catch me. Why should I come down and stop the fun?"

The outlaws stared at him. The leader scowled.

"Fun?" growled the leader. "Are you trying to tell us you did all that running around for fun?"

"Why, sure," said Bill, laughing again, just to drive the fact home, "you didn't think I was scared of you, did you?"

They blinked at him.

"What do you mean?" growled the leader. "You weren't scared?"

"Scared? Who? Me?" said Bill heartily, leaning a little farther out of his hole to talk. "We Shorties aren't scared of anything on two legs or four. Or anything else!"

"Oh? Then how come you don't come down from that hole now?" demanded one of the other outlaws.

"Why, naturally," said Bill, "there's six or seven of you and only one of me. If it wasn't for that—"

"Hey, what's up?" boomed a new voice, interrupting him. Bill raised his eyes to look beyond the outlaw group and the outlaws themselves turned about to stare. Strolling out of the woods was the tallest, leanest Dilbian Bill had seen so far. He was unarmed, but he was as much taller than the general height of the sword-bearing outlaws as they were taller than Thing-or-Two, and his fur was a light, rusty-brown in color.

"Some of your business, Uplander?" growled the outlaw leader.

"Why, not if you say it's not," responded the newcomer

17

genially, strolling up to the group. "But you look like you got something cornered up in Tin Ear's roof, there, and——"

"It's a Shorty," growled the outlaw leader, turning to look once more at Bill, and apparently accepting the newcomer without further protest. "He's got up in there and if you try climbing up, holding on with your finger and toenails, he shoves you off. And he just sits up there laughing at us."

"That a fact?" said the tall Dilbian. "Well, I know how I'd get him out of there."

"You?" snorted he leader. "Who says you could get him down if we can't?"

"Why, because I wouldn't have to climb," said the tall Dilbian, easily. "You see, I'm just a hair or two bigger than the rest of you. Want me to try?"

"You can try for all I care," grumbled the leader, and the rest of the outlaws muttered agreement. On the ground, Tin Ear was beginning to sit up and look about himself, somewhat dazedly. "But it won't do any good."

"Think so?" said the tall Dilbian, unruffled. "Let me just take a little look, first." He moved to directly below Bill's bolthole. "Look out up there, Shorty—here I come!"

With these last words he crouched suddenly, then sprang, flinging up his unbelievably long arms at the same instant. Bill ducked back from the entrance, instinctively, as with a thud, ten powerful, furry fingers appeared, hooked over the bottom log of his entrance. A second later and the face of the newcomer rose to stare in interestedly at him.

Still holding himself by his grip on the entrance, the tall Dilbian performed the further muscular feat of sticking his head partway into the hole. Bill braced himself to resist capture. But, astonishingly, what came from the intruder was nothing more than a hoarse whisper.

"Listen! You're the Pick-and-Shovel Shorty?"

"Well—uh," Bill whispered back, confused. "My Shorty name's actually Bill Waltham, but they warned me I'd be given——"

"Sure!" whispered the Dilbian impatiently. "That's what I

18

said. You're Pick-and-Shovel. Now, listen. I'm going to get them to back off. When they do, you take a leap out of there, and I'll get you away from them. Understand?"

"Yes, but—"

Bill found himself talking to empty air. A thud from the ground outside signaled that his interviewer had dropped to earth. Bill crept forward and looked out. Below him, the tall Dilbian was muttering to a close huddle of the oulaws, all of them with their heads down. Apparently the muttering was supposed to be confidential, but the words of it came clearly to Bill's ears.

". . . You got to be tricky with these Shorties," the tall Dilbian was saying. "Now, I told him I'd talk you all into going away and leaving him alone. So the rest of you go hide around the corners of the building, and when he climbs down, I'll get between him and the corner of the house here, and the rest of you can run out and catch him. Got it?"

The outlaws muttered gleeful agreement. Heads were lifted.

"Well," yawned the outlaw leader, in a loud voice, pointedly not looking up in Bill's direction, "guess we better be moseying along back to the valley. Let's go, men."

All pretending elaborate unconcern, the outlaws wandered off around the other front corner of the house leaving their pile of loot behind them; and a moment later Bill could plainly hear the heavy thud of a number of Dilbian feet, running around the back of the building to just out of his sight behind the corner below him, and stopping there.

"Well, Shorty," said the tall Dilbian in loud tones looking up at Bill. "Like I told you, they've all gone back to the valley"—his voice suddenly dropped to an undertone, and he held out his two enormous paws—"all right, Pick-and-Shovel, come on! Jump!"

Bill, who had been crouching poised in the entrance of his hiding place, hesitated, torn over the decision of whether to believe what the tall Dilbian had said to him or believe what the same individual had just told the outlaws below. He

19

remembered however, the hypnoed fact that Dilbians would go to almost any lengths to avoid the lie direct, although perfectly willing to twist the truth through any contortions necessary to produce the same effect.

The tall Dilbian had said he would get Bill away from the outlaws. Having said it, he was almost duty-bound to perform at least the letter of his promise. Besides, Bill remembered in the nick of time, the outlaws had first addressed the newcomer as "Uplander"—and Bill's information had it that there was little love lost between Uplanders, or mountain-dwelling Dilbians, and the Lowlanders.

Bill jumped.

The big hands of the outlaw fielded him with the skill of an offensive end in professional football. And a second later they were running.

Or rather, the Dilbian was running, and Bill was joggling up and down in his grasp.

Behind them, Bill could hear the sudden, furious shouts of the outlaws. Craning his head around a pumping hairy elbow, Bill saw the outlaws swarming out from behind the farmhouse in pursuit. At the same time he felt himself lifted up over the shoulder of the tall Dilbian.

"Climb—on to my back—" grunted that individual, between strides. "Sit on the dingus, there! It's the same one I used for the Half-Pint-Posted. Then I can get down to some serious moving!"

Staring down over the furry shoulder, Bill saw something like a crude saddle anchored between the straps crossing the Dilbian's back. Hanging on tight to the thick neck beside him, he climbed on over the shoulder and, turning around, got himself seated down on the saddle. He grabbed the shoulder straps for added support and anchored his legs in the back straps below.

"All set," he said, finally, the words jolted out of his mouth into the other's ear.

"All right," grunted the other. "Now we leave them eating dust. Watch a real man travel, Pick-and-Shovel!"

The rhythm of the tall native's stride changed—it was a difference like that between the trot and the gallop of a horse. Bill, clinging to the straps, looked back and saw they were drawing away almost magically from their pursuers. In fact, even as he watched, some of the outlaws began to slow down to a walk and drop out of the chase.

"They're giving up!" he said in the ear of his mount.

"Sure, they would," answered that individual. "I knew they'd see it right off—they couldn't catch me. No one can catch me, Pick-and-Shovel. Never could, never will— Lowlander, Uplander, nobody!"

He slowed to a steady, swinging walk. Bill looked shrewdly at the back of the furry head eight inches in front of his own nose.

"You're the Hill Bluffer, aren't you?" he inquired.

"Who else?" snorted the other. Bill got the idea that the Hill Bluffer would have been impressed only if Bill had failed to recognize him. The Dilbian went into a half-chant. "Hill Bluffer, that's my name and fame! Anything on two feet walk away from me? Not over solid ground or living rock! When I look at a hill, it knows it's beat, and it lays out flat for my trampling feet!"

"Er—yes," said Bill.

"You're lucky to get me," stated the Hill Bluffer in a more conversational tone, but with no show of false modesty. "Just luck you did. When the other Shorties decided to bring you in here, they looked me up right away. Could I take a leave of absence from carrying the mail between Humrog Village and Wildwood Peak, and come down to the Lowlands here to take care of another Shorty? Well, it wasn't an easy thing to do, but I just happened to have an experienced substitute handy to take over the mail route. So I came on down. The ten pounds of nails was all right, but it didn't have much to do with it."

"It didn't?" asked Bill.

The Hill Bluffer snorted. It sounded like a small factory

explosion and shook Bill upon his saddle perch like a small earthquake.

"Of course not!" said the Hill Bluffer. "That's good pay, but a man wants more than that. This was a matter of reputation. After having taken care of a Shorty once before, could I let another one get himself into all kinds of trouble down here without me? Of course not!"

"Well . . . thanks," said Bill. "I appreciate it."

"You'll appreciate it more by the time you're done," said the Hill Bluffer cheerfully. "Not that you'd have needed me just for protection against these fat-muscled, weak-livered Lowland folk with their sticks and their knives and their swords and their shields and such-like. Can you beat it? No, it wasn't protection you needed down here, Pick-and-Shovel. It was experience, and a good, clean-thinking tough cat of a mountain man like myself to back it up. Well, here we are at Muddy Nose Village."

Here, in fact, they were.

Now he looked up and saw, indeed, that they were beginning to travel down the miry main street of some kind of native settlement village. Bill could see how the village had gotten its name.

At first, as they moved between the two rows of log buildings that lined the street, they attracted little attention. But soon they were spotted by the various other Dilbians Bill saw lounging around the fronts of the buildings, and deep bass shouts began to summon other local inhabitants from the interior of the structures. Bill found himself and the Hill Bluffer being bombarded by questions, most of them humorous, and few of them polite, as to his identity and his immediate intentions now that he had arrived at his destination.

He had, however, no chance to answer, for the Hill Bluffer strode swiftly on, grandly ignoring the tumult around them, like an aristocrat taking a stroll among peasants whom it would be beneath his dignity to notice. Bill tried to imitate the postman's indifference. The Bluffer came at last to the far end of the village street, and to a rather wider, more modern-looking log structure there, which sat back a little ways from the other buildings of the village. Bill, finding his wits sharpened by events since he had landed on this world, noticed that the door to this final building was cut in the generous proportions necessary to admit a Dilbian, even a Dilbian as tall as the Hill Bluffer. But, by contrast, the windows in the building were cut down low enough so that a human being would be able to look out of them.

"All right. Here we are," he said, halting. "Light down, Pick-and-Shovel, and get whatever Shorty-type gear you'll need. Then you can get the story straight from Sweet Thing herself, and we'll be off to Outlaw Valley to see about getting Bone Breaker to turn loose Dirty Teeth."

Bill slid down from the broad, furry back, relieved to have his feet on a solid surface once more. He found himself standing in a pleasantly sunlit sort of reception room with some Dilbian sized benches around the walls and a good deal of empty space between them. He looked toward a half-open door, which evidently led deeper into the building.

"What?" he answered, as the Hill Bluffer's last words registered on him. "Wait a minute. I don't think I better go anyplace right away. I'll be expected to stay here until I talk to the Resident and his—I mean—the other Shorty who's staying here."

"Are you deaf, Pick-and-Shovel?" boomed the Hill Bluffer, exasperated.

Surprised, Bill turned to face him.

"Didn't you hear what I was just saying to you?" demanded the Bluffer. "You can't just sit down here and wait for either Dirty Teeth or the Tricky Teacher. Don't you Shorties ever know anything about each other? You can sit here all you want, but neither one of *them's* going to show up."

Bill stared at the tall Dilbian. His scrambling mind finally evoked the hypnoed information that Tricky Teacher was the Dilbian name of the Resident, Lafe Greentree, and that Dirty Teeth was the name the natives had pinned on Greentree's

23

female trainee-assistant—apparently because she had been observed brushing her teeth one day and the Dilbians had jumped to the obvious conclusion that anyone who cleaned their teeth like that as a regular practice must have strong need to do so. But even with this additional knowledge, the Bluffer's last words made no sense.

"Why not?" Bill was reduced to asking, finally.

"Why, because the Tricky Teacher broke his leg a couple of days ago, and a box like the one that always drops out of the sky to bring you Shorties and haul you away took him off to get it fixed!" said the Bluffer, exasperatedly. "That left Dirty Teeth in charge, and of course she had to go out to Outlaw Valley and get mixed up in this hassle between Sweet Thing and Bone Breaker—just like a female. And of course, once he got her in the valley, Bone Breaker just kept her there to make Sweet Thing come to her senses. Well, you Shorties can't let an outlaw like Bone Breaker hang on to one of your females like that and think the farmers around here are going to pay any attention to you when you try to teach them tricks with those picks and shovels and plows and things you brought them!"

He broke off and stared down at Bill from his lean ten feet of height.

"—So, what you've got to do is get going right now out to Outlaw Valley and get Dirty Teeth back. With the Tricky Teacher gone, there's no one else to do it," the Bluffer said. "And we better get moving soon as you've talked to Sweet Thing if we want to get in today. Those outlaws bar the gates to their valley at sundown, and anyone trying to get in or out gets himself chopped. Well, what's holding you?" roared the Bluffer as Bill still stood there. "You're not going to let a Lowlander outlaw hang on to one of your females like that and do nothing about it? You're going after her, aren't you?"

Chapter 3

"No," said Bill automatically.

It was an instinctive reply. Out of the welter of odd names and odder statements that the Hill Bluffer had just been throwing at him, the only thing that stood out clearly was that Bill was being asked to do something besides instruct Dilbians in how to use agricultural implements. Apparently Lafe Greentree had broken his leg and had been taken off-planet for medical treatment, leaving Anita Lyme in charge. And evidently she had interfered, where she should not, in native affairs, and been made a prisoner.

The Hill Bluffer roared, jerking Bill's attention back to the tall Dilbian.

"*No!*" exploded the Hill Bluffer incredulously. Bill with some relief—he had been ready to start running again—realized that the other was not expressing fury so much as he was expressing outrage. "*No*, he says! Here, a female Shorty's got herself captured, and you say you won't go after her! Why, if I'd known you weren't anything like the Half-Pint-Posted, I'd never had let myself in for this job! I'd never even have considered it!"

"Half-Pint-Posted?" echoed Bill, as the Dilbian paused for breath.

"Of course!" snorted the Bluffer. "He was just a Shorty too, but did he hesitate to take on the Streamside Terror? I ask you?"

"I don't know," answered Bill, half-deafened by the other's voice in this enclosed space. "Who's the Streamside Terror?"

25

"Why, just the toughest Upland hill-and-alley brawler between Humrog Village and Wildwood Peak!" said the Bluffer. "Just the roughest—why, the Terror'd chew this Bone Breaker outlaw up for breakfast—" The Bluffer's voice abruptly lowered, and became judicious, "not that Bone Breaker's an easy match, of course. It's just that he's used to fighting with that blade and shield of his in the sissy Lowland fashion. Barehanded, I'll bet the Terror could take him any day. And the Half-Pint-Posted took the Terror."

Bill's mind staggered under the impact of this additional, improbable information.

"You mean this Shorty—a human like me," said Bill, "fought this Streamside Terror you talk about, without weapons?"

"Didn't I say so?" demanded the Bluffer. "Bare-handed and man-to-man. Not only that, but beside a mountain creek—the Terror's favorite spot. And Half-Pint licked him."

"How do you know—" Bill was beginning, when the Bluffer interrupted him.

"How do I know?" shouted the Bluffer in fresh outrage. "Didn't I carry Half-Pint on my back until we caught up with the Terror? Didn't I stand by him and watch while they tangled? Are you questioning my word, Pick-and-Shovel—the word of the official postman between Humrog Village and Wildwood Peak?"

"No—no, of course not," said Bill, still bewildered, "It's just that I hadn't heard—about it before now." As he spoke, his mind was racing. There must be more to it than the Bluffer was telling. Probably there was some kind of gimmick that had kept the match from being the simple massacre of a human being that by rights it would have had to have been.

Also—a new thought struck him—if Greenleaf was actually gone and his assistant was honestly in trouble, then he did indeed have a responsibility to do whatever was necessary to get her out of it. At least, to begin with, he could go and talk to this Dilbian who had taken her, and who evidently was an individual of importance among the outlaws—if not their chief. If nothing else, he could stall until the Resident returned. An ordinary broken leg should not keep the man away from his job much more than the three or four days of the round trip required to take him to a hospital ship and bring him back here.

Bill scrambled about in his mind for words to explain his first refusal to go to Outlaw Valley to help Dirty Teeth. He was neither a quick nor easy liar and excuses did not come readily to him. Luckily, at that moment he remembered that underneath the wild improbabilities of the situation here on Dilbia, there still existed the prosaic organization of any off-world project. Project Spacepaw might be the most fouled-up human endeavor ever to take place beyond Earth's orbit around the Sun, but behind it there had to exist the ordinary official machinery of equipment and regulation.

"Now, listen to me!" he said to the Hill Bluffer. "I'm as good a Shorty as this Half-Pint-Posted or any other one of us you've met; and I'm not going to let one of my own people be held against her will if I can help it. But you've got to remember I'm not the head Shorty here. Before I go dashing off to Outlaw Valley, I've got to see if the Tricky Teacher left me any message telling me what to do. If he did, I've got to do what he said. If he didn't, then I can do things my own way. You're just going to have to wait until I see if he left that message."

"Well, why didn't you say so?" demanded the Hill Bluffer, obviously relieved. "You don't have to explain things twice to an official postman, where something like a message is concerned. If the Tricky Teacher left you a piece of mail to read before you started out, that comes before anything. Though what he should've done was give it to me to deliver to you. It wouldn't have cost him anything extra, and that way he'd be sure you got it right off. Of course," said the Hill Bluffer, suddenly interrupting himself, "come to think of it, he couldn't. Because I just got here yesterday and he was already gone; and probably he didn't want to trust it to any of

27

these Lowlanders. Why, one of them's just as liable to lose it down a well, or go off and leave it lying someplace—"

He checked himself again.

"Anyway, you go read your message, Pick-and-Shovel," he said, "and I'll go dig up Sweet Thing and bring her back here."

He headed toward the door.

"Just a minute," Bill called after him. "Who's Sweet Thing, anyway?"

"Thought you knew," replied the Bluffer, surprised, opening the door. "More Jam's daughter, of course—More Jam's the innkeeper here in town. Passable enough female, I suppose, but like any Lowland woman, talk your head off, even if she hadn't been listening to those crazy notions of Dirty Teeth. Well, see you in a few minutes—"

Out he went. Bill spun around and headed back through the halfway open door into the living quarters of the Residency.

He knew what he was looking for first, whether Greenleaf or Anita Lyme had actually left him a message or not. Somewhere in this building there would be the official daily log of the project—and the odds were strongest he would find it in the room holding the off-planet communications equipment and project records.

It took him four or five minutes of opening doors before he discovered the room for which he searched. It was a square, white-walled room with office equipment and the two banks of consoles which severally operated the Residency computing equipment and the off-planet communications equipment. On one of the room's two desks, he saw the heavy, black-bound book which would be the project log. He sat down hastily at the desk and flipped it open, searching for the latest entries.

He found them within seconds, but they proved to be unusually uninformative, merely listing equipment loaned to the farmers and the times and subjects of conferences between either Greenleaf or Anita Lyme and the local natives.

28

There was none of the diary-like chattiness that isolated project members usually added to log entries in situations like this on Dilbia, and which might have told Bill a great deal more than he now knew about Greenleaf and the girl. Three days ago, there was a brief entry in Greenleaf's upright, hard-stroked hand:

... fell from ladder climbing to replace blown-away roofing shakes on Residency roof above north wall. Broke leg. Have called for medical assistance.

The next entry, the following day, was in a sloping, more feminine hand.

0800 hours, local time. Resident Greenleaf evacuated by shuttle from nearby courier ship, for transportation to closest available hospital ship, for treatment of broken leg.

1030 hours. Leaving for conference with Bone Breaker at Outlaw Valley.

Anita Lyme, Trainee Assistant

That was the last entry in the log, two days ago. There was no message for Bill from either Greenleaf or Anita, though it was highly irregular of the girl to go off without leaving one. Unless, that is, she had honestly expected to be back the same day.

Bill closed the log, got to his feet, and stepped over to the communications equipment. It was a standard console, arranged to put whoever used the equipment in touch with a relay station orbiting the planet, which would in turn rebroadcast the message at multilight velocity to its interstellar destination. Bill had been checked out on its use, as he had been checked out on most general equipment in use on off-world projects. He flipped the power switch and pressed the microphone button.

Nothing happened. The power light on the console did not go on. The microphone did not give out the signal hum that announced it as being in operating condition.

The set was dead.

For a second, Bill stared at it. Then, quickly, he ran over the console, flipping check switches and trying to locate the

29

malfunction. But nothing responded. His hands flew to the toggle-nuts holding the face of the panel in place. Somewhere in the building there would be test equipment and with it, given time, even he ought to be able to trace down what was keeping the set from operating.

"PICK-AND-SHOVEL!"

It was the voice of the Hill Bluffer, roaring for him from the reception room. A second later, it was reinforced by a lighter toned, female Dilbian voice, also calling him. Grimly, Bill dropped his hands and turned away from the console. Fixing the communications equipment would have to wait.

He went rapidly out of the room and down the hall toward the front of the building. A moment later, he stepped into the reception room and found the Bluffer there with his female companion, who was the first to break off shouting for Bill as he came through the door.

"Well, there you are, Pick-and-Shovel!" said Sweet Thing— for this short, compact newcomer could only be that Dilbian female whom the Bluffer had gone to get, thought Bill. "It's high time you got here to Muddy Nose!"

"You knew I was coming?" asked Bill, in the sudden silence as the Bluffer stopped his shouting in turn and nodded genially at Bill.

"Why, of course we knew you were coming!" said Sweet Thing sharply. "Didn't *She* say *She* was sending for you? Of course *She* did. She knew how to handle the situation even if no one else did. As *She* said, the time had come to strike a blow for our rights. What *She* said was—"

"Let him get a word in edgewise, will you?" roared the Bluffer, for Bill had valiantly been trying to speak in the face of this torrent of talk.

"Who's *She*?" asked Bill hurriedly into the moment of silence that followed Sweet Thing's snort.

"*She?*" answered Sweet Thing, on a rising note. "Why Dirty Teeth, of course! *She* who has roused us at last to strike for our rights against men who have been telling us what to do all the time!"

30

The Hill Bluffer snorted.

Sweet Thing snorted.

"Wait—" said Bill hastily, before the situation could degenerate into a private argument between the two Dilbians. "What I want to know is, why is Dirty Teeth being held by Bone Breaker, in the first place?"

"Why, because *She's* the champion of us women!" said Sweet Thing swiftly. "It comes from listening to Fatties, that's what it does! Bone Breaker wants to force me to go live in that robber's roost of his. Well I won't do it! You can tell him so. Not if he should chop Dirty Teeth up for fish bait. I've got my principles!"

Once more, Sweet Thing's nose elevated itself toward the ceiling.

Bill had felt his heart lurch a little bit at the mention of Dirty Teeth being chopped up for fish bait. The matter seemed to be more serious than he had thought at first. What listening to "Fatties"—the Dilbian name for Hemnoids—had to do with it, was another mystery. Ignoring that for the moment, however, Bill decided to stick to his main line of questioning.

"You mean the only thing that will save Dirty Teeth is if you go live in this Outlaw Valley?" Bill demanded.

"Of course not!" retorted Sweet Thing. "All you have to do is go and take Dirty Teeth back from him. Why do you think *She* sent for you?"

"Well, as a matter of fact ..." Bill's voice trailed off. He had been about to protest that it had not been Dirty Teeth at all who was responsible for his being here. Just in time, it had occurred to him that the situation was complicated enough already. There was no telling what harm he might do if he revealed that he was not specially appointed by this girl, who appeared to have become something of a local heroine to Sweet Thing, if not to the other females of Muddy Nose. "You say I just go in and get her?"

"Well, I'd certainly teach him a lesson while you're about it—Bone Breaker, I mean," said Sweet Thing. "Imagine the

31

idea of holding prisoner someone like Dirty Teeth! It's just what you'd expect of some scruffy outlaw. Tell him you'll hit him one for me, too!"

"Hit him one—I don't understand—" Bill was beginning, when Sweet Thing exploded.

"Well, I don't see what there is not to understand!" she cried angrily. "I've been explaining and explaining until even a Shorty like you ought to be able to follow it. I won't marry that Bone Breaker unless he gives up his outlaw ways and settles down to being a farmer here in Muddy Nose, like you Shorties say everybody in the Lowlands should do. It's all nonsense about a girl having to go where her husband says. It's only women like Thing-or-Two that pretend to believe the world's coming to an end if any of the old customs get changed. Hah! Why she's really all for the old customs is that if she can get me out of the Inn, she'd have a right as female relative next-of-kin to move into it as inn-keepress in my place. She'd drive my poor old daddy crazy in a week! No, no—Dirty Teeth explained it all to us! We've just as much right to say where we're going to settle down as the men have! Bone Breaker's as bad as the rest, but he really made a mistake when he decided to make Dirty Teeth a prisoner out in the valley. I wish I could see his face when you do it!"

"Do what?" demanded Bill, baffled.

"Challenge him, of course!" snapped Sweet Thing, turning on her heel and opening the street door. "Naturally, he's not going to give Dirty Teeth back to you unless you fight him for her and win, like the Half-Pint-Posted did with that mountain man who ran off with a Shorty female. So you better get out there to the valley and do it. I've waited long enough for Bone Breaker as it is, and it's a cinch there's no one else around Muddy Nose with nerve enough to take him on!"

She went out, slamming the door behind her.

A second later, it opened again, and she stuck her nose back in.

"Don't worry about having to get him all riled up before

you challenge him," Sweet Thing added. "He knows what you're coming out there for. I sent word for him to expect you a couple of days ago."

Chapter 4

Sweet Thing's nose disappeared. The door slammed shut again. Bill stared at it, with his head swimming. If there was one thing he had absolutely no intention of doing, it was challenging the head man, or whatever, of outlaws like those from whom he had run and hidden in Tin Ear's farmyard earlier in the day.

"Well, so you see," said the Hill Bluffer behind him heavily. Bill turned to look at the postman and the Bluffer nodded at the closed door. "Crazy as a spring storm. And with a father who thinks more of his belly than he does of his daughter, or she wouldn't be able to get away with these wild, Shorty ideas—"

He broke off, glancing at Bill apologetically.

"—No offense to you, of course, Pick-and-Shovel," he rumbled. "As for Sweet Thing's ideas—"

"Wait a minute," interrupted Bill hastily. "Can't the village get together and help someone like Tin Ear—"

"Well, now, that's an idea for you!" said the Hill Bluffer indignantly. "Sure, if a neighbor yells for help, you might run over and give him a hand—when you hear him yell. But put yourself and all of your family into blood-feud for someone who's no kin at all? Well, a man'd be crazy to do that. After all, these are pretty honorable outlaws. Bone Breaker sees to that. They take their outlaw-tax out of what the Muddy

33

Nosers can spare—they don't go taking what the local people have to have to stay alive. If they did that, then I suppose the Muddy Nosers would get together in blood-feud, if they had to declare themselves a clan, temporarily to do that. We've got to get going to make that valley before the gates are closed." He turned his massive, furry shoulders to Bill and squatted down. "Climb on, Pick-and-Shovel."

Bill hesitated only a second, and then climbed into the saddle on the postman's back. Listening to Sweet Thing, he had come to the conclusion that whatever he did, he could not avoid at least going to the valley and talking to the outlaw chief. In the absence of orders from his superiors he had no choice. But he certainly had no intention of challenging Bone Breaker, no matter what Sweet Thing thought. What he could and would do, would be to spin out negotiations until Greenleaf got back, which would certainly be within four or five days at most.

"—Of course," said the Bluffer, unexpectedly breaking the silence as the trees closed about them, "naturally, that's why the Tricky Teacher hasn't been having much success getting these Lowlanders to use all these tools and things you Shorties have brought in."

Bill, by this time, was beginning to get used to the unexpectedness of Dilbian conversation. It required only a little thought on his part to realize that the Bluffer was continuing the conversation begun inside the Residency after Sweet Thing's departure.

"What's why?" Bill asked, therefore, interested.

"Why, the fact there's no point in these farmers learning all sorts of new tricks so they can grow more food," answered the Bluffer. "The outlaws just take anything extra, anyway. The more extra food they raised, the more extra outlaws they'd just be supporting."

"How far is it to the valley?" Bill asked.

"Just a step or two," answered the Bluffer economically.

However, a step or two by the Bluffer's standards seemed to be somewhat more of a distance than the term implied to human ears. For better than half an hour, the Bluffer strode rapidly into rougher and rougher country. The Dilbian sun was close to the tops of the hills and peaks ahead of them, when the Bluffer at last made an abrupt turn and plunged downward into what looked like an ordinary ravine, but which suddenly opened up around a corner to reveal, ahead and below them down a narrow ravine, a parklike, green valey, walled in all other directions by near-vertical cliffs of bare stone from fifty to a hundred feet in height. Softly green-carpeted with the local grass, the valley glowed in the late afternoon sun, the black log walls of a cluster of buildings at its far end soaking up the late light.

That light fell also on a literal wall made of logs about thirty feet high, some fifty yards ahead down the path. This wall was pierced by a heavy wooden door, now ajar but flanked by two Dilbians wearing not only the straplike harness and swords Bill had seen on those at Tin Ear's farm, but with heavy, square, wooden shields hanging from their left shoulders, as well. Sweet Thing's words about challenging Bone Breaker came uncomfortably back into Bill's mind.

The Hill Bluffer, however, had evidently come here with no sense of caution. As he approached the two at the gate, he bellowed at the two outlaws on watch.

"All right, out of the way! We've got business with Bone Breaker!"

The guards, however, made no move to step aside. Their nine-foot heights and a combined weight of probably over three-quarters of a ton, continued to bar the entrance. The Bluffer necessarily came to a halt before them.

"Step aside, I say!" he shouted.

"Says who?" demanded the taller of the guards.

"Says me!" roared the Bluffer. "Don't pretend you don't know who I am. The official postman's got right of entry to any town, village, or camp! So clear out of my way and let us through!"

"You aren't being a postman now," retorted the Dilbian who had spoken before. "Right now you're nothing but a plain, ordinary mountain man, wanting into private property. Did anybody send for you?"

"Send for us?" the Bluffer's voice rose to a roar of rage, and Bill could feel the big back and shoulder muscle of the Dilbian bunching ominously under him. "This is the Pick-and-Shovel Shorty who's here to tangle with Bone Breaker if necessary!"

"Him? Tangle with Bone Breaker!" the guard who had been talking burst into guffaws. "Hor, hor, hor!" His companion joined in.

"So you think that's funny!" snarled the Bluffer. "There were a few of you valley reivers at Tin Ear's farm earlier today who got made to look pretty silly. And lucky for them, that was all that happened—" The Bluffer's voice took on an ominous tone. "Remember it was a Shorty just like him that took the Streamside Terror!"

Startlingly enough to Bill, this reminder seemed to take the wind out of the sails of the two guards' merriment. Apparently, if Bill found it impossible to believe that a Shorty could outfight a Dilbian, these two did not think so. Their laughter died and they cast uneasy glances over the Bluffer's shoulder at Bill.

"Huh!" said the talkative one, with a feeble effort at a sneer. "The Streamside Terror. An Uplander!"

Bill felt the saddle heave beneath him as the Bluffer took a deep breath. But before that breath could emerge in words, the talkative guard abruptly stood aside.

"Well, who cares?" he growled. "Let's let 'em go in, Three Fingers. Bone Breaker will take care of them, all right!"

"High time!" snarled the Bluffer. But without staying to argue anymore, he set himself in motion through the gate, and a second later was striding forward over the lush slope of grass toward the log buildings in the distance, all these things now reddened by the setting sun.

As they drew closer, Bill saw that there was considerable difference in the size of some of the buildings. In fact, the whole conglomeration looked rather like a skiing chalet, with a number of guest cottages scattered around behind it. The main building, a long one-story structure, stood squarely athwart their path, the big double doors of its principal entrance thrown wide open to reveal a perfectly black, unlighted interior. As the Bluffer approached the building Bill could smell the odor of roasting meat, as well as several other unidentifiable vegetable odors. Evidently it was the hour of the evening meal, which Bill's hypnoed information told him was served about this time of day among the Dilbians. Once inside, the Bluffer stepped out of line with the open doorway, and stopped abruptly; evidently to let his eyes adjust to the inner dark.

Bill's eyes were also adjusting. Gradually, out of the gloom, there took shape a long narrow chamber with bare rafters overhead, and a large stone fireplace filled with crackling logs in spite of the warmth of the closing day, set in the end wall to their right. There was a small, square table with four stools set before the fireplace, just as there were other. long tables flanked by benches stretching away from it down the length of the hall. But what drew Bill's eyes like a magnet to the table with four stools in front of the fireplace was not the tall Dilbian with coal-black fur sitting on one of the stools, talking, but his partner in conversation, sitting across from him.

This other was not a Dilbian. Swathed in dark, shimmering cloth, his rotund body was scarcely half a head shorter than that of the Dilbian. Standing, Bill guessed that he could be scarcely less than eight feet tall, a foot or so below the average height of a male Dilbian. His face, like his body, bulged in creases of what appeared to be fat. But Bill knew that they were nothing of the kind. Seated, talking to the black-furred Dilbian was a member of that alien race which was most strongly in competition with the humans for influence with the natives on worlds like Dilbia, and for living space in general between the stars.

The being to whom the black-furred Dilbian was speaking was a Hemnoid, and his apparent fat was the result of the powerful muscles required by a race which had evolved on a world with half again the gravity of Earth.

Abruptly and belatedly, the meaning of Sweet Thing's obscure reference to taking the advice of Fatties became clear to Bill. A cold feeling like a cramp made itself felt at the pit of his stomach.

It was Bone Breaker, apparently, who had been taking the advice of Fatties—or of this one Fatty in particular. Unexpectedly, Bill found himself facing a Hemnoid in exactly the sort of ticklish interracial situation that the Human-Hemnoid treaty of noninterference in native Dilbian affairs had been signed to prevent. Too late now, he realized that he had intruded on the type of incident that should be dealt with by no human below the rank of a Resident in the Diplomatic Service. Let alone a trainee-assistant in mechanical engineering who was like a fish out of water in being assigned to an agricultural project. And let alone a trainee-assistant who had been unable to contact his superiors by off-planet communications, and who was operating totally without authority and on his own initiative.

"Turn around!" Bill hissed frantically in the Hill Bluffer's ear. "I've got to get out of here!"

"Out? What for?" said the Bluffer, surprised. "Anyway, it's too late now."

"Too late—?"

Bill never finished echoing the Bluffer's words.

From just outside the door behind him there came a sound like that of a large, untuned, metal gong being struck. A voice shouted:

"Sun's down! Close the gates."

There was only a second or two of pause, and then floating back from the far distance of the valley entrance with a clarity that only the lung-power of a Dilbian could provide with such pressure, came the answering cry:

"The gates are closed!"

Chapter 5

The long, drawn-out cry from the valley gate had barely died away, before the Hill Bluffer was in motion, heading toward the short table in front of the fireplace. Bill opened his mouth to protest, then quickly shut it again. Now he saw that the room was crowded with Dilbians of all sizes, and probably of both sexes, both standing about and seated at the various benches. At first this crowd had not noticed the Bluffer and Bill, standing just inside the doorway. But as they began to move toward the small, square table at the head of the room, before the fireplace, they drew all eyes upon them, and silence spread out through the room like ripples from a stone flung into a pond. By the time the Bluffer reached the table where the Hemnoid and the black-furred Dilbian sat, that silence was absolute.

The Bluffer stopped. He looked down at the seated Hemnoid and the seated Dilbian.

"Evening, Bone Breaker," he said to the Dilbian, and transferred his gaze to the Hemnoid. "Evening, Barrel Belly."

"Evening to you, Postman," replied Bone Breaker. His unbelievably deep, bass voice had an echoing, resonant quality that made it seem to ring all around them. The outlaw chief was, Bill saw, almost as outsize for a Dilbian as was the Hill Bluffer. Probably not quite as tall as the Bluffer, judged Bill, as he tried to estimate from the seated figure of the outlaw, but heavier in the body, and certainly wider in the shoulders. A shiver trickled coldly down Bill's back. There

39

was an air of competence and authority about this one Dilbian that was strangely at odds with the appearance of other members of that same race that Bill had met so far. The eyes looking at him now out of the midnight black of the furry face had a brilliant, penetrating quality. Could someone like this be holding prisoner a human being for such emotional and obvious reasons as Sweet Thing had attributed to him?

But he had no chance to ponder the question. Because the Hemnoid was, he found, already talking to him, gazing up at him over the Bluffer's furry shoulder, and speaking in a voice which, while not so deep as those of the Dilbians, had the ponderous, liquid quality of some heavy oil, pouring out of an enormous jug.

"Mula-*ay*, at your service," gurgled the Hemnoid with a darkly sinister sort of cheerfulness. He was speaking Dilbian, and the fact he did so, alerted Bill to answer in the same language—and not fall into the social mistake of speaking out in either human or Hemnoid, of which latter alien tongue he also owned a hypnoed knowledge.

"Or, 'Barrel Belly,' as our friends here call me," went on Mula-*ay*. "I'm a journalist, here to do a series of articles on these delightful people. What brings you among them, my young, human friend?"

"Bill Waltham," answered Bill cautiously. "I'm here as part of our agricultural project at Muddy Nose." Mula-*ay* might indeed be a journalist, but it was almost certain he was also a Hemnoid secret agent—that was the Hemnoid way.

"Just part of it?" Mula-*ay* gave a syrupy chuckle as he answered, like a hogshead of molasses being emptied into a deep tank. There was a note of derision in his chuckling. A note that seemed to invite everyone else to join him in laughing over some joke at Bill's expense. This in itself might mean something—or it might not. A love of cruelty was part of the Hemnoid character, as Bill knew. It was a racial characteristic which the Hemnoid culture praised, rather than condemned. Nonetheless, it was not pleasant to be the butt of Mula-*ay*'s joke, whatever it was. Feeling suddenly ridiculous,

Bill took his feet out of the back straps of the Bluffer's harness and slid down to stand on the floor.

Now on his feet and facing both the seated Mula-*ay* and Bone Breaker, Bill found he could look slightly down into the face of the Hemnoid, although his eyes glanced level with the eyes of Bone Breaker.

"Have a place at my table, Pick-and-Shovel," rumbled the outlaw chief. His tone was formal, so that the words came out very like a command. "You too, Postman."

Without hesitation, the Bluffer dropped down on one of the unoccupied stools. Bill walked around and hoisted himself up on the other empty seat. He found himself with Bone Breaker close at his right elbow; while at his left elbow, with only a few feet between them, sat the gross form of Mula-*ay*, his Buddha-like face still creased in a derisive smile. Opposite, Bill's single ally, the Hill Bluffer, seemed far away and removed from the action.

With the fire lashing its red flames into the air at one side of them, throwing ruddy gleams among the sooty shadows of the bare rafters above them and the outsize figures surrounding him, there came on Bill suddenly a feeling of having somehow stumbled into a nether world, peopled by dark giants and strange monsters. A momentary feeling of helplessness washed through him. All around him, the situation seemed too big for him physically, emotionally, and even professionally. He broke out rashly and directly to Bone Breaker, speaking across a corner of the table.

"I understand you've got a Shorty here—a Shorty named Dirty Teeth!"

For a long second, the outlaw merely looked at him.

"Why, yes," answered Bone Breaker. Then, with strange mildness, "She did wander in here the other day and I believe she's still around. Seems I remember she told me yesterday she didn't plan to leave for a while—whether I liked it or not."

He continued to gaze at Bill, as Bill sat, momentarily shaken both by his own lack of caution and by Bone Breaker's astonishing answer. Now, while Bill was still trying to collect his scattered wits, Bone Breaker spoke again.

"But let's not get into that now, Pick-and-Shovel," said the outlaw chief, still in that tone of surprising mildness. "It's just time for the food and drink. Sit back and make yourself comfortable. We'll have dinner first. Then we can talk."

Mula-*ay*, Bill saw, was still grinning at him, evidently hugely enjoying Bill's confusion and discomfiture.

"Well . . . thanks," said Bill to Bone Breaker.

A couple of Dilbian females were just at this moment coming to the table with huge platters of what appeared to be either boiled or roasted meat, enormous irregular chunks of brown material that seemed to be some kind of bread, and large wooden drinking containers.

"What's the matter, Pick-and-Shovel?" Bone Breaker inquired mildly, as the wooden vessels were being poured full of a dark brown liquid, which Bill's nose told him was probably some form of native beer. "Nothing wrong with the food and drink, is there? Dig in."

"Quite right," Mula-*ay* echoed the Dilbian with an oily chuckle, cramming his own large mouth full of bread and meat and lifting the wooden tankard to wash the mouthful down. "Best food for miles around."

"Not quite, Barrel Belly," replied Bone Breaker, turning his deceptive mildness this time upon the Hemnoid. "I thought I told you. Sweet Thing is the best cook in these parts."

"Oh yes—yes," agreed the Hemnoid hastily, swallowing with a gulp, and beaming hugely at the outlaw, "of course. How could it have slipped my mind? Good as this is, it isn't a patch on what Sweet Thing could cook. Why, sure!"

Bone Breaker, Bill thought, must possess an iron fist within the velvet glove of this apparent mildness of his, judging by the reaction of the Hemnoid. Now the black-furred outlaw's eyes were coming back to Bill. Bill hastily picked up a chunk of meat and began gnawing on it. Oh well, he thought, nothing ventured, nothing gained.

Conversation in general had ceased, not merely at their own head table, but about the hall, as the Dilbians present settled down to the serious business of eating. Their industry in performing that task was awesome enough from a human's point of view. Bill had never thought of himself as a particularly light eater—in fact, at Survival School, he had been accused of just the opposite. But compared to these Dilbians, and to the Hemnoid at his left elbow, his performance as a trencherman was so insignificant as to seem ridiculous.

To begin with, somewhere between six and eight pounds of boiled meat had been dumped upon his wooden plate, along with what looked like about the equivalent of two loaves of bread. The wooden flagon alongside his plate looked as if it could hold at least a quart or two of liquid, and it had been generously filled.

After a first attempt at trying to keep up with the over-sized appetites and capacities of those around him, Bill gave up. He scattered the food around on his plate as much as possible to make it look as if he had eaten, and resigned himself to pretending to be busy with the drinking flagon, which, as it became more and more empty, got easier to handle.

He had just, somewhat to his own surprise, managed at last to drain the final mouthful of liquid from this oversized utensil and set it back down on the table, when to his dismay he saw Bone Breaker turn and lift a pawlike hand. One of the serving Dilbians came over and refilled the flagon.

Bill gulped.

"Very good. Very good," gurgled Mula-*ay*, tossing off at a gulp his own refilled flagon, which if anything was a little bit bigger than Bill's. "Our Shorty is quite an eater and drinker"— he added in a deprecating tone—"for a Shorty."

"Man don't lick the world by filling his belly," growled the Hill Bluffer.

An instinct warned Bill against glancing appreciatively in the Bluffer's direction. Nonetheless, he warmed inside, at this evidence of support by the lanky Dilbian.

"But a man's got to lick the world sometime," said the Hemnoid, chuckling richly as if this was some rare kind of joke. "Isn't that so, Pick-and-Shovel?"

Bill checked himself on the verge of answering, and picked up his heavy drinking utensil in order to gain time.

"Well . . ." he said, and put the vessel to his lips.

As he pretended to swallow, over the circular wooden rim of the container, he unexpectedly caught sight of a small, slim, non-Dilbian figure moving along next to a far wall, until it reached the big double doors which still stood open to the twilight without. It passed through those doors and was gone. But not before Bill, staring after it over the rim of his drinking vessel, had identified the figure as human—and female, at that.

Hastily, he replaced the drinking container on the table, turning to Bone Breaker.

"Wasn't that—" he had to think a moment to remember the Dilbian name for her, "Dirty Teeth, I just saw going out the door?"

The huge Dilbian outlaw chief stared back down at Bill with dark, unreadable eyes.

"Why, I don't know, Pick-and-Shovel," answered Bone Breaker. "Did you say you saw her?"

"That's right," replied Bill, a little grimly, "she just went out the doors there. You didn't see her? You're facing that way."

"Why," said Bone Breaker mildly, "I don't remember seeing her. But as I said, she's around here some place. It could have been her. Why don't you take a look for yourself, if you want?"

"I think I'll do just that," replied Bill. He swung around on the stool and dropped to the floor. To his discomfort and dismay, he discovered that the dangling of his legs in midair over the sharp edge of the stool had put the right leg to sleep. A sensation of pins and needles was shooting through it now, and it felt numb and unreliable. Trying not to hobble, he turned and headed toward the big, open, double door.

Finally he reached the wide-open doors and stepped thankfully into the twilight outside. Looking first right and then left he saw that even the guards who had been lounging there were gone now. For a moment, as his gaze swept the gloaming that was settling down over the barricaded valley, a feeling of annoyance began to kindle in him. He could not discover anywhere that slim, girlish figure he had seen passing within the hall. Then abruptly his eyes located her—hardly more than a dark shadow against the darkening loom of the wall of an outbuilding some fifty feet away.

He went down the steps at a bound and headed toward her at a run, just as she turned the corner of the outbuilding and disappeared.

The soft turf all but absorbed the sound of his thudding boots as he ran. He reached the corner of the building and came swiftly around it. Suddenly, he was almost on top of her, for she had been merely idling on her way, it appeared, her head down as if she was deep in thought.

What do you say in a situation like this, wondered Bill, as he hastily put on the brakes; and she, still deep in thought, continued to wander on, evidently without having heard him. He searched his mind for her real name, but all that would come up from his memory in this winded moment was the nickname of Dirty Teeth that the Dilbians had given her. Finally, in desperation, he compromised.

"Hey!" he said, moving up behind her.

She jumped, and turned. From a distance of only a few feet away, in the growing dimness of the twilight, he was able to make out that her face was oval and fine-boned, her hair was brown and smooth, fitting her head almost like a helmet, and her eyes were startling green and wide. They widened still further at the sight of him.

"Oh, here you are!" she cried in English. "For heaven's sake, what do you mean by coming here, of all places? Didn't you know any better than to charge into a delicate situation like this, the moment you landed, like a bull into a china shop?"

45

Chapter 6

Bill stared at Anita Lyme, wordlessly.

He was not wordless because she had left him with nothing to say. He was wordless because he had too many things to say at once, and they were all fighting each other in his mind for first use of his tongue. If he had been the stuttering kind, he would have stuttered—with incredulity and plain, downright fury.

"Now, wait!" he managed to say at last, "you got yourself into this place, here—"

"—And I knew what I was doing! You don't!" she snapped back, neatly stealing the conversational ball from his grip. "You're just lucky I was here to get you out of it. If I hadn't heard from the outlaw females about Sweet Thing's message to Bone Breaker that you were coming, you'd have been committed to a duel with Bone Breaker right now! Do you know why you aren't? Because the moment I heard, I went to Bone Breaker and told him that I was enjoying my visit here with the females and I wasn't going to leave for anybody! You couldn't very well fight over my being here after that!"

"No," said Bill grimly. "But as it happens, I wasn't planning to. Meanwhile, you're still stuck here, Greenleaf is off-planet, and I'm left with a Residency and a project I've been drafted to and don't know anything about. I'm not one of your agricultural or sociological trainee-assistants. My field's mechanical engineering. What do I do—"

"Well, you find that out for yourself," she said. "Just call Lafe and ask him—"

"The communications equipment's dead. It won't work."

She stared at him.

"It can't be," she said at last. "You just didn't get it turned on right."

"Of course I got it turned on right!" said Bill stiffly. "It's not working, I tell you!"

"Of course it's working. It has to work! Go back and try it again. And that's the point—" she said, checking herself suddenly. "The point is, you shouldn't ever have come here in the first place. Common sense should have told you—"

"Sweet Thing said you needed rescuing from Bone Breaker."

"Did you have to believe her, just like that? Honestly!" said Anita, on an exasperated note. "You should have immediately called Lafe—"

"I tried to. I tell you—" said Bill, almost between his teeth, "the communications equipment doesn't work!"

"I tell you it does! It worked when I left for the valley here, two days ago—and what could have happened to it since? Wait—" Anita held out a hand in the gathering dusk to stop him as he was about to explode into speech. She lowered her own voice to a more reasonable tone. "Look, let's not fight about it. The situation here is too important. The point is, I've saved you from fighting Bone Breaker. Now, the thing for you to do is get back to the village as fast as you can, and stay there. Get busy at your real job."

"What real job?" ejaculated Bill, staring at her.

"Organizing the villagers to stand up all together to the outlaws, of course!"

"What!"

"That's right." She lowered her voice still further, until it barely carried to his ears. "Listen to me—ah—Mr. Waltham—"

"Call me Pick-and-Shov—I mean, Bill," answered Bill,

47

lowering his own voice in turn. "What are we whispering for?"

She glanced around them at the gathering dusk.

"That Hemnoid understands English as well as you or I understand Hemnoid," she murmured. "Let me explain a few things to you about Project Spacepaw—Bill."

"I wish you would," said Bill, with deep emotion.

"Oh, stop it! There's no need to keep getting a chip on your shoulder!" said Anita. "Listen to me now. This started out here as a perfectly ordinary agricultural project, taking advantage of the fact that when the original Human-Hemnoid Non-Interference Treaty on Dilbia was signed, neither the Hemnoids nor we knew that there were any sizable Dilbian communities that weren't organized and disciplined by the clan structure you find among the Dilbians in the mountains—where ninety percent of the native population lives."

"I know that," interrupted Bill. "I spent five days on the way here wearing a hypno-helmet. I can even quote the part about the project aims. *The project name 'Spacepaw,' refers to the hope of giving technology a foothold among the Dilbians—literally translated into Dilbian, it comes out meaning 'helping hand from the stars'—except that since the Dilbians consider themselves to be the ones who have hands—Shorties and the Fatties are referred to as having 'paws.'* I already know all about that. But I was sent here to teach the natives how to use farm tools, not to organize a—" he fumbled for a word.

"Civil defense force!" supplied Anita.

"Civil defense . . ." he goggled at her through the increasing darkness.

"Why not? That's as good a name for it as any!" she whispered, briskly. "Now, will you listen and learn a few things you *don't* know? I said this *started out* like an ordinary project. The Lowland Dilbians here at Muddy Nose come from fifty or sixty different Upland clans. They don't have the clan organization, therefore, and they don't have any

Grandfathers of the Clan, to exert a conservative control over the way they think and act. Also, they don't have the Upland Dilbian's idea that it's sissy to use tools or weapons. So it looked like they were just the community to let us demonstrate to the mountain Dilbians that tools and technology in general could raise more crops, build better buildings, and everything else—start them on the road to modern civilization."

"And, incidentally, make them closer friends of ours than they are of the Hemnoids," put in Bill skeptically.

"That, too, of course," said Anita. "At least, if the Dilbians have some knowledge of modern technology, they'll be better able to understand the psychological difference between us and the Hemnoids. We're betting that if we can raise their mean technological level, they'll want to be partners with us. The Hemnoids don't want them to become technologically sophisticated. They'd rather take the Dilbians into the Hemnoid sphere of influence, now while they're still safely primitive and they'd have to be technologically dependent."

"You were going," pointed out Bill, "to tell me something I didn't know."

"I am, if you'll listen!" whispered Anita fiercely. "When we started to make a success of this project, the Hemnoids moved to counter it. They sent in Mula-*ay*, one of their best agents—"

"Agents?" echoed Bill. He had suspected it, of course, but finding himself undeniably up against a highly trained alien agent sent an abruptly cold shiver snaking its way between his shoulder blades.

"That's what I said. Agent. And Mula-*ay* didn't lose any time in taking advantage of the one local condition which could frustrate the project. He moved in with the outlaws, here, and pointed out to them that the more the villagers could produce from their farms, the more surplus the outlaws would be able to take from them. The outlaws only take what the farmers can spare, you know. Dilbian custom is very strict on that, even without Grandfathers—"

"I know," muttered Bill impatiently. "Why wasn't I told about the Hemnoid being here and being an agent, though? None of the hypnoed information mentioned it."

"Lafe was supposed to brief you after you got here—that's what he told me, anyway," she said, in so low a voice that he could hardly hear her. "The Hemnoids are too good at intercepting and decoding interstellar transmissions for the information I'm giving you now to be sent out for inclusion in ordinary hypno tapes. The point is that word of what Mula-*ay* told the outlaws got back from the outlaws to the villagers, and the villagers began to ask themselves what was the point of using tools, if making a better living simply meant making a better living for the outlaws. You see, the outlaws go around collecting their so-called tax and the Muddy Nosers can't stop them."

"Why not?" asked Bill. "There must be more of them than there are of outlaws—"

"That's what I've been trying to tell you," whispered Anita. "There *are* more of them than there are of outlaws. But without a clan structure they won't combine, and the outlaws raid one farm at a time and take whatever the farmer has to spare. The farmer doesn't even fight for his property—for one thing he's always outnumbered. For another, most of them rather admire the outlaws."

"Admire them!"

"That's right," said Anita. "They complain about how the outlaws take things from them, but when they're telling you about it, you can see they're halfway proud of having been robbed. It's been a sort of romantic interlude, a holiday in their lives—"

"Yes," said Bill, suddenly thoughtful. He remembered Tin Ear's drunken but happy grin as he had sat at the table, being forced to swallow his own beer.

"The point is," wound up Anita, "agriculture isn't going to be improved around Muddy Nose as long as this nest of outlaws continues to exist. We've got a stalemate here—outlaws balanced off against villagers, the Hemnoid influence

50

balanced off against ours. Well, I've had some success with bringing the local females around to a human point of view. Lafe told me our superiors think maybe someone—er, mechanically oriented—like you, could have some success with the village males. So—as I say, you go back and try to organize them into a civil defense force—"

"I see," said Bill. "Just like that, I suppose?"

"You don't have to sneer at the very notion," she retorted. In fact, a note of enthusiasm was beginning to kindle in her own voice as she talked—almost as if, Bill thought, she was falling in love with her own idea. "All the village males really need is a leader. You can be that—only, of course, you'll need to operate from behind the scenes. But why don't you talk to the village blacksmith to begin with? His name's Flat Fingers. He's big enough and strong enough to be a match for Bone Breaker himself, if they went at it without weapons. You get him on your side—"

"All right. Hold on a minute!" interrupted Bill. "I don't know what this business of raising a civil defense force has to do with the situation, but it's not the reason I came here. For your information, I was drafted while I was en route to a terraforming project on Deneb Seventeen, and what I was drafted for was to instruct the Muddy Nose villagers in the use of farming tools. In short, those were my orders and no one in authority has changed them. Until someone does—"

"*So!*"

It was the first time Bill had ever actually heard the word hissed. He stopped his own flow of words out of sheer surprise.

"So—you're one of those, are you!" Anita's voice was bitterly accusing. "You don't really care a thing about your work out between the stars! All you want to do is put in your two years and get your credit so that you can enter a university back home and get a general instead of a restricted professional license when you graduate! You don't care what happens to the project you work on, or the job it's trying to do—"

"Now hold on—" began Bill.

"—You don't care about anything but putting in your tim the easiest way possible—"

"If you want to know," began Bill, "the way I feel abou the terraforming of a whole world, with—"

"—and to blazes with anyone else concerned, human o native! Well, it happens I *do* care about the Dilbians—I car too much to let the Hemnoids stand in the way of thei developing into an expanding, technological society and join ing us and the Hemnoids not just as poor country cousin but as an independent, self-sufficient, space-going race—"

"If you'll listen a minute, I didn't mean to say—"

"So nobody's given you any orders, have they?" furiousl whispered a spot in the by-now pitch-darkness, twelve inche in front of and eight inches below Bill's nose. "Well, we'll jus fix that! You're a trainee-assistant, aren't you?"

"Of course," he said, when he was able to get the word out.

"And I'm a trainee-assistant. Right? But which one of u was here first?"

"You, of course," said Bill. "But—"

"Then who's senior at this post? *Me.* You go back to th village tonight—"

"You know I can't get back tonight!" said Bill desperately "The gates were closed at sundown!"

"Well, they'll be opened up again, if Bone Breaker say so—ask him!" snapped Anita. "Then go back to the villag tonight and stay there and start organizing the villagers t defend themselves against the outlaws! That's not a sugges tion I'm giving you, it's an *order*—from *me* as your superior Now go do it, and good night, Mr. Pickham—I mean, Mr Billham—I mean—oh, *good night!*"

There was a feminine snort of rage almost Dilbian in it intensity, and Bill heard the sound of shod human fee stamping off across the turf away from him in the blackness.

Bill stood where he was, stunned. It was part and parcel o the ridiculously unorthodox way in which things had bee

52

going ever since he had landed on Dilbia that he should find himself at the orders of a female trainee-assistant who apparently was stark, raving unreasonable on the subject of the local natives. Now what? Should he follow Anita's orders, organize the Dilbians of Muddy Nose—even if he was able to accomplish that—into a fighting force, and end up being tried under out-space law for unwarranted interference with natives' affairs on Dilbia? Or should he go back to the village, instruct the locals in the uses of picks and shovels, and end up being tried under out-space law for refusing to obey an order of his immediate superior?

Chapter 7

It was too much to figure out now. Bill gave up. Tomorrow, he would think the whole matter through. Meanwhile, there was the business of getting back to the village tonight—and into a human-style bed at the Residency, which he was far from unwilling to do. Maybe Anita was right about his only having to ask Bone Breaker to let himself and the Bluffer out after hours.

He turned about uncertainly, peering through the night, and to his relief, discovered the lights shining out of the windows of the outlaw buildings like beacons, a little way off. He went toward them, and as he got close, he discovered that he was coming up on the rear of the main building. He swung out around the closer end of it and headed toward the front entrance.

As Bill approached, he saw a number of Dilbian figures standing in front of the entrance steps—among them, standing a little apart, was the obese-looking figure of one who could only be the Hemnoid, Mula-*ay,* and with him two unusually tall Dilbians, one taller and thinner than the other, who should be Bone Breaker and the Hill Bluffer. Bill went up to them. As he got close, the large moon poked itself farther and farther above the mountain peak, and the silvery illumination in the fortified valley increased—so that by the time he stopped before all three of them, he was able to see their expressions clearly.

"Well, well, here he is," chuckled Mula-*ay* richly. "Did you find your little female, Pick-and-Shovel?"

"I spoke to her," replied Bill shortly. He turned toward the outlaw chief. "She suggested I could ask you whether you wouldn't let the Hill Bluffer and myself out of the gate, even if it has been closed for the night. I'd like to get back to the village before morning."

"She did?" answered Bone Breaker, with that same deceptive mildness of tone. It was impossible for Bill to tell whether the Dilbian was intending to agree or refuse to let Bill and the Bluffer leave. The Hill Bluffer chuckled—for no reason apparent to Bill. Mula-*ay* chuckled again, also.

"You mean," Mula-*ay* said, "you're going to go off and leave the little creature here, after all?"

Bill felt his ears beginning to grow hot.

"For the moment," he said, "yes. But I'll be back, if necessary."

"There you are!" said the Hill Bluffer happily. "Didn't I say it? He'll be back. And I'll bring him!"

"Anytime, Pick-and-Shovel," rumbled Bone Breaker mildly. "Just so it's in the daytime."

"Of course I'll come in the daytime," he said. "I wouldn't be leaving now, but after talking to—ah—Dirty Teeth, we decided—that is, I decided—to get back to the village tonight."

"And why not?" trumpeted the Bluffer, in something very like a challenging tone of voice.

"No reason at all," said Bone Breaker mildly. "Take all the

time you want. Come on, the two of you, and I'll see the gate opened and both of you let out."

The outlaw chief headed off toward the end of the valley where the wall and the gates were. The Hill Bluffer absently started after him, and Bill was forced to run in an undignified fashion after the Dilbian postman and jerked at the belt of his harness in order to alert the Bluffer to the fact that Bill could not keep up with his strides.

"Oh?—sorry, Pick-and-Shovel," chuckled the Bluffer, as if his attention had wandered. He paused to scoop up Bill in his two big paws and plump him down in the saddle on his back. "You kind of slipped my mind for the moment . . . are you all set, up there?"

Bill replied in the affirmative and the Hill Bluffer once more started off after the Bone Breaker.

For the first time, Bill began to realize what kind of favor the Bone Breaker was doing by letting him out after hours. Opening the gate was far from a simple procedure. First the guards had to find torches of resinous wood and light them. Then with the help of Bone Breaker and the Hill Bluffer they removed two heavy cross-beams from the inner side of the gates. Finally, with a great deal of heaving, puffing, and shoving, the gates were forced to rumble open, squeaking and roaring as they each traversed on a sort of millstone arrangement, with one round wooden wheel rotating upon the flat surface of another. At last, however, the gates stood open.

"Well, good night and good traveling, Bluffer. You too, Pick-and-Shovel," said Bone Breaker.

Bill and the Bluffer returned the good night, and the Bluffer headed out into the patch of outer darkness beyond the gates and the reach of the flickering torches. As that darkness swallowed them up, Bill could hear the gates once more rumbling shut on the millwheel-like arrangement behind them, and over this rode a powerful shout, which could only have come from the lungs of Bone Breaker.

"Remember, Pick-and-Shovel!" he heard. *"In the daylight!"*

"What's the matter, Pick-and-Shovel," growled the Bluffer underneath Bill. "Aren't you going to promise him?"

"Oh—" said Bill, startled. He raised up in his stirrups, turned his head, and shouted back as loudly as he could. "I promise—by daylight, Bone Breaker!"

The Bluffer chuckled. Behind them, Bill could see the outlaw chief nodding in satisfaction. Bill turned his head back toward the front, and sank down into his saddle, adjusting himself to the sway and plunge of the big body of the Hill Bluffer, striding beneath him. The lanky Dilbian postman said nothing except to chuckle once or twice to himself. Since Bill was too tired to inquire what the joke was, neither one of them said anything further, until they were once more treading the main street of Muddy Nose Village and the Residency loomed before them in the moonlight.

"All right, light down here," said the Bluffer, stopping abruptly before the Residency's front door. Bill complied.

"Are you staying here—" Bill began, but the Bluffer was ahead of him.

"I'm off down to the Village Inn, myself," the Dilbian replied. "If you want me, that's where you'll find me—from now until dawn, that is," grumbled the Hill Bluffer.

"Well—ah—I'll probably have lots of things to keep me busy early in the morning here—"

"You can say that, all right!" interrupted the Bluffer. "They say this blacksmith called Flat Fingers, here in the village, is a pretty good workman, but it's my guess you're going to have to stand over him all the time he's at it. Well, I'll stand there right beside you. We'll mosey up to his forge tomorrow morning and see what kind of promises we can get out of him."

"Flat Fingers?" echoed Bill, puzzled. "Blacksmith? What would I be wanting a blacksmith for?"

The Bluffer chuckled slyly.

"Why, to make you one of those sissy Lowlander fighting tools they call a sword—and a shield, of course! You didn't think they had things like that just lying around so you could

56

go pick one up when you needed it? You Shorties take too much for granted."

"Sword?" echoed Bill, by this time thoroughly confused. "Shield?"

"I don't blame you," said the Hill Bluffer, but chuckling again. "It'd gall me to the very bone, too, to have to fight with gadgets like that. But there's no choice." He paused, peering down at Bill in a way that was almost sly. "After all, you were the one who challenged Bone Breaker, so he's got choice of place and style—and you can bet he isn't going to tangle without his blade and buckler. Trust a Lowlander for that."

Bill stood, frozen, staring upward at the big furry shape of the Dilbian, looming over him.

"*I* challenged the Bone Breaker to a fight with swords?" he managed to get out, finally.

The Hill Bluffer released his inner glee in a sudden roar of laughter that shattered the sleeping silence of the darkened village.

"Thought you'd missed out on the chance, didn't you?" he sputtered, finally calming down. "I could have told you different as soon as we left the valley, but I thought I'd let you chew on your hard luck for a while first. Didn't I tell you you were lucky to have me? The minute I heard Bone Breaker say Dirty Teeth was staying there because she wanted to, I saw what was up. She'd got some female notion about not wanting you to tangle with Bone Breaker. That was it, right? So later on after you'd gone out to talk to her, I got Bone Breaker alone in a corner and put in a few good words."

"Good words . . . ?" echoed Bill, an uneasy suspicion beginning to form in his mind.

"You can bet I did," said the Bluffer. "I said it was a real shame you and he weren't going to be able to tangle after all—especially as you'd said you'd find it interesting, and I was sure he felt the same way. I pointed out that after all we didn't have to have a real spelled-out challenge, just as long as folks thought there'd been one. I said he could tell his

57

folks you'd said to me that it was a lucky thing Dirty Teeth didn't need rescuing, because you could have taken him with one paw tied behind your back."

Bill gulped.

"And he could say," went on the Bluffer gleefully, "that the minute he'd heard this from me he told me that he'd never believed the story about the Half-Pint-Posted and the Streamside Terror—that he didn't believe any Shorty could last two seconds with a man like him—and he didn't mind if I passed the word along to you. And I did, and you challenged him, naturally, right away, swords or anything he wanted."

"Swords . . . " said Bill dazedly.

"I know how you feel," said the Bluffer with sudden sympathy. "Kind of sickening, isn't it, when a man's still got the teeth and nails he was born with? Anyway, we can get you one made, and the duel's on. Everybody knows about it by now. That's why Bone Breaker and I arranged for him to holler after you through the gate to come back in daylight, and I nudged you to holler back you would, meaning you'd be around to tangle as soon as it was convenient, in daylight and in front of witnesses. But I agree with you about those swords. It's sure a measly way to fight."

The Hill Bluffer sighed heavily.

"Of course, maybe I shouldn't worry about it," he said brightening. "Maybe you Shorties *like* fighting with tools. You seem to use them for just about everything else. Well, grab yourself a good night's sleep—and I'll see you at dawn!"

Chapter 8

Bill awoke from a confused dream of rolling thunder, as in a heavy thunderstorm, in which Kodiak bears had risen up on their hind legs, put on armor, and begun a sort of medieval tournament which he was being compelled to join. Then he became more fully awake and realized that the thunder was the roaring of a Dilbian voice, shouting Bill's own Dilbian name of Pick-and-Shovel, and that the nightmare was no dream but merely the dream-twisted facts of his previous day on Dilbia.

He opened his eyes to the sight of one of the Residency's spare bedrooms. Scrambling out of bed, he pulled on his pants and stumbled down the hall in his bare feet to open a door and step into the reception room at the front of the Residency. Standing in the middle of the room and still shouting for him was a Dilbian. But it was not the Hill Bluffer, as Bill had automatically assumed it would be. Instead, it was the strangest-looking member of Dilbia's native race that Bill had so far encountered.

He was the widest being on two legs that Bill had ever seen, in the flesh or in any reproduction of any alien race humans had discovered. Bill had so far adjusted to the size of the Dilbians in his one day among them that he had felt prepared for anything the race might present him with. But the individual he looked at now was beyond belief.

He was a Dilbian who made Mula-*ay* look skinny. This, in spite of the fact that he must have been a good head taller than the Hemnoid. What he must weigh was beyond the

59

power of Bill's imagination to guess. Certainly, at least double the poundage of the ordinary Dilbian male. So furry and round was he, that he had a jovial, if monstrous teddy-bear look to him; but this impression was immediately diluted by the fact that, hearing Bill come through the door, the fat Dilbian whirled to face him, literally on tiptoe, like a ballet dancer, as if his enormous weight was nothing at all.

"Well, well, there you are, Pick-and-Shovel!" he beamed, chortling in a voice like the booming of some enormous kettledrum. "I had a hunch if I just stood still and yelled about for you, a bit, you'd come running sooner or later."

"Grnpf!" growled Bill, deep in his throat. He was only half awake, and he had never been one to wake up in an immediate good humor. On top of this, having been summoned from sleep, and down the long cold floor of a hallway in his bare feet, by someone who seemed to be using the same technique a human might use to call a dog or cat to him, did not improve his morning temper. "I thought you were the Bluffer!"

"The postman?" the laughter of the roly-poly Dilbian shook the rafters. "Do I look like that skinny mountain cat? No. no——" His laughter subsided, his humor fled, and his voice took on a wistful note. "No bluffing of hills for me, Pick-and-Shovel. Not these many years. It's all I can do to waddle from place to place, nowadays. You see why?"

He gazed down at his vast stomach and patted it tenderly, heaving a heavy sigh.

"I suppose you'd guess from the looks of me that I enjoyed my food, wouldn't you, Pick-and-Shovel?" he said sadly.

Bill scowled at him. Then, remembering the duty he owed as a trainee-assistant assigned to this area, he managed to check the instinctive agreement that was about to burst from his lips.

"Well, I—ah—" he began uncomfortably.

"No, no," sighed the Dilbian. "I know you what you think. And I don't blame you. People herebouts have probably told you about poor old More Jam."

60

"More Jam?" echoed Bill frowning. He had heard that name somewhere before.

"That's right. I'm the innkeeper here," said More Jam. "You've already talked to my little girl. Yes, that's exactly who I am, Sweet Thing's poor old father; a widower these last ten years—would you believe it?"

"Sorry to hear it," muttered Bill, caught between confusion and embarrassment.

"An old, worn-out widower," mourned More Jam, sitting down disconsolately on one of the room's benches that were designed for Dilbians—which, however, in spite of its design, creaked alarmingly underneath him as his weight settled upon it. He sighed heavily. "You wouldn't think it to look at me now, would you, Pick-and-Shovel? But I wasn't always the decrepit shell of a man you see before you. Once—years ago—I was the champion Lowland wrestler."

"Long ago?" echoed Bill, somewhat suspiciously. He was waking up, automatically, remembering Dilbian verbal ploys. The unkind suspicion began to kindle in his mind that More Jam was protesting his weakness and age a bit too much to be truthful. He remembered the lightness and quickness with which the rotund Dilbian had spun about on his toes as Bill entered the room. If More Jam could still move that mass of flesh he called a body with that much speed and agility, he could hardly be quite as decrepit and ancient as he claimed.

Not only that, thought Bill, watching the native now through narrowed eyes, but Bill's experiences on Dilbia so far had begun to breed in him a healthy tendency to take a large grain of salt with anything one of them claimed about himself.

"Tell me," Bill said now, becoming once more uncomfortably conscious of the iciness of the boards under his bare feet, "what did you want to see me about?"

More Jam sighed again—if possible, even more sadly than he had managed to sigh before.

"It's about that daughter of mine, Sweet Thing," he answered heavily. "The apple of my eye, and the burden of my declining years. But why don't you pull up a bench, Pick-and-Shovel, and we can go into this matter in detail?"

"Well—all right," said Bill. "But if you wait a moment or two, I'd like to get some clothes on."

"Clothes?" said More Jam, looking genuinely surprised. "Oh, those contraptions you Shorties cover yourselves up with. You and the Fatties. Never could understand that—but go ahead, don't mind me. I'll just wait here until you're ready."

"Thanks. Won't be a minute," said Bill gratefully.

He ducked back through the door and down the hall back into his bedroom, where he proceeded to get the rest of his clothing on. Now at least dressed and shod—he returned to the reception room where More Jam was waiting.

Before he had fully traversed the hall, and long before he had opened the door to the reception room, a booming of Dilbian voices informed him that More Jam was no longer alone. Even with this warning, however, he was not prepared for the sight that greeted his eyes as he stepped back into that room. Two more Dilbians had appeared. One of them was the Hill Bluffer. Another was a Dilbian with grayish-black, rather singed-looking hair on his forearms, who was fully as large as Bone Breaker. It was not, thought Bill as he stepped into the room without being noticed at all by the three natives, that any of them were larger than he might have expected. It was just that all three of them together seemed to fill the reception room well past the overcrowding point. Not only this, but the sound of their three voices, all talking at once, was deafening.

"There he is!" said the Hill Bluffer proudly, being the first to notice him. "Pick-and-Shovel, meet Flat Fingers—the blacksmith in the village here. The one I was telling you about."

"That him, hey?" boomed the blacksmith in a decidedly hoarse voice. He squinted down at Bill. "Why if I was to make him a regular blade, it'd be bigger than he was! And a shield—why if I was to make him a shield and it fell over on top of him, he'd plumb disappear!"

"You too, huh?" roared the Bluffer, making Bill's ears ring. "Didn't you ever hear about the Shorty that took the Streamside Terror? Didn't I tell you about him?"

"I heard. And you told me several times." Flat Fingers rubbed his bearlike nose thoughtfully. "Still and all, it stands to reason. I say a regulation sword and shield's too big for him. Who's the expert here, you or me? I've been shoeing horses and arming men and mending kettles for fifteen years, and what I say is, a regular blade and buckler's too big for him. And that's that!"

"All right!" shouted Bill quickly, before the Hill Bluffer could renew the argument. "I don't care what size my sword and shield are. It doesn't make any difference!"

"There!" boomed the Bluffer turning on the blacksmith. "I guess that shows you what these sissy fighting weapons of you Lowlanders are worth! Even a Shorty doesn't care what they're like, when he has to use them! I'd like to see some of you iron-carriers wander up into the mountains bare-handed some of these days and try your luck man-to-man in my district. Why, if I wasn't on official duty, more or less, with Pick-and-Shovel here—"

"Ahem!" More Jam interrupted at this point by clearing his throat delicately—delicately, that is, for a Dilbian. However, the sound effectively stopped the Bluffer and brought his eyes around toward the wide-bodied individual.

"Far be it from me to go sticking my oar into another fellow's argument," said More Jam sadly. "Particularly seeing as how I'm old and decrepit and fat, and have a weak stomach and I've long forgotten what it was like back in my wrestling days—"

"Come on now, More Jam," protested Flat Fingers. "We all know you aren't all that old and sickly."

"Nice of you to say so, Flat Fingers," quavered More Jam, "but the truth is with this weak stomach of mine, that can't hardly eat anything but a little jam and bread or something like that—though I do try to force down some regular meat and other things just to keep myself alive—I'm lucky if I can leave the house. But it's true—" He looked sidelong at the Hill Bluffer, "that once I'd have taken on any mountain man, bare-handed."

"No one's putting *you* down, More Jam," rumbled the Hill Bluffer. "*You* never used to tangle with a lot of sharpened iron about you!"

"True, true," sighed More Jam. "And true it is, that our younger generation has kind of gotten away from the old way of doing things. Just like it's true that I never had anything in the way of a weapon about me—that time I happened to be up in the mountains and ran into One Man."

He pronounced this name with a peculiar emphasis, and Bill saw both the blacksmith and the Hill Bluffer stiffen to attention. The Hill Bluffer stared at him.

"*You* tangled with One Man?" the Bluffer said, almost in a tone of awe. "Why, nobody ever went up against One Man alone. Nobody!" He glanced aside at Bill. "There never has been anybody like One Man, Pick-and-Shovel," he explained. "He's a mountain man like myself, and he's called One Man because in spite of being an orphan, with no kin to help, he once held feud with a whole clan, just by himself—and won!"

The Hill Bluffer turned back to More Jam almost accusingly.

"You *never* tangled with One Man!" he repeated.

More Jam sighed regretfully.

"No, as a matter of fact, I never did, the way things worked out," he rumbled thoughtfully. "I'd heard of him, up there in the mountains, of course. Just as he'd heard of me, down here in the Lowlands. Then one time we just happened to run into each other in the foothills back a ways from here, and we got a look at each other for the first time."

More Jam paused, to sigh again. Flat Fingers and the Hill Bluffer were staring at him.

"Well, go on More Jam!" boomed Flat Fingers, after a moment of stillness. "You met him you say—and you didn't tangle?"

"Well, no, as it happened. We didn't," said More Jam; and his eyes swung about to catch and hold the eyes of Bill with a particular intensity. "It's quite a little story—and as a matter of fact, that's what brought me up here this morning to talk to Pick-and-Shovel. I got to remembering that story, and it began preying on my mind—the strange things that could happen to keep a couple of bucks from tangling, in spite of all their being primed and hardly able to wait to do it!"

Chapter 9

"You mean—?" the Bluffer stared down at More Jam. "In spite of both of you being in the same place and eager to go, something happened to keep the fight from coming off?"

"Well, yes. In fact a couple of things happened . . ." said More Jam, rubbing his nose thoughtfully. "The place One Man and I happened to run into each other was a place called Shale River Ford—"

"I know it. Good day's walk from here," said the Bluffer promptly.

"Yes, I guess you would know it, Postman," said More Jam. "Well, there was a sort of celebration of some kind going on when we both landed there at the same time—I forget what it was. But the minute the folk there saw One Man and I had run into each other, at last, they asked us to put off our little bout until the next day. So they could get word out to all their friends and kin to come watch. Well, now, we couldn't be so impolite as to say no—but what am I thinking about?"

More Jam broke off suddenly in mid-sentence, his gaze returning to Flat Fingers and the Bluffer.

"Here I am yarning away like the old dodder-head I am," said More Jam, "never thinking you two men must have come over here to talk some kind of important business with Pick-and-Shovel. Well, I won't hold you up a moment longer. You go right ahead with your business and I'll hold my story for another day."

"No business. That is, nothing that can't wait," broke in the blacksmith hastily. "Go on with the story. I never heard it before."

"Well, maybe I've got a duty to let everyone know about what happened, at that," said More Jam thoughtfully. "Though, as I say, I just wandered down here to tell it to Pick-and-Shovel, and actually it's more for him than for telling back up in the mountains anyway. I was just saying . . . where was I?"

"The Shale River Forders had asked you and One Man to hold off the fight until the next day," prompted the Hill Bluffer.

"Oh, yes . . . well, as I said earlier, it was really a couple of things that happened to keep us from tangling." More Jam's eyes drifted around to hold Bill's strangely once more. "One to each of us, you might say. You see, as long as we had to wait until the next day, there was no reason we shouldn't have a party the night before. So the Shale River Ford people got a rousing time going. Well, after a bit, One Man and I went for a walk outside, so we could have a chance to hear each other talk. You know how it is when you meet somebody in the same line of business, so to speak . . ."

More Jam glanced at Flat Fingers and the Hill Bluffer. The blacksmith and postman nodded with the seriousness of dedicated professionals, each in their own lines of business.

"Happened, we had quite a talk," continued More Jam. "I might say we even got to know each other pretty well. We finally split up and headed for a good night's rest, each of us looking forward to the fight the next morning, of course."

"Of course," rumbled Flat Fingers.

"But then it happened," said More Jam. He gazed sadly at the Bluffer and at Flat Fingers, and then, unaccountably, his eyes wandered slowly back again to meet the eyes of Bill.

"It?" demanded the Bluffer.

"Would you believe it," demanded More Jam, staring at Bill, "after I'd left One Man—it was a pitch-black night out, of course—on the way back to the Inn, I bumped into someone who told me that my maternal grandmother had just died back down here at Muddy Nose?"

"Your grandmother?" began Flat Fingers, wrinkling his nose in puzzlement. "But I thought—"

"Well, of course," went on More Jam smoothly, ignoring the blacksmith and keeping his gaze on Bill, "no ordinary person would ever have thought of trying to get from where I was all the way back to Muddy Nose to pay my last respects to my grandmother, and still make the trip back again in time for the fight the next day. No ordinary person, as I say. But in those days I was in pretty good shape, what with one thing and another. And I didn't hesitate for a minute. I just took off."

"But your grandmother—" Flat Fingers was attempting again, when More Jam smoothly interrupted him once more.

"—Wasn't dead at all as it turned out, of course," said More Jam, his eyes still fixed on Bill's. "As folks around here know, she lived to be a hundred and ten. It was just some kind of a rumor that this stranger had picked up and passed on. And of course, it was so dark out when he told me that I didn't know what he looked like. So I was never able to find him again."

"Good thing for him I bet!" muttered Flat Fingers. "So you went all the way home and didn't get back in time for the fight? Was that it, More Jam?"

"Not exactly," said More Jam. "As I say, I was in pretty good shape in those days. I turned right around when I found out the truth, and headed back toward the foothills. And I made it back, too. I got back to Shale River Ford just as dawn was breaking. But you know, when I hit the door of the Inn, I sort of collapsed. I just fell down and passed out. It was plain for one and all to see that after a round trip like that, I was in no condition to fight."

"True enough," said the Hill Bluffer, with an expert traveler's judiciousness.

"So that's why you didn't fight One Man?" interposed Flat Fingers.

"Well . . . yes, and no," said More Jam mildly. "You see a funny thing had happened to him, too—I found out after I woke up. Just as One Man was heading back to the Inn, himself, the night before, after talking to me—I told you how dark it was out—"

"You told us," put in Flat Fingers.

"Well, dark out as it was," said More Jam, "One Man didn't see this hole in the ground. And he stepped right into it and twisted his ankle. Broke it, I think, although it was kind of hard to tell; his legs were so muscley. Of course," added More Jam, deprecatingly, with a glance at Flat Fingers and the Bluffer, "nobody was about to call One Man a liar if he said he thought his ankle was broken."

"Ha!" snorted the Bluffer. "That's right enough!"

"And, of course," added More Jam mildly, "nobody would think of doubting *my* word that I'd actually had somebody come up to me in the dark who I couldn't see, and tell me a false rumor about my grandmother being dead."

"I'd like to see them try it!" growled Flat Fingers. "That'd be something to see!"

"So. one way and another," wound up More Jam, his gaze returning to Bill, "neither One Man nor I was fit to have that fight after all. And the way it worked out, we never did meet again. Though I hear he's still alive, up there in the mountains."

"He sure is," said the Hill Bluffer. "Says he's all worn out now and decrepit! Him—decrepit!" The Bluffer snorted again, disbelievingly.

"You shouldn't jump to conclusions though, Postman," put

in More Jam, almost primly. "You young men in the prime of life, you don't know what it's like when your bones start creaking and groaning. Why, some people might even look at me and think I might have as much of a shadow of my own old strength left. But I tell you, if it wasn't for my daughter's cooking—and my stomach's so delicate nowdays I can't handle anything else—I'd have been dead long ago. You may not believe One Man's being cut down by age, but an old hulk like me knows better."

The Bluffer muttered something, but not loudly enough, or in a tone disbelieving enough, to emerge as obvious challenge to the innkeeper's statement.

"But there you have it, Pick-and-Shovel," said More Jam sadly, turning back to Bill. "That story of mine, of how I had my chance at One Man and then missed out on it—through no fault of my own—has been preying on my mind for a couple of days, now. I just figured I had to step up here and tell you about it, so it could be a caution to you. I know you can't hardly wait to get at Bone Breaker, just like I couldn't hardly wait to get at One Man, and vice-versa. But things you wouldn't believe can crop up to interfere with the most promising tangle in the world."

He sighed heavily, apparently remembering Shale River Ford.

"So I just wanted to put you on your guard," he went on. "Something just might come up that'd threaten to keep you from meeting Bone Breaker for that duel. But if it does, let me tell you, you only have to turn and call for More Jam for anything his old carcass can manage by way of help. Because it means a lot to me, your taking Bone Breaker, it really does."

"It does?" said Bill puzzled. "Why to you, in particular?"

"Why, because of this delicate stomach of mine," said More Jam, patting the stomach in question tenderly. "Oh, I know some folks in Muddy Nose think I'm going against tradition, when I back up my little daughter in refusing to let herself be taken off to Outlaw Valley to live. But if Bone

Breaker takes her away, who's going to cook for poor old More Jam? I can't move out there with her and turn outlaw at my time of life—even if my old bones would stand the hardships. On the other hand, if he'd do like she wants and settle down here in Muddy Nose, I know I'd always have a bench at their table. Or maybe he'd even want to go into the inn business with me. So, as I say, if you ever find yourself in a position where you have to think about not tangling with Bone Breaker—for his sake, of course—just stop and think instead about More Jam, and see if it doesn't help!"

He closed his eyes, patted his mountainous stomach again, very tenderly, and fell silent. Bill stared at him, baffled.

"All right, Pick-and-Shovel!" said the blacksmith's voice.

Bill turned to find Flat Fingers stooping over him with a leather cord in his two, huge furry hands.

"Hold your arm out, there," rumbled the big Dilbian, "and I'll get you measured for your little blade and buckler—though much good they're likely to be to you—"

Bill's mind had been whirling ever since More Jam had finished talking. What it was spinning about, mostly, was the strange glances the rotund Dilbian had kept shooting at him while telling the story about his own near-fight with the mountain champion, One Man. Clearly, More Jam had been trying to convey some sort of message. But what was it? Bill tried to make some kind of connection between the story of the near-duel and what Anita Lyme had said to him the evening before. Maybe there was more to this business of organizing the villagers to defy the outlaws than he had thought. On the other hand, clearly More Jam was offering to be an ally of some sort. Anita had suggested that he get the blacksmith on his side. But just how was he supposed to do that? Flat Fingers obviously had a pretty low opinion of Shorties, physically at least. The blacksmith was not likely to accept as a leader someone with whom he was not impressed, and how could Bill impress him—particularly, physically? Offhand, he could think of nothing in which he could even begin to put up a showing against one of the huge, male

Dilbians. He certainly could not outrun them, nor outjump them, nor—.

Bill's mind broke off in mid-thought. A bit of information about the level of Dilbian science and technology from the hypnoed information had just sat up and clamored for attention in the back of his head. Dilbians, he remembered suddenly, had never heard of a block-and-tackle. He turned to the blacksmith, and taking advantage of a split-second pause in the argument between that individual and the Bluffer, he threw in a few words of his own.

"So you don't think much of me?" he said.

The attention of both Dilbians returned to him. The blacksmith burst into sudden, thunderous laughter.

"No offense to you either, Pick-and-Shovel," he said, still laughing. "But you really don't expect me to take you for being the equal of a real full-grown man. Now, do you?"

"Well, no," retorted Bill, drawling the words out. "I kind of hoped you'd take me for something better than a real man—one like you, for instance!"

The blacksmith stared at him. For a moment, Bill thought that he had overdone the brashness and insult, which, the hypnoed information in his head had informed him, passed for everyday manners of conversation among the Dilbians. Then the Hill Bluffer broke the silence in his turn with a booming and triumphant laugh.

"Hor, hor, hor!" bellowed the Hill Bluffer, giving the blacksmith a mighty slap between the shoulder blades. "How do you like that? I told you! I told you!—and here you were thinking he was just as meek and mild as some little kid's pet!"

The swat on the back, which would probably have broken Bill in two, plus the Hill Bluffer's words, apparently woke the blacksmith out of the stunned condition into which Bill's words had thrown him.

"You?" he said incredulously. "Better than *me*?"

"Well, we don't have to fight about it to find out," said

71

Bill, with the best show of indifference he could manage. "I suppose you think you can lift something pretty heavy?"

"Me? Lift?" Flat Fingers' hoarse voice almost stuck in his throat under the combination of his astonishment and outrage. "Why I could lift twenty times what you could lift, Shorty!"

"I don't think so," said Bill calmly.

"Why, you—" stuttered the blacksmith, balling a huge furry fist ominously. The Hill Bluffer shouldered between him and Bill. "You actually want to try—" words failed Flat Fingers. He tried again. "You want to try to outlift me?"

Bill had a sudden inspiration—born of the fact of the Dilbians being strict about the letter of the law, while playing free and loose with the spirit of it.

"Well, of course," said Bill in a deprecating voice, and borrowing a page from More Jam's technique, "I'm just a Shorty, and I'd never have the nerve to suggest that I might be able to *outlift* you ordinarily. But I just might be able to *outdo* you at it if I had to, and I'm ready to prove it by moving something you can't move!"

Flat Fingers stared at him again.

"Why, he's sick!" said the blacksmith in a hushed voice, at last turning to the Hill Bluffer. "The poor little feller's gone completely out of his head!"

"Think so, do you?" said the Hill Bluffer smugly. "Suppose we all just go up to that forge of yours, get something heavy, and find out!"

"Uh—not right away," said Bill hastily. "I've got a few things to do around here, first. How about just after lunch?"

"Suits me . . ." said the blacksmith, shaking his head and still looking at Bill peculiarly, as if Bill had come down with some strange disease. "After lunch will do fine, Pick-and-Shovel. Just wander up to the forge, and you'll find me there. Now, hold out your arm."

Shaking his head, he proceeded to measure Bill, making knots in the cord to mark the various lengths he took. Then,

72

without a further word, he turned toward the door and went out.

"Don't worry about a thing, Pick-and-Shovel!" said the Hill Bluffer reassuringly, as he turned to follow the black-smith. "I'm out to spread the word, myself. I'll see that the whole village is there to watch; as well as everybody else who's close enough to get here by midday."

He, in his turn, went out. The door crashed shut behind him and Bill found himself left alone with More Jam, who seemed to have fallen asleep on his bench. He turned swiftly and went back through the inner door to the rear rooms of the Residency.

He wasted no time—for the moment, even on the matter of his upcoming weight-lifting contest with the blacksmith. Instead, he went directly to the communications room and bent to work removing the console panel. Once it was off, he started the process of checking the components of the equipment, one by one.

Dismantling and checking took time. Bill began to perspire gently as that time crawled by, and unit after unit that he examined had its small quartz window intact. The perspiration did not cease when he finally reached the end of his checking without finding any unit out of order.

It was impossible—but there was only one other place to look.

As rapidly as possible, he reassembled the equipment units and replaced the console panel. Then he started to trace the power cable leading from the wall beside the console.

His search led him out and down the corridor until at last he stepped into a large room in the rear of the Residency, packed with storage cases. The cables there led to a so-called lifetime battery set. It was simply not possible that one such battery set could fail, or have its stored power exhausted in the ordinary lifetime of a project like this one at Muddy Nose—and Bill's hypnoed information told him that this project was less than three years old. But when he came close to the battery set, he saw why the communications equipment was not working.

The power cable leading to the communications equipment had been disengaged from its battery set terminals.

It had not been wrenched or broken off. Someone had used a power wrench to unscrew the heavy connection clamps.

—And no Dilbian would know how to operate a power wrench, even if he or she recognized the purpose for which the tool had been designed.

Hastily, Bill found a power wrench among a rack of tools in one corner of the storage room which seemed to have been fitted up as a workshop area. There were not only hand tools there, but a hand-laser welding torch and a programed, all-purpose lathe. With the wrench, he reconnected the power cable and ran back to the Communications Room. This time, when he sat down before the control console and keyed it into action, the ready light glowed amber on the panel in front of him. A second later, a computer's mechanical voice, somewhat blurred by static, spoke to him from the overhead grill of the speaker.

"Station MRK-3. Station MRK-3 . . ." said the voice. "This is Overseer Unit Station 49. Repeat, this is Overseer Unit Station 49. I am receiving your signal, Station MRK-3. I am receiving your signal. Is this the Resident at Muddy Nose Village, Dilbia?"

"Overseer Unit Station 49, this is Station MRK-3," replied Bill, speaking into the microphone grill of the console before him. "This is the Residency at Muddy Nose Village, Dilbia. But I am not the Resident. Repeat, not the Resident. I am trainee-assistant William Waltham, just arrived at this Residency yesterday. The only other Trainee-Assistant here is unavailable, and I understand the Resident has been taken off-planet for medical attention for a broken leg. Can you locate him, please? I would like to talk to him over this relay. If he cannot be located will you connect me with my next available superior? Will you connect me with the Resident or my next available superior officer? Over to you, Overseer Unit Station 49."

"This is Overseer Unit Station 49. This is Overseer Unit Station 49. Your message received, Station MRK-3, Trainee-Assistant William Waltham. We can relay your communication only to Hospital Spaceship Paar. Repeat, communication from your transmitting point can be relayed only to Spaceship Paar. Please hold. Repeat, please hold. We are relaying your call to Hospital Spaceship Paar."

Overhead, the voice ceased. Bill settled back to wait.

"Station MRK-3, Muddy Nose Village, Dilbia, Trainee-Assistant William Waltham, this is Hospital Spaceship Paar, Information Center, accepting your call on behalf of Patient Lafe Greentree. This is Hospital Spaceship Paar—" It repeated the statement several times. Then it continued. "Are you there, William Waltham at Station MRK-3?"

"This is Trainee-Assistant William Waltham at Station MRK-3," replied Bill. "Receiving you clearly, Hospital Spaceship Paar, Information Center. Please go on."

"This is Hospital Spaceship Paar Information Center Computer Unit, answering for Patient Lafe Greentree."

"May I speak to Mr. Greentree, please?" asked Bill.

There was a slightly longer than usual time lag, before the Computer Unit answered again. "Patient Greentree," it announced, "is not able to communicate at the moment. Repeat, the patient is not able to communicate. You may speak with the Computer Unit which now addresses you."

"But I have to speak with him," protested Bill. "If I can't speak with him, will you relay my call to my next nearest superior?"

"Patient Greentree is unable to speak," replied the voice after the usual pause. "I have no authority to relay your call to anyone else. You may speak with the Computer Unit now addressing you."

"Computer Unit! Listen!" said Bill desperately. "Listen to me. This is an emergency. *Emergency! Mayday! Emergency!* Please bypass normal programing, and connect me at once

75

with my nearest superior. If you cannot connect me with my nearest superior, please connect me with any other human aboard the Hospital Spaceship! I repeat, this is an emergency. Bypass your usual programing!"

Again, there was a longer than usual pause. Then the Computer Unit's voice replied once more.

"Negative. I regret, but the response must be negative. This is a military ship. I cannot bypass programing without instructions from proper authority. You show no such authority. I cannot, therefore, bypass programing. I cannot let you speak to Patient Greentree. If you wish, I can give you the latest bulletin on Patient Greentree's condition. That is all."

Bill stared, tight-jawed, at the communications equipment. Like any other trainee-assistant he had been taught to operate such sub-time communicators. But of course he had not yet been informed on local code calls and bypass authorization procedures. That information would have to come to him in the normal course from the Resident himself. He was exactly in the position of a man who picks up a phone and finds himself connected with an automatic answering service, stubbornly repeating its recorded message over and over again.

"All right," he said, finally, defeated. "Tell me how Resident Greentree is, and how soon he'll be coming back to his duty post, here."

He waited.

"Patient Greentree's condition is stated as good," said the machine. "The period of his hospitalization remains indefinite. I have no information on when he will be returning to his post. That is the extent of the information I can give you about this patient."

"Acknowledged," said Bill grimly. "Ceasing communication."

"Ceasing communication with you, Station MRK-3," said the speaker.

It fell silent.

Numbly and automatically, Bill reached out to shut off the power to the equipment. After it was shut off, he sat where he was, staring at the unlighted console. The suspicion which had first stirred in him yesterday when he had arrived to find a deserted Residency was now confirmed and grown into a practical certainty.

Something was crooked in the state of affairs on Dilbia, particularly within the general vicinity of Muddy Nose Village; and no more evidence was needed to make it clear that he was the man on the spot, in more ways than one. If he had only had time to check the communications equipment out thoroughly on his arrival, he would never have left the Residency without discovering that crookedness before he got himself irretrievably involved in local affairs.

The power cable, detached by either Hemnold or human hands, had kept him in ignorance of his actual isolation here just long enough for him to get himself into trouble. As it stood now, he was cut off from outside human aid, cut off even from his immediate superior, Greentree, and faced not only with a captive co-worker, plus a highly trained and experienced enemy agent, but the prospect of a duel which meant death as certainly as stepping off the top of one of the vertical cliffs walling in Outlaw Valley.

One thing was certain. Whatever other aims there might be in the mind or minds of those who had planned this situation for him, one thing was certain. His own death or destruction was part of the general plan. It would ruin any scheme if he was left alive to testify to what had happened to him. Possibly Anita's death was scheduled, too, for the same reason.

He was faced with essentially certain death, in a situation involving aliens with which he was unfamiliar, on a world for which he had not been trained; and he was left to his own devices. From here on out, he must save himself as best he could, and with no help from off-planet.

—Which just about threw out all the rules.

Chapter 10

Bill did not sit for long, thinking in front of the console. A glance at his watch woke him to the fact that he had less than four hours until the noon meal, and it was right after that meal that he had promised to outdo the village blacksmith. It was high time he was getting busy. He got up from his chair before the power console panel of the communications equipment, and went out of the room. He headed toward the storeroom containing the battery set at the back of the Residency, where he hoped he would find what he needed.

Bill had very little trouble finding what he looked for first. He discovered a coil of quarter-inch rope among the farming tools, and measured out and cut off forty feet of it. Then he started to look for a second item—an item he was pretty sure he would not find.

Indeed, he did not. What he was looking for was nothing less than a ready-made block-and-tackle. But after some forty minutes had gone by without his finding one, he realized he could spend no more time looking for it. He would have to make his own block-and-tackle.

This was not as difficult as it might have seemed to someone with both a theoretical and practical knowledge of such a simple machine. Earlier, as he had stepped into the dim storeroom with its warehouselike smells of plastic wrappings and paper boxes, he had identified a self-programing lathe over against the wall in the one corner that seemed to be a general work area, fitted out with several machines and a multitude of tools racked and hung about the walls.

Now he hunted for some metal stock, but was not able to find what he wanted. He would have to use something else. The outer walls of the Residency, like the walls of most Dilbian buildings, were made of heavy logs. Detaching a power saw from the tool rack on the work-area wall, Bill took it over to a doorway in the back wall of the building. Opening the door, he used the power saw to cut off a four-foot section of one of the logs that ended against the frame of the doorway.

Bill took the log back to the lathe and cut it up into four sections, approximately one foot in length and a foot in diameter. Then he put the sections aside, and turned on the programing screen of the lathe. Picking up the stylus he began to sketch on the screen the pulley-wheel sections that he wanted to construct.

The parts took shape with approximate accuracy in three dimensions, and the programing section of the lathe took it from there. Eventually a red light lit up below the screen, revealing the black letters of the word "*ready.*" Bill pressed the replay button, and before him on the screen there appeared completed and corrected, three-dimensional blueprints of the components for a block-and-tackle.

The lathe was now prepared to go to work. Bill fed his log sections to it, one by one, and ended up fifteen minutes later with twelve lathe-turned, wooden parts which he proceeded to join into two separate units by wood-weld processing. The first unit consisted of two double pulleys welded together, or four movable pulleys. This was the fixed block and had a brake and lock as well as a heavy wooden hook welded to the top of it. The other unit was the movable block which contained three pulleys. The two units, combined with the rope, together should give Bill a block-and-tackle with a lifting power of seven times whatever pull he could put upon the fall rope. Flat Fingers, being a little bigger than most Dilbians, outweighed Bill by—Bill calculated—about five to one. In other words, the village blacksmith could probably lift about his own body weight of nine hundred pounds. However, the block-and-tackle Bill had constructed gave him a seven-times advantage. Therefore, if he could put upon the rope he would be holding a pull equal to *his* own human body weight of a hundred and sixty-five pounds, he should be able to lift well over a half-ton. Bill looked at what he had constructed, feeling satisfied.

He looked at his wristwatch. The hands, recalibrated to Dilbian time, stood at about half an hour short of noon. He was reminded, suddenly, that he had had no breakfast, and no evening meal the day before except for the Dilbian fare he had choked down in Outlaw Valley. He remembered seeing a well-stocked kitchen in his earlier exploration of the Residency. He turned away from the block-and-tackle, leaving it where it was on the workbench, and opened the doorway to the hallway leading back to the living quarters of the building. The hallway was dim, but as he stepped into it he thought he saw a flicker of movement from behind the door as it opened before him.

But that was all he saw. For a second later a smashing blow on the back of his head sent him tumbling down and away into spark-shot darkness.

When he opened his eyes again, it was at first with the confused impression that he was still asleep in his bed at the Residency. Then he became conscious of a headache that gradually increased in intensity until it seemed to fit his head like a skullcap, and, following this, he was made aware of a sickly taste in his nose and mouth, as if he had been inhaling some sort of anesthetic gas.

Cautiously he opened his eyes. He found himself seated in a small woodland clearing, by the banks of a stream about fifteen or twenty feet wide. The dell was completely walled about by underbrush, beyond which could be seen the trunks and the trees of the forest.

He blinked. For before him, seated crosslegged like an enormous Buddha on the ground with his robe spread around him, was Mula-*ay*. Seeing himself recognized, the Hemnoid produced one of his rich, gurgling chuckles.

"Welcome back to the land of the living, ah—Pick-and-Shovel," said Mula-*ay* cheerfully. "I was beginning to wonder if you were ever going to come to."

"What do you mean, knocking me on the head and bringing me here—" Bill was beginning, when the thunder of his own voice and the working of his own jaw muscles so jarred his skullcap of headache pain that he was forced to stop.

"I?" replied Mula-*ay*, in a tone of mild, if unctuous surprise, folding his hands comfortably upon his cloth-swathed belly. "How can you suspect me of such a thing? I give you my word I was simply out for a stroll through these woods, and noticed you tied up here."

"Tied up—?" began Bill, too jolted by the words to pay attention to the stab of pain that the effort of speaking sent through his skull, from back to front. He became aware that his hands were pulled around behind him, and a moment's experimentation revealed that his wrists were tied together on the opposite side of the narrow tree trunk that was serving him for a backrest.

"You can't get away with this sort of thing!" he stormed at Mula-*ay*. "You know no Dilbian would do something like this. You're breaking the Human-Hemnoid treaty on Dilbia. Your own superiors will have your hide for this!"

"Come now, my young friend," chuckled Mula-*ay*. "As I say—my superiors are reasonable individuals. And where are the witnesses who can call me a liar? I was merely wandering through the woods and happened to see you here, and sat down to wait for you to wake up."

"If that's true," said Bill, his headache by this time completely disregarded, "how about untying my hands and turning me loose?"

"Well, now, I don't know if I could do anything like that!" said Mula-*ay* thoughtfully. "That might be interference in native affairs—expressly forbidden, as you yourself point out, by the Hemnoid-Human agreements. For all I know you've been caught in the act of committing some crime, and the local inhabitants have tied you up here, until you can be taken back to face their native justice." He shook his head. "No, no, my dear Pick-and-Shovel. I couldn't take it on myself to untie you—much, of course, as I'd like to."

"You can't get away with claiming something like that!" exploded Bill. "You—" He became aware abruptly of a sheer look of enjoyment on the round face opposite him, and checked himself with sudden understanding. He was rewarded by seeing a slight shade of disappointment overshadow the smile with which Mula-*ay* had been regarding him up until now.

"All right," said Bill, as coolly as he could. "You've had your fun. Now suppose you tell me what this is all about. I suppose you want to make some kind of deal with me, and your idea in kidnapping me and tying me up here is to start me out at a disadvantage. Is that right?"

Mula-*ay* chuckled again and rubbed his large hands together.

"Very good," he said. "Oh, very, *very* good, young Pick-and-Shovel! If you'd only had a little more training and experience, you might have made quite a decent undercover agent—for a human, that is. Of course, that was the last thing your superiors wanted, in this case—someone with training and experience. Oh, the last thing!"

He chuckled once more.

"Cut it out!" said Bill in a level voice. "I told you, you've had all the enjoyment out of me you are going to have. Quit hinting and come right out with whatever it is you've got to say. I'm not going to squirm just to please you."

Mula-*ay* shook his head, and his smile evaporated.

"You really *are* uninformed, aren't you, Pick-and-Shovel?" he said seriously. "Your knowledge of my race is only that kind of half-rumor that circulates among humans who have never done anything but listen to tall tales about Hemnoids. Do you seriously think that my business here on Dilbia would allow me to engage in that special and demanding art form among my people which you humans consider to be merely the exercise of a taste for deliberate cruelty? To be sure, I'm mildly pleased by your responses when they verge on *sana*, as our great art is known among us. But any serious consideration of such is impossible in this time and place."

"Oh, is that a fact?" said Bill ironically.

"Indeed," said Mula-*ay*, in a tone of great seriousness, "it *is* so. Let me try to draw you a parallel out of your own human experience. You humans have a response called *empathy*—the emotional ability to put yourself in another's skin and echo in your own feelings what that other is feeling. As you know empathy, we Hemnoids do not have it. But our *sana* is a comparable response, among us, even though you humans would consider it quite the opposite. *Sana,* like empathy, is a response that puts two individuals into a special relationship with one another. Like your empathy, it requires a powerful involvement on the part of the individual engaging in it."

"Only you don't happen to feel like engaging in it right now, I suppose?"

"Your skepticism," said Mula-*ay* steadily, "shows a closed mind. You humans do not empathize lightly, and neither do we engage in *sana* easily or casually. I would no more consider you a subject of *sana* on the basis of our casual acquaintance here, than you would be likely to empathize with—say—Bone Breaker, or any of the Dilbians, on the slight basis of the acquaintanceship you have had with them so far."

Bill stared at the Hemnoid. Mula-*ay* was apparently being as frank and honest as it was possible for him to be, in his own terms. And the Hemnoid's argument was convincing. Only, just at that moment, something inside Bill suddenly clamored like an alarm bell in denial of something Mula-*ay* had just said.

"So—you understand," Mula-*ay* was going on, "and you can put your own interior human fears to rest on that subject. Just as," Mula-*ay* chuckled again briefly, "you can abandon the idea that I brought you here to make some kind of deal with you. My dear young human, you are not one of those with whom deals are made. You are only a pawn in the game here on Dilbia—an unconscious pawn, at that."

He stopped speaking and sat beaming at Bill.

"I see," said Bill, while the back of his mind was still busily digging, trying to identify the note of misstatement he had sensed in Mula-*ay*'s earlier explanation. Suddenly he wanted very much to hear more from the Hemnoid. "I'm supposed to ask you why I'm here, then? Well, consider I've asked it."

"Oh, but you haven't, you know," chuckled Mula-*ay*, gazing upward at the fleecy clouds spotting the blue sky above the treetops surrounding their clearing.

"All right!" said Bill. "Why did my superiors send me here—according to you?"

"Why," Mula-*ay* brought his gaze back from the clouds to Bill's face, "to get you killed by Bone Breaker in a duel, of course!"

Bill stared at him. But Mula-*ay* did not seem ready to offer any more conversation without prompting.

"Oh, sure!" said Bill at last. "Do you think I'll believe that?"

"Eventually. Eventually, you will . . ." murmured Mula-*ay*, still watching Bill's face. "Once you let the idea sink in and consider the fact that you are alone here, with no communication off-planet to your superiors. Yes, I know about that. And committed to the duel I mentioned. Don't you think it strangely coincidental that the Resident should be off-planet with a broken leg just when you get here, and that your young female associate should be an involuntary house-guest, so to speak, in Outlaw Valley? Don't you think it strange that you should be placed in the almost identical position of that earlier young human whom the Dilbians called the Half-Pint-Posted, who had a hand-to-hand battle with a native champion in another locality? Come, come now, Pick-and-Shovel; surely your intelligence is too adequate to blink those facts away!"

In fact ... in spite of himself a distinctly cold feeling was forming somewhere under Bill's breastbone. The facts were overwhelming—and they were the very facts he had been facing as he had sat in front of the communications console earlier this day. It was unbelievable that there could exist an official human conspiracy to get Bill himself killed. But nonetheless the facts were there and ...

"Why?" said Bill, as if to himself. "What reason could they have? It doesn't make sense!"

"Oh, but it does, Pick-and-Shovel," said Mula-*ay*. "The situation here between Resident Greentree and myself has become—how shall I put it—stalemated." Mula-*ay* chuckled again, softly, as he used the very word Anita had used to Bill the night before. "There's no further gain to be gotten from this Muddy Nose Project for you humans. The local farmers won't accept your help, and the outlaws under Bone Breaker are only enjoying the situation—with my modest help."

He beamed at Bill.

"The best thing for your superiors, in fact," he went on, "is to close this ill-planned project before it turns even more sour. But how to do that without losing face, both with the Dilbians and on an interstellar level? It would be like acknowledging we Hemnoids have won a round here at Muddy Nose. The answer, of course, is to close the project—but first to find a suitable excuse for doing so. And what would make the most suitable excuse?"

He stopped and beamed once more at Bill.

"All right," said Bill grimly. "I'll ask. What would?"

"Why, for some untrained, unfortunate youngster to join the project, and—through no fault of his own, but through a series of unlucky accidents—make an irretrievable mess of the situation with the local Dilbians. To the extent, in fact, of getting himself involved in a duel and killed by the local champion, Bone Breaker."

Mula-*ay* stopped and chuckled so heartily that his whole heavy shape shook.

"What a perfect situation that would be!" he said. "For

one thing, it would require the humans to close down the project and withdraw its personnel, temporarily—of course, it would never be started up again, nor would they return. For another, there would be no loss of face with the Dilbians; for, even though their foolish young man got himself killed, still he *did* show the combativeness necessary to tangle with Bone Breaker, and therefore the Shorties' record for personal courage on this world would not be impaired."

Bill stared at him.

"You seem pretty sure I'm bound to lose," he said although the cold feeling was back under his breastbone again. "The Half-Pint-Posted didn't."

Mula-*ay* chuckled, undisturbed.

"To be perfectly frank, Pick-and-Shovel," he said, "that is one small caper pulled off by you humans that we haven't been able to figure out, yet. But we have no doubt—and you need have no doubt either—that there was something more at work in that victory than simply one of you small creatures outgrappling a Dilbian. In fact, you hardly need the assurance of our belief. I ask you—can you picture a human who could win such a victory, without some unseen, unethical advantage?"

It was true, Bill could not. The cold feeling under his breastbone increased.

"No, no . . ." Mula-*ay* shook his head. "The very thought of a human winning any physical fair fight between himself and a Dilbian is unthinkable to the point of ridiculousness. But don't worry, little Pick-and-Shovel. I'm going to save you from your cruel and heartless superiors, as well as from Bone Breaker."

Bill stared at him.

"You . . . ?" he began, and then remembered to hide his emotions just in time.

"To be sure," said Mula-*ay*, rising softly to his feet and cocking his ear toward the noises of the forest behind him. "And here, unless I am mistaken, comes the means of that rescue, now. Reassure yourself, Bone Breaker won't kill you."

"Oh, he won't?" said Bill, speaking as coldly and unconcernedly as he could. For at that moment, he had heard what Mula-*ay* had just heard. It was the noise of heavy Dilbian feet approaching.

"No, indeed," said Mula-*ay*, "you will lose your duel and your life, instead, to the most feeble and decrepit Dilbian that the local area provides. Let your superiors try to save face, after that—following your foolish challenge of the best fighter for miles around!"

He half-turned from Bill. At that moment there burst into the clearing two female Dilbians and a scrawny, tottering male so old that his body fur was gone in patches. Of the two females with him, one was short and plump—and disturbingly familiar-looking, and the other was younger, somewhat statuesque of build, and almost tall enough to be a male.

They came to a halt, their eyes roaming the little dell, and fastened all together on Bill.

"There he is!" said the old male with a (for a Dilbian) high-pitched cackle of satisfaction. "Right where we want him!" And he rubbed his hands with glee.

"I leave you in good hands, Pick-and-Shovel," murmured Mula-*ay*. With a wink and a nod, but no words spoken, in the direction of the three Dilbians who had just arrived, he glided softly off into the surrounding brush and disappeared.

Chapter 11

"All right, Pick-and-Shovel," said the aged Dilbian male, as the three of them reached him and stopped, standing over him, "are you ready to stand trial, hey? Are you ready to submit yourself to the judgment of a Grandfather—"

A snort from the tall, young-looking female interrupted him. He turned angrily on her.

"Don't you go getting smart with me, Perfectly Delightful!" he shouted. "Got grandchildren, haven't I? I got just as good right to be a Grandfather as anyone!"

"Thank goodness," replied Perfectly Delightful, with the Dilbian equivalent of a ladylike sniff, "at least I'm not one of them!"

"Perfectly Delightful," said the older, plumper female sternly, in a voice which Bill suddenly recognized from the episode in Tin Ear's farmyard, "you leave Grandpa Squeaky alone! He's here to do a job, that's all. If you keep bothering him, he'll never be able to do it!"

Grandpa Squeaky burst into sneering laughter.

"That's right, Thing-or-Two!" he cackled. "Tell the young biddy a thing or two! Go ahead! Thinks she's so good-looking she can get away with murder! Well, it may work with the young squirts, but it doesn't work with old Grandpa Squeaky. And judging by the way things have been going, it hasn't worked too well with Bone Breaker, either! The last I heard," he added in a jeering tone, "he was still hankering after Sweet Thing!"

"Is that so!" cried Perfectly Delightful, on a rising note, furiously turning upon the aged male, who slipped behind the stout body of Thing-or-Two with prudent alacrity. "Some people," spat out Perfectly Delightful, "will say anything! And some other people will repeat it! But that doesn't change things. It's *me* Bone Breaker's always liked best."

She lifted her head and craned her neck, looking down rather complacently at herself. "After all," she went on in a calmer tone, "I *am* Perfectly Delightful. Everyone's always said so. Is it sensible that a tall, powerful man like Bone Breaker would want some little chunky creature like Sweet Thing? Oh, she can *cook* all right. I don't deny that. I believe in giving everyone their due. But there's more to life than eating, you know."

"Never mind that now, Perfectly Delightful!" snapped the

older female. "We aren't here to talk about Bone Breaker. We're here to settle this Shorty's hash. Bear in mind, both of you, if you please, that it's the ancient and honorable customs of our village that's at stake here. We're not going to keep this Shorty from helping Sweet Thing get Bone Breaker, just to please *you*, Perfectly Delightful!"

"Hey, never mind that!" broke in Grandpa Squeaky, jittering with what appeared to be eagerness. "Let me at him, hey? I'll judge him! I'll rule on what's to be done with him!"

Grandpa Squeaky approached Bill and bent down until his breath fanned the hair on Bill's forehead. Bill held his breath— for Grandpa Squeaky, it seemed, had a rather bad case of halitosis.

"Hey, you Shorty! Pick-and-Shovel!" demanded Grandpa Squeaky.

"What is it?" demanded Bill, turning his face away. To his relief, the aged Dilbian stood upright, removing both his face and his breath to a bearable distance.

"Answers to his name, all right," commented Grandpa Squeaky to the two females. "That takes care of the part about who he is."

"Why don't we find a rock and hit him on the head?" queried Perfectly Delightful, in a pleasant tone of voice.

"Go on, I say!" insisted Thing-or-Two to Grandpa Squeaky. Grandpa Squeaky swallowed, and obeyed.

"Here, you, Pick-and-Shovel," he said, "you come in here, helping Dirty Teeth and the Tricky Teacher upset all our honorable old ways of living. We let you get away with that, and you think you can get away with even worse. Now, didn't you take Sweet Thing's side against a fine young buck like Bone Breaker, encouraging a young female to dispute where her husband-to-be wants her to live? Didn't you interfere, hey, in something that wasn't your concern? And besides, didn't you go and challenge our village blacksmith to a weight-lifting contest at noon today?"

"Certainly I did!" retorted Bill. "And I was just about to head for his forge—"

"Never mind about that!" interrupted Thing-or-Two. "Go on, Grandpa Squeaky."

"I'll find a rock in a minute, and then we can shut him up," put in Perfectly Delightful brightly. She was searching around among the grassy open area of the dell.

"Sure you did!" said Grandpa Squeaky. "And then you sneaked off to the woods here and hid out, so you wouldn't have to face him—I mean Flat Fingers—thereby injuring the honor of our village."

"Hey!" shouted Bill. "What do you mean, sneaked off? Can't you see my hands are tied behind me here?"

"Nonsense! Go on," said Thing-or-Two, as Grandpa Squeaky showed signs of being baffled, once more.

"But his hands—" began Grandpa Squeaky uncertainly, turning toward Thing-or-Two.

"Nonsense, I tell you!" retorted Thing-or-Two. "You can't see his hands from where you're standing, can you? So you've only got his word for it, haven't you? And you aren't going to take the word of a moral wrecker, who thinks our young women can start telling their future husbands how to come and go and where they're supposed to live after they're married? Well, are you?"

"Of course not," said Grandpa Squeaky. He straightened up, squared his shoulders, and addressed Bill once more in a rather more grand manner. "This acting Grandfather—me, that is—finds you guilty as all get out on all counts. Accordingly, he sentences you—this acting Grandfather, who's me—to have your head chopped and your body left at that Residency building for the next Shorty that comes along to take care of."

He dropped his grand manner for a more colloquial one.

"I left the axes back in the woods a-ways. I'll go get them now."

Grandpa Squeaky turned away toward the brush, just as Perfectly Delightful came up with a rock the size of a small cantaloupe.

"Knock him on the head with this," she suggested helpfully, "that way he can't dodge around—"

"No, we don't!" snapped Thing-or-Two. "Grandpa Squeaky's got to chop him, and nobody'll believe it was a fair fight if we've got a dead Shorty with a large bump on his head—"

"Wait!" shouted Bill, desperation adding volume to his voice. "Are you all crazy? You can't go killing me, just like that—"

"Why, sure we can, Pick-and-Shovel," interrupted Grandpa Squeaky, staggering back under the double load of a pair of heavy Dilbian axes, massive, with triangular heads made of gray, native iron. "It's not as if you don't have a chance. Seeing I'm just an acting Grandfather, I'm giving you a chance to fight for your life, instead of just chopping you like that. I'll take one ax and you can have the other. Here!"

He dropped one ax in front of Bill, and its handle thudded to the earth six inches from Bill's crossed legs.

"What do you mean?" cried Bill. "I told you, I'm tied up! Can't you see my hands are tied—"

"What do you mean, tied?" demanded Thing-or-Two. Looking at the older Dilbian female, Bill discovered that she had her eyes tightly shut. "I don't see any ropes on his hands. Do you, Perfectly Delightful?"

"Neither do I!" exclaimed Perfectly Delightful, shutting her own eyes. "You know what I think? I think the Shorty's scared. He's just scared—that's why he won't pick up the ax."

"All right, Pick-and-Shovel!" piped Grandpa Squeaky, doing a kind of feeble war dance, tottering around with his own ax. "What's the matter, hey? Scared of me, hey? Come on and face up to me like a man! The witnesses don't see any ropes on your hands—" Hastily, he shut his own eyes. "Neither do I! Grab your ax, if you've got the guts to face me, or I'll start to chop you anyway. This is your last chance, Pick-and-Shovel—"

At that moment, however, he was interrupted by a voice. It burst upon them all like a shout of thunder.

"WHAT ARE YOU DOING WITH MY SHORTY?"

For a second the three Dilbians facing Bill stiffened in mid-movement. Then they spun about to face in the direction from which the voice had come, and, in turning, moved enough apart so that Bill could see between them.

Breaking into the clearing through the brush at its edge was another Dilbian, a female, shorter than either Perfectly Delightful or Thing-or-Two. For a moment, he had no idea who this was, though the voice that had just shouted at them rang on his ear with accents of familiarity. He was suddenly aware, however, that he seemed to have found a friend, if not a rescuer, and that was all that was important at the moment.

Then Thing-or-Two unconsciously, if conveniently, came to his aid.

"Sweet Thing!" the older Dilbian female exploded, on an indrawn, snarling note.

"You just bet it's me!' snarled Sweet Thing in return, advancing into the clearing. She stopped some fifteen feet from the other three. She did not put her hands on her hips, but Bill got the strong impression that if this had been a Dilbian gesture, she certainly would have done so. "And here you are with my Shorty!" Her eyes scorched them all, but ended upon Grandpa Squeaky. *"You!"*

"Hey, now," protested Grandpa Squeaky, with a perceptible quaver in his voice. A quaver of tremulous old age which contrasted markedly with his energy of a moment before.

"What were you doing to Pick-and-Shovel?"

"None of your business!" snapped Thing-or-Two.

"Pick-and-Shovel!" called Sweet Thing. "What were they doing to you here?"

"They seemed to be putting me on trial—or something," shouted Bill back. He found himself wondering how he could have originally have wondered, on first seeing Sweet Thing, what made her attractive to the outlaw. Right now she was looking decidedly beautiful to him. In fact, the only individual who could have looked much more beautiful would have been Lafe Greentree, himself, with a cast on his broken leg if necessary, but with a handgun in his fist. "This Grandfather here—"

He tried to point at Grandpa Squeaky with his head, but both the pointing and the finishing of the sentence were unnecessary.

"Grandfather!" cried Sweet Thing, scorching Grandpa Squeaky with her eyes again. "*You,* a Grandfather!" She laughed scornfully. "A fine, squeaking Grandfather you'd make, with your nose in a beer cup all day long! You, a Grandfather! Wait'll I tell my father! I'll just tell More Jam that you've been pretending to be a Grandfather—"

"No!" cried Squeaky Grandpa, agonized. "Sweet Thing, you wouldn't do that to an old man? You wouldn't tell your father about a little harmless joke like this? You wouldn't—"

"You better get out of here fast, then," said Sweet Thing ominously.

"I'm going—I'm going—" Squeaky Grandpa lost no time in putting his words into action. He was across the clearing and into the brush, in a sort of tottering rush before he had finished repeating himself the second time. Sweet Thing's eye swung to the other two females. These, however, did not show the satisfactory sort of response that Grandpa Squeaky had exhibited.

"For your information, Sweet Thing," said Thing-or-Two grimly, "you can tell your father about this every day and twice on Sunday, and much it'll mean to me!"

"How much will it mean to you, though," said Sweet Thing, in a surprisingly gentle voice, "when my father tells the whole village how you've been making fun of them by putting up poor old Grandpa Squeaky to act like he's the sort they might pick for a Grandfather? Don't you think that might bother you just the least little bit?"

"Why—" Thing-or-Two broke off sharply. She hesitated. "Why, they'd never believe such a thing. Never in a lifetime!"

Nonetheless, Bill noted, a good deal of the fire had gone out of her tone of voice.

"They won't believe it?" echoed Sweet Thing in a voice filled with innocent wonder. "Not even when More Jam tells them he saw it with his own two eyes?"

"Saw it?" Thing-or-Two darted a sudden, nervous glance around her at the silent brush enclosing the dell. Her voice stiffened. "More Jam wouldn't lie to the whole village. He wouldn't do such a thing!"

"Not if I just refused to cook for him until he did?" queried Sweet Thing, in the same innocent and wondering tone. "Of course, Thing-or-Two, you're a lot older than I am and you know best. But I should think that if I really told my father I wouldn't do any more cooking for him, that he wouldn't hesitate about telling everybody what he really saw with his own two eyes here in this clearing."

Thing-or-Two stared angrily back at the younger female. But after a second, the stiffness seemed to leak out of her. She snorted angrily—but also she began to move. With her head in the air, she marched across the clearing and into the brush, and Bill heard her moving away from them. He looked back at Sweet Thing, who was now facing Perfectly Delightful, the only one of the original three conspirators left in the dell.

"You can go, too," said Sweet Thing, in a voice that suddenly had become very ugly.

"Oh, I don't know," replied Perfectly Delightful lightly. "Everybody knows what an obedient young girl I am. Naturally I had to do what my elders said—like when Thing-or-Two and Grandpa Squeaky told me to come along here."

"They aren't telling you what to do now," said Sweet Thing.

"Oh, I don't know," repeated Perfectly Delightful, gazing absently at the same white clouds drifting overhead that had earlier interested Mula-*ay*—but without failing to watch Sweet Thing at the same time out of the corners of her eyes. "They told me earlier to see that Pick-and-Shovel, here, didn't get loose and run away. They haven't told me anything to change that. They've just gone off. Maybe they're going to be back a little later. Or maybe they figured I'd stay here and guard the Shorty for them. I really don't know what else I can do," said Perfectly Delightful, helplessly withdrawing her eyes from the clouds at last and fixing them firmly on Sweet Thing, "but stay right here and see that nobody tampers with this Shorty."

As Perfectly Delightful had been talking, Sweet Thing had begun to move forward slowly. However, as she came to just beyond arm's reach of the other young Dilbian female, she began to circle to her right. So it was that Perfectly Delightful, while still speaking, began to turn so as to face Sweet Thing. Gradually, they were beginning to circle each other like a couple of wrestlers, and after Perfectly Delightful had stopped talking, they continued to circle in silence for a number of seconds.

Bill, watching in fascination with his hands tied behind the tree trunk, was made suddenly aware of the fact that he was unable to get out of the way in case trouble should erupt. It was true that Perfectly Delightful, though tall for a female, would hardly have been able to raise the crown of her head above the point of the Hill Bluffer's shoulder, and that Sweet Thing was a head and a half shorter than her opponent. Nonetheless, either one would have considerably outweighed and outmuscled any two good-sized professional human wrestlers, and they seemed to possess the same willingness as Dilbian males to get down to physical brass tacks when a question was in dispute. Added to this was the fact that the nails on their hands and feet were rather more like bear claws, and their teeth rather more like the teeth of grizzlies than those of humans. So that in sum, the situation was one that made Bill devoutly wish he was on the other side of the tree to which he was tied.

The two had been circling for some little time, shoulders hunched, heads outthrust, arms half flexed at the elbow, when Perfectly Delightful broke the tense silence with a musical laugh.

"So you think this is funny?" inquired Sweet Thing lightly, but without at all pausing in her movement, or relaxing her attitude.

"Oh this? Not necessarily," replied Perfectly Delightful merrily—but equally without pausing or relaxing. "It just crossed my mind what a stubby little thing you are, and I imagined how you must look through the Bone Breaker's eyes."

"Oh, I don't think he finds me so stubby," replied Sweet Thing conversationally. "Maybe you won't find me so stubby either." And she laughed merrily in her turn.

They continued to circle, now almost within arm's reach of each other.

"But, really," protested Perfectly Delightful. "To be stubby is bad enough, but can you imagine what you'll look like with an ear torn off, too?"

For the first time, Bill became uncomfortably aware of how much taller and heavier Perfectly Delightful was than Sweet Thing. Up until now, he had been concerned with himself mainly as an anchored spectator of what might happen. Now, suddenly, his imagination galloped ahead a little further and began to consider what should happen if Perfectly Delightful should end up the victor in any combat that should occur.

"But I plan to keep my ears, both of them," Sweet Thing was saying sweetly. "I expect to have both my ears for many years after today—pardon me, I meant to say, after you have lost your teeth. You know, I've often heard my father and other men talking about how funny a woman looks with her teeth knocked out."

"Oh, you have, have you!" retorted Perfectly Delightful shortly. Evidently, in the contest between the two to see who should lose her temper first, Perfectly Delightful was beginning to crack. "If you get close enough to my teeth to try knocking them out, you'll wish you hadn't!"

Meanwhile, in a cold sweat, Bill was struggling for the first time and seriously to see if he could not wriggle his hands loose from the rather thick rope that seemed to be tying them together. He had been tied rather tightly, but he now discovered the thickness of the rope was such in comparison with the size of his wrists that it might be possible for him to slide his right hand free. Evidently, the smallness of the human wrist compared to the Hemnoid one was something that Mula-*ay* had not taken into account. He managed to get his right hand halfway out through its bonds—but there it stuck.

Agonizedly, he looked back at the center of the dell, where the two were still circling each other and trading insults. The tempers of both were sparking now and sarcasm had given way to direct, untranslatable Dilbian epithets.

"*Snig!*" Perfectly Delightful was hissing at Sweet Thing.

"*Pilf!*" Sweet Thing was snarling back at Perfectly Delightful.

Suddenly, far off in the woods, came the sound of possible rescue, falling sweetly upon Bill's ears. It was the stentorian shout of a male Dilbian. It was more than that. It was the voice of the Hill Bluffer, shouting.

"*Pick-and-Shovel! Pick-and-Shovel—where are you?*"

"Here!" roared back Bill, with all the volume his chest and throat could muster. "Here! This way! I'm over here!"

"I hear you!" floated back the shout of the Bluffer. "Keep yelling, Pick-and-Shovel, and I'll get there in a moment! Just keep shouting!"

Bill opened his mouth to do so. But before he had the chance to make a sound, his shouting to the Bluffer had become as impossible as it was unnecessary as a source of sound to guide the postman to him.

The period of insults between Sweet Thing and Perfectly Delightful had come to an end. With a sound like that of an old-fashioned Western movie brawl between at least half-a-dozen homesteaders and as many cattlemen, Sweet Thing and Perfectly Delightful had closed in battle in the center of the clearing.

Chapter 12

Bill shrank back against his tree. There was little else he could do but make himself as small as possible and watch the action. The action, however, turned out to be wonderful to behold.

Not at first. At first, all Bill saw was a rolling tangle of furry bodies, arms and legs, glinting claws and flashing teeth, rolling this way and that on the ground—and occasionally threatening to roll in his direction. But then the whole tangle rolled over the bank of a little stream running through the clearing and splashed into the water; at which point it immediately separated into two individuals. But the battle was not ended. Sweet Thing and Perfectly Delightful wasted no time climbing out onto the bank and joining in combat again.

Only this time there was a difference. Apparently, the first time around, Sweet Thing had been too worked up to use whatever knowledge she had about fighting. Now, cooled off by her dip in the stream, she proceeded to demonstrate that she knew more than enough to compensate for the difference between her size and the size of Perfectly Delightful. Before Bill's astonished gaze, Sweet Thing proceeded to demonstrate something very like a judo chop to the lower ribs, a forearm smash to Perfectly Delightful's jaw, a knee in the stomach, and finally a shoulder throw that flipped Perfectly Delightful completely over in the air and brought her down flat with an earth-shaking thud on her back in the grass.

It was at this point that the Hill Bluffer burst out of the

surrounding bushes and accidentally ran directly into Sweet Thing.

Sweet Thing, either blinded by rage, or perhaps confusing the Bluffer with some ally of Perfectly Delightful's, threw her arms around the postman and attempted to execute the same shoulder throw with him. This time though, the results were not so satisfactory. Sweet Thing was trained and willing enough, but in the Hill Bluffer she had taken hold of an opponent even longer-limbed than Bone Breaker himself. She was in somewhat the same position, it occurred to Bill, as a five-foot woman attempting to throw down a man six and a half feet tall. The theory was excellent, but the practice ran into problems involving the weight and length of the intended victim.

Sweet Thing did manage to get one of the Bluffer's long legs off the ground and toppled him off balance. However, one of the Bluffer's equally long arms propped him off the ground, keeping him from falling even while she still had him in only a half-thrown position and a second later the postman had more or less gently pried her arms loose from their grip upon him, and was holding her by the biceps, out at the length of his own arms and facing away from him.

This should have settled matters, since Sweet Thing was no longer in a position to do any damage with teeth, nails, arms, or legs. But so intense was her fighting fury by this time that she literally ran off the ground into the air in her efforts to get loose, and the Bluffer was forced to trip her, get her down on the ground, and sit on her, pinning her arms so that she could not reach back and grab him.

Bill continued to look on, awed. Sweet Thing, no longer able to make effective use of any of her other natural weapons, had fallen back upon her tongue. She was busy telling the Bluffer what she would do to him the moment he turned her loose. It was a question that also interested Bill. It was all very well for the Bluffer to have Sweet Thing immobilized as she was at the moment. But sooner or later he would have to let her up—and what would happen then?

". . . My father . . . Bone Breaker . . . limb-from limb . . ." Sweet Thing was informing the lanky postman. Bill did not see how the Upland Dilbian could possibly get out of his present awkward situation with life and limb intact. But he was about to learn that Dilbian emotional responses were somewhat adaptable in these circumstances. The Bluffer waited patiently until Sweet Thing paused for breath, and then said, apparently, exactly the right thing.

"I've really got to ask you to forgive me for interrupting that beautiful fight of yours," he observed genially. "Where'd a girl like you learn to tangle like that?"

There was a long moment of silence from Sweet Thing. Then she spoke.

"More Jam," she said in a much calmer and obviously pleased voice. "Don't you remember? My father was champion Lowland wrestler."

"Why, of course," said the Bluffer, letting her up, "that explains it."

Sweet Thing bounced hastily to her feet.

"Where is she?" Her face fell. "Oh, she got away."

Bill, also looked around the clearing. It was a fact. Perfectly Delightful had disappeared.

"Oh well," said Sweet Thing philosophically. "She'll be around. I can catch her anytime I want to."

She and the Hill Bluffer both turned to look at Bill.

"How about untying me?" demanded Bill.

"Why, sure," said the Bluffer. He walked around behind the tree to which Bill was anchored, and began untying the ropes binding his wrists together.

Bill endured, without really feeling, the rather bruising and painful business that the Hill Bluffer's big fingers made of clumsily jerking loose the knots that tied Bill's hands. His mind was busy, and once he was on his feet, he had a question for both of the two Dilbians facing him.

"How did you happen to find me?" he asked.

"Well, I don't know how *he* did," said Sweet Thing, sniffing slightly, "but Thing-or-Two and Perfectly Delightful

100

had been looking too pleased for words all day long, so I knew something was going on. When they and Grandpa Squeaky ducked off into the woods instead of joining everybody else up at the forge, I just followed them. I lost them in the woods for a few minutes, but I just poked around—and here they were, with you."

"So that's what it was," said the Hill Bluffer, looking down at her admiringly. "Your old dad, More Jam, came rolling up to me when I was waiting at the forge.

" 'Word in your ear, Postman,' he said to me, and led me off behind a shed. 'Haven't seen that daughter of mine around any place, have you?' he asked me.

" 'No,' I said, 'Why should I?'

" 'Because it's all a little peculiar, that's all,' said More Jam, sort of thoughtful. 'I just saw Perfectly Delightful and Thing-or-Two, with Grandpa Squeaky, sliding off into the brush a few moments ago, and that daughter of mine right behind them. Naturally, I didn't pay much attention, except that it was just about time for me to have a little, hot something to settle this delicate stomach of mine, and Sweet Thing might not be around to fix it for me—' and he patted his stomach, the way he does. 'It sure is peculiar, particularly when you figure that Pick-and-Shovel ought to have shown up at the blacksmith's by this time.'

"Well," said the Bluffer, looking meaningfully at Bill, "it'd been on my mind, too, that it was high time you were showing up at the forge. So I asked him where he'd seen all this going on—and in what direction Sweet Thing and the others had taken off. Then I went down to the Residency and looked for you. But you weren't there. So I just took off in the woods the way I'd been told everybody else'd gone, and after a while I figured it wouldn't do any harm to sort of yell your name a bit and see if you answered. Well," wound up the Bluffer, "you did. And here I am."

"I see," said Bill. "I wonder how it was More Jam just happened to be watching, to see what he did?"

Sweet Thing and the Hill Bluffer stared back down at Bill with noses wrinkled in every evidence of puzzlement.

"Guess he just happened to, Pick-and-Shovel," said the Bluffer.

"I see," said Bill again. There were a number of questions that were coming to his mind right now that he would like to have answered by Sweet Thing and the Bluffer—particularly by the Bluffer. But he remembered that he had unfinished business back at the village.

"Better let me get back up in that saddle," he said to the Bluffer now. "I'm a good three hours overdue at the forge."

The Bluffer stared at him in consternation, as did Sweet Thing. There was a moment of silence.

"Why, Pick-and-Shovel," said the Bluffer, finally, "you can't go back there now!"

Bill stared up at him.

"Why not?"

"Why? Well, because you—just can't!" said the Bluffer in a shocked tone of voice. "Why, they'd laugh you out of town if you showed up now, Pick-and-Shovel. Here you went and set up a weight-lifting contest, and then you didn't show up for it when the time came."

"But it wasn't my fault I wasn't there," said Bill. Tersely, he told them about being hit on the head and brought into the woods and tied up by the Hemnoid. However, to his surprise, when he finished, the long looks on the faces of Sweet Thing and the Bluffer did not lift. The Bluffer shook his head slowly.

"I might've figured it was something like that," said the Bluffer heavily. "But it doesn't make any difference, Pick-and-Shovel. No doubt you had a good reason for not being there on time—but the point is you *didn't* show up. How're folks to be sure you didn't just duck out of it and make this whole story up as an excuse? I believe you, because I know something about the kind of guts you Shorties've got. But these Muddy Nosers aren't going to believe you. They'll figure you probably knew you couldn't outlift Flat Fingers, so you just didn't show up."

"Well, I'll outlift him now," said Bill.

But the Bluffer still shook his head.

"You don't understand, Pick-and-Shovel," he said. "Flat Fingers isn't going to stick his neck out by agreeing to lift weights with you again. He did once and you ducked out— all right, I know it wasn't your fault. But he's going to be thinking—suppose he agrees to lift again, and you duck out a second time, or fall down and play sick, or something? If it happens twice in a row that you get out of it, people are going to start laughing at him for letting himself be fooled that way."

The Bluffer shook his head.

"No, I wouldn't go back to the village right now if I were you, Pick-and-Shovel," he said. "What you and I better figure on doing is camping out here in the woods for a few days. I'll go in and get your sword and shield made by the blacksmith—that's business, he won't mind making those. Then, when you've got these weapon things of yours, you can go and have the duel with Bone Breaker, and after you win that maybe they'll let you back in Muddy Nose Village without falling over and rolling way down the street, laughing, every time they see you."

"So," observed Bill grimly. "Barrel Belly managed to get me in bad with the villagers, after all, did he? Your rescuing me didn't help at all, then, did it?"

Both the postman and Sweet Thing looked uncomfortable. Sweet Thing, however, was quick to recover.

"Well, why don't you think of something, then?" she demanded. "You Shorties are all supposed to be so tricky and sneaky! Tricky Teacher was supposed to be so smart at thinking up things and getting around people; but where is he when *She* needs him? Not here, that's where he is! Instead, you're here, Pick-and-Shovel. So why don't you think up something? I know why! It's because you're a male Shorty.

103

She'd think of something, if *She* were here. I know *She* would. *She——*"

The continued emphatic repetition of the word "She" was doing little to improve Bills temper which had already been worn rather threadbare by events. The single thought that was in his mind at the moment was that palm trees would be flourishing on the Weddell pack ice of Antartica, back on Earth, before he would let any combination of events keep him out of Muddy Nose Village. He interrupted Sweet Thing roughly.

"All right," he retorted. "I've thought of something. Let's head for the village."

Chapter 13

The Hill Bluffer still hesitated.

"Are you sure you know what you're doing, Pick-and-Shovel?" he asked. "Like I say, Flat Fingers won't lift weights with you now——"

"That's what he thinks!" said Bill.

The Hill Bluffer lit up suddenly.

"You mean you figured out a way to make him?" said the Bluffer, happily. "Why didn't you say so?" He turned on Sweet Thing. "There, how do you like that? You and your female Shorties!"

Sweet Thing sniffed disdainfully.

"Oh, well," she said. "*She* would have thought of it right away."

"Climb up in the saddle, Pick-and-Shovel," said the Hill

Bluffer, ignoring this, and turning his back on Bill. "And we'll get going."

Bill scaled the Bluffer's back by means of the straps of the Dilbian's harness, and seated himself. The three of them started back through the woods toward the village.

As they went along, the heads of Dilbians out on the street turned to look at them, and the sounds of comments, ribald and otherwise, began to float to Bill's ears. He held on to the straps of the Bluffer's harness, before him, looking neither to right nor left. He noticed that Sweet Thing and the Hill Bluffer were not particularly pleased, either—even though they themselves were not the target of the jeers and catcalls that pursued them as a group. The Bluffer snorted once or twice under his breath. Sweet Thing stopped once and swung half-around, as if ready to turn back and give battle to those who were criticizing. More Jam was not to be seen, Bill noted.

However, in due time they ran the long gauntlet of the street and arrived at the blacksmith's property. Flat Fingers paid no attention to them as they came up. He studiously avoided looking at Bill, and only grunted in response to the greeting of the Hill Bluffer.

"Well," said Bill, as cheerfully as he could manage, in the Bluffer's ear, "I'll get down here."

Flat Fingers was busy at the forge, beating rather savagely upon a piece of red-hot iron. The Bluffer was seated on the bench and Sweet Thing was standing near the Bluffer. Just outside the shed where they all stood, a crowd of villagers was beginning to gather. These stood and watched; silently, but grinning widely, and obviously expecting the worst. Bill felt a return of the coldness inside him he had felt with Mula-*ay*. However, he smiled and turned his back on them with as much an appearance of unconcern as he could muster.

"Well," he said loudly to the Bluffer, ignoring the blacksmith, who had now ceased hammering and thrust the beaten piece of red-hot iron, hissing, into a dark and dirty-looking barrel of water alongside the forge, "so this is Flat Fingers' place, is it?"

"That's right, Pick-and-Shovel," replied the Bluffer curiously.

Bill did not say anything more immediately. Instead he began to wander among the piles of wood and iron that were stacked up under the shed roof, stopping here to finger a broken candlestick—there to run his finger along the edge of a broken sword. Flat Fingers, having laid aside the piece of iron he had been working on before, now had picked up what apparently was a broken barrel hoop and was scowling at it.

"Mighty interesting around here," commented Bill loudly, examining the rafters of the shed overhead. They were very stout rafters indeed, made of logs and a good twelve feet in the air, well out of his reach unless he climbed up on a stack of five- and six-foot lengths of foot-diameter logs—firewood, probably—that were piled up a little distance from him. He drifted over to the logs and began to examine them. Then he turned back to Sweet Thing and pulling her head down to approximately the level of his own mouth, spoke quietly into her ear for a second. Sweet Thing went off through the crowd, followed by the curious stares of those nearby, who watched her disappear in through the front door of the Residency. They might have gone on watching, if Bill had not started talking again and drawn their attention back to him.

"Yes," he said thoughtfully, staring at the logs. "It's a shame I couldn't get here in time to have that weight-lifting contest with the blacksmith."

"Sure was!" spoke up a voice from the crowd, producing a chorus of bass-voiced laughter.

"Yes, a real shame," went on Bill, ignoring the reaction and nodding at the Hill Bluffer. "It would've been something to see."

He looked over at Flat Fingers, who had moodily shoved

106

both the broken ends of the hoop into the bed of coals at his forge and was grimly pumping the bellows attached to it.

"Yes . . ." went on Bill, fingering one of the logs and trying to estimate its weight. It was about five feet long and looked as if it might weigh pretty close to a hundred pounds. The logs underneath it were similar in size, and their weight should be about the same, "An appointment like that's an *appointment*. If you miss it, that's that. I wouldn't insult Flat Fingers by suggesting he lift weights with me now, since I already missed one chance at it."

"That's playing it safe, Shorty!" boomed another voice from the observing crowd, and a new burst of laughter followed.

"No," said Bill thoughtfully. "That'd look like I might be trying to pull the same trick all over again. So I guess there isn't much for me to do——" He broke off as Sweet Thing shouldered her way importantly back through the crowd, the block-and-tackle Bill had made slung over one shoulder. There was a hum of interest at the sight of her, and it; but she ignored the reaction. She came up to Bill and dumped the block-and-tackle into his arms.

"There!" said Sweet Thing. She went over and sat down on the bench beside the Hill Bluffer, as if she had just done something remarkable to put everyone in their place. The crowd stared with interest at Bill and the block-and-tackle. Even Flat Fingers, over by the forge, shot a surreptitious glance in Bill's direction.

"On the other hand," went on Bill, as if to himself, but loud enough to be heard by everyone standing around, "I suppose I could just lift something around here, anyway, and sort of leave it lying where I've lifted it, and maybe Flat Fingers would notice it later—and maybe he wouldn't."

With these last words, thrown away in the best style of More Jam, Bill climbed up on the small pile of logs and tossed one end of the rope attached to the block-and-tackle over one of the rafters, and then tested it to see if it would slip easily. The rafter, being itself a smooth round section of log with all the bark peeled off, allowed the rope to slide around it almost as well as if it, too, was a pulley.

Bill climbed down, took the rope at the bottom end of the block-and-tackle, and ran a loop around five of the logs. He slid the loop to their center, and tied it down tight there, with the lower block of the tackle perhaps six inches above the tie. He then secured the upper part of the block-and-tackle by a separate rope to the beam itself, and once more flung over the rafter the long, operating end of the rope running into the sheaves of the block-and-tackle.

The crowd had quieted down and had been watching in interested silence while he went through these maneuvers. Out of the corner of his eye, Bill could see Flat Fingers, also watching.

"Well," he said, when he was done, "let's see if I can lift those five pieces of wood, now."

He took a good grip and started to draw down upon the rope to the block-and-tackle running over the rafter overhead. The rope creaked and moved. The wooden pulleys of the block-and-tackle also creaked and whined under the strain. The rope from the pulley moved jerkily through his hands, but at first the five logs did not seem to move.

"You got to try harder than that, Shorty!" whooped a voice from the crowd, followed by another burst of laughter—but then the laughter broke off suddenly. For, as all those who were watching could see, the tied-together bundle of logs had stirred and jerked. Abruptly, they were no longer resting on the logs below, but visibly swaying in the air, a fraction of an inch above them. A few more heaves on the rope by Bill, who was beginning to perspire, and the five logs swung obviously into the air above the pile beneath.

There was a deep-voiced babble of amazement and approval from the group around. Leaving the logs swinging there, held by the brake in the block-and-tackle itself that prevented the line from running out again in reverse order, Bill dusted his hands and walked over to the Bluffer. The onlookers quieted to hear what might be said.

"What do you think, Hill Bluffer," Bill asked conversationally. "You think a man the size of Flat Fingers could lift that?"

The Bluffer squinted thoughtfully at the bundle of five logs.

"Yes," he said at last, "I'd have to say I'd think he could, Pick-and-Shovel."

"Well, I'll guess I'll have to add another log or two," said Bill. He went back to the pile and let the bundle back down. Then he loosened the ropes about the five logs, wrestled another into position on top of them, tightened the loop, and using the block-and-tackle, proceeded to lift the heavier load. Once more he went back to the Bluffer.

"What do you think now, Hill Bluffer?" he asked. "You think Flat Fingers could lift that much?" He spoke airily, but the back of his neck was creeping slightly with the knowledge that Flat Fingers was standing only half a dozen feet behind him, taking it all in. The closeness of the blacksmith, however, did not seem to bother the Bluffer. He took his time about once more examining the bundle of logs.

"If you want my opinion, Pick-and-Shovel," he said at last, judiciously, "I think the blacksmith could lift that much and—say, two more logs, as well."

"Would you say he could lift that much and *three* more logs?" asked Bill.

The Bluffer considered.

"Well," he drawled finally. "I'd have to say no, I don't think he could."

"Suppose I added four logs to that stack," said Bill. "You'd be pretty sure then he wouldn't be able to lift them?"

"Sure I'd be sure," said the Bluffer promptly.

"Well, I'll just add those other four logs on, then," said Bill.

He went back to the stack of logs and did so. As he took hold of the rope running over the rafter to the block-and-tackle, and began to put his weight on it, a trace of uneasiness crept into him for the first time. There was over half a

109

ton of dead weight at the other end. The block-and-tackle might be able to lift it—but the question was, could he? For one thing, the added weight was making the friction between the rope and the rafter over which it ran a not inconsiderable item to be dealt with. At his first tug, it seemed as if the load would not move. Then—Bill remembering the fury that had been born in him back in the woods into which Mula-*ay* had kidnapped him. He set his teeth, wound his hands in the rope—and *pulled*.

For a long second, nothing happened. Then the rope gave, first a little, then a little more. Soon he was able to change his grip and the rope began coming steadily down toward him. Still, he did not count the battle won until a sudden gasp from the crowd behind him told him that the stack of ten logs had finally swung free and clear of the pile below it, visibly into the air.

Gratefully, he let go of the rope, and turned to look. Sure enough, the load he had just lifted showed daylight between it and the top of the log pile.

"Well, there it is," said Bill mildly. "I guess I did manage to lift a little bit, after all."

He dusted his hands together, turned back, and released the brake on the block-and-tackle. The load it was supporting fell with a crash back on to the top of the stack beneath. Bill surreptitiously locked the brake in place with a thrust of his thumb against the rachet he had provided for that purpose. Then he turned back and walked over to the bench where the Hill Bluffer was still sitting.

"Well," Bill said, "I guess you and I might as well be wandering back on down to the Residency. I just wanted to show what I could do if I had a mind to do it. But I can't really expect Flat Fingers to go and try and lift that same weight, too. So I'll just leave it there; and we'll be going—"

The Bluffer had gotten to his feet, and Bill had already turned toward the Residency when an angry snarl behind him turned him back.

"Just a minute there, Pick-and-Shovel!" snapped the blacksmith. He strode over to the rope still hanging from the opposite side of the beam from which the block-and-tackle itself depended, and grasped it firmly in his two huge, furry hands.

Then, without warning, he threw all his weight upon it. The rope twanged, suddenly taut—and alarm leaped inside Bill. The rope he had chosen was perfectly adequate to the task of lifting the load he had just lifted—otherwise it would have broken. But he knew how a rope that will not break under a steady pull will part under a sudden jerk that snaps it. For a moment, hearing the bass-viol note of the rope as it straightened out, Bill was sure that this was what had happened in Flat Fingers' huge hands.

But then he saw that the rope had held. Not only that, but although the great shoulder muscles under the black fur of Flat Fingers were bunching heroically, and the block-and-tackle was creaking painfully, the load was not lifting.

The line was now as taut and straight as a bar of iron. The whole body of the blacksmith vibrated with the effort he was making. But, as the long seconds slipped away, it became obvious he was not going to be able to do it.

A single, jeering laugh rang out from the surrounding crowd. With a speed of reflex that seemed unbelievable in one so big, Flat Fingers suddenly let go of the rope, spun around and took three long strides into the crowd, to reappear a second later dragging forward by the neck and arm a somewhat smaller, male Dilbian. Having got the other out where there was room to swing him, the blacksmith shook him like a terrier shaking a rat.

"You want to try it, Fat Lip? You and one of your friends, together, want to try to lift it?" roared Flat Fingers.

He let the other go, and Fat Lip staggered for a moment before gaining his feet. Then, however, licking his lips, he took a look at the rope, and turned to shout a name into the crowd.

In response to that name another Dilbian of about the

same size came forward. Together, grinning, they hauled on the rope.

However, for them as for the blacksmith, the lock held the brake on the block-and-tackle in place. Instead of the rope running through the pulleys as it had for Bill, they—like Flat Fingers—were reduced to trying to lift by main strength the dead weight not only of the logs but of the block-and-tackle itself. They did not succeed. In fact, a third Dilbian was needed to help them before the bundle of logs could be swayed, creakingly, up into the air.

A mutter, a rumble, a general sound of awe ran through the crowd. They stared at Bill with strange eyes.

"Well, Blacksmith!" said the Bluffer, with something very like a crow of triumph in his voice. "I guess that settles it?"

"Not quite, Postman!" replied the blacksmith. He had stepped back to the forge and picked up a rather long sharp knife from a small table near it. Now, approaching the tied-up bundle of logs, and shoving the three who had lifted it out of his way, he cut the rope above the block-and-tackle and below it, tossed it aside and retied the cut end of the lifting rope directly to the rope binding the load together. Then he stepped back, and turned to Bill.

"All right, Pick-and-Shovel," he said ominously. "Let's see you lift it now."

Bill did not move. But his heart felt as if it had just stopped beating.

"Why should I?" he asked.

"I'll tell you why!" said Flat Fingers. He reached down and picked up the block-and-tackle in one large hand and shoved it before Bill's eyes. "Did you think a professional man like me could have something like this pulled right under his nose and not know what's going on? The only reason you could lift those logs was because you used *this*! This gadget, right here!" He shook it, fiercely, almost in Bill's face. "I don't know how you made it work for you, and not work for me—but this is how come you managed to lift those logs!"

"That's right," said Bill calmly. The sweat was prickling under his collar.

"Hey!" cried the Hill Bluffer in alarm. "Pick-and-Shovel, you aren't saying—"

"Let him answer me, first," rumbled the blacksmith dangerously. In the mask of his furry face, his eyes were suddenly red and bloodshot.

"I said," repeated Bill distinctly, "of course I did. As you all know"—he turned toward the crowd of Dilbians just outside the shed—"my main job here is to teach you all how to use the tools that us Shorties brought you in order to make your farming less work, and make it produce more crops. Well, I just thought I'd give you a little example of what one of our gadgets can do."

He pointed at the block-and-tackle, which the blacksmith still held.

"That's one of them," he said, "and you just saw how easy it made lifting those logs. Now wouldn't you all like to have a gadget like that—"

"Hold on!" snarled Flat Fingers ominously. "Never mind changing the subject, Pick-and-Shovel! You set up a weight-lifting contest. You claimed you could outlift me. But when it came down to it, you used this. You *cheated!*"

The word rang out loudly on the warm afternoon air. From the crowd around there was dead silence. The accusation, Bill knew, was the ultimate one among Dilbians.

It was the old story of the spirit versus the letter of the law, again. What held true for laws held true also for verbal contracts and personal promises. Bill had conceived the block-and-tackle as a clever way of discharging an apparently impossible promise. But what Flat Fingers was saying was that Bill had promised one thing but delivered another.

There was all the Dilbian world of difference between the two things. What Bill had intended to pull off was something clever—and therefore praiseworthy. What Flat Fingers was claiming was anathema to all Dilbians.

The absolute inviolability of the letter of the law was the

113

cement holding the Dilbian culture together. It was the one thing on which farmers, outlaws, Lowland and Upland Dilbians agreed instinctively. Not even the Hill Bluffer would stand by Bill if it was agreed that he had done what the blacksmith said. The penalty for *cheating* was death.

The crowd about the forge was silent, waiting for Bill's reply.

Chapter 14

Silently, Bill blessed the inspiration that had come to him earlier when he had originally begun to challenge the blacksmith. That inspiration should get him out of his present fix now, he told himself firmly. But in spite of that inner firmness, he felt his stomach sink inside him as he looked around at the grim, furry faces ringing him in. He forced himself to maintain his casual voice, and the careless smile on his face.

"Oh, I wouldn't say that," he said lightly. He turned and looked into the crowd. "Where's More Jam?"

"What's More Jam got to do with it?" growled Flat Fingers, behind him.

"Why, just that he was there when you and I had our little talk," answered Bill, without turning. "He's my witness. Where *is* More Jam?"

"Coming!" huffed a voice from the back of the crowd. And a moment later, More Jam himself shoved his way through the front ranks and joined Bill and the others under the shed roof.

"Well, now, Pick-and-Shovel," he said. "You were passing the shout for me?"

"Yes, I was," said Bill. "You were over at the Residency this morning and maybe you were listening when I had my little talk with Flat Fingers. I wonder if you could think back and see if you remember just what I said I'd meet him here at noon to do? Did I say I'd *outlift* him?"

"Let's see, now," rumbled More Jam. "As I remember it, what Pick-and-Shovel here said was—*'I'm just a Shorty and I'd never have the nerve to suggest that I might be able to outlift you ordinarily. But I just might be able to outdo you at it if I had to, and I'm ready to prove it by moving something you can't move.'*"

More Jam cocked his head at the blacksmith.

"Sorry not to be able to back a fellow townsman up, Flat Fingers," said Sweet Thing's father sadly, "but that's what Pick-and-Shovel said, all right. And he suggested that you get together after lunch and you said 'Suits me . . .'" More Jam continued, repeating the conversation with as much accuracy as if he had been a recording machine.

Bill let a slow, silent sigh of relief escape him. The Dilbians, he knew, had the rather elementary written language that made the Bluffer's job as postman possible and necessary. But Bill had gambled on the fact that, like most primitive cultures, it was the Dilbian custom and habit to depend on the memories of living witnesses to any agreement or transaction.

However, the verdict, Bill noted, was not in yet. The crowd was still silent.

Bill's breath checked in his chest once more—but just then a swelling wave of thunderous, bass-voiced Dilbian laughter began to rise and ring about Bill's ears from every direction. Everybody was laughing—even, finally, Flat Fingers himself. In fact, the blacksmith showed an alarming intention of slapping Bill on the back in congratulation—an intention Bill only frustrated by hastily backing up against the stout belly of More Jam.

"Well, well, well!" chortled the towering blacksmith finally, as the laughter began to die down. "You sure are a sneaky little Shorty, at that—and I'm the first man to admit it! No offense about my flying off the handle and saying you cheated, I hope? If you feel we ought to tangle about it, right now—"

"No, no—no offense!" said Bill quickly. "None at all!"

General sounds of approval from the surrounding crowd greeted this magnanimous attitude on Bill's part. By this time the shed was completely hemmed in by the villagers. It occurred to Bill that this might be a good time to try to get them on his side against the outlaws, striking while the iron was hot, so to speak. He stepped up on a pile of logs.

"Er—people of Muddy Nose," said Bill. For a second, his voice threatened to stick in his throat. For all the crowd's present good humor, Bill could not forget the ominous quiet that had hung over them a moment earlier when the blacksmith had accused him of cheating. It was a little like public speaking to a convocation of grizzlies. Nevertheless, Bill fell back upon his innate stubbornness and determination, and went doggedly ahead with what he had intended to say.

"—As you all know," he said, "my main job here is to help all of you to make your farms turn out bigger and better crops. But as you all know, too, I haven't been able to do anything about this yet because I've been tied up with a problem about Dirty Teeth and a bunch of outlaws headed by Bone Breaker—whom you all know well.

"But I'm sure you can all understand how this could keep me busy," went on Bill, "because these same outlaws have been keeping you people here around Muddy Nose busy for some time.

"So, I just wanted to mention that perhaps the time has come for you and me to join forces and see about settling the hash of these outlaws once and for all," said Bill. "When I first landed in this community, I was given to understand that you might not be too interested in following a Shorty that wanted to do away with the community menace up in Outlaw

116

Valley. I can understand that—you didn't know anything about me. But now, though I do say it myself who shouldn't—you've seen me have this little competition here with your village blacksmith, who's as good a man as they come—"

Bill paused to wave in Flat Fingers' direction, and Flat Fingers scowled from right to left—that being the male Dilbian way of taking a bow when referred to on public occasion.

"At any rate, I thought that maybe now we might get together and start to make some plans about cleaning out the outlaws . . ." For the first time, Bill began to be conscious of a good-natured, but rather obvious, lack of response from the crowd before him. In fact, from his elevated position on top of the logs, he now saw some of the outer members of his audience beginning to turn away and amble off.

"Believe me," he said, raising his voice and speaking as earnestly and forcefully as he could, "Muddy Nose Village can't get better and richer and stronger until those outlaws are settled. So what I thought was that we might get together a town meeting . . ."

The crowd, however, was visibly breaking up. Individually and in small groups they began to scatter, turning their backs on Bill and drifting off into the body of the village. Bill continued to talk on, almost desperately. But it was plainly a losing cause. Very shortly, his audience was down to its hard core. That is to say—Sweet Thing, More Jam, the Hill Bluffer, and Flat Fingers. Feeling foolish, Bill stopped talking and climbed down from the pile.

"I guess I don't convince people very well," he said in honest bewilderment to those who remained.

"Don't say that!" said Flat Fingers strongly. "You convinced *me*, Pick-and-Shovel! And I'm as good as any three other men in the village, any day—" He checked himself, looking apologetically at Sweet Thing's male parent. "—men my own age, that is."

"Why thanks, Blacksmith," said More Jam with a heavy sigh. "Nice of you not to include me—though of course I'm only a shadow of my former self." He turned his head to Bill, however, and his voice became serious. "In fact, you've got a friend in me too, Pick-and-Shovel—just as I told you yesterday. But that doesn't change things. If you figured this village to fall in line behind you in a feud with the outlaws, you should've known better."

"You sure should have!" interrupted the Bluffer emphatically. "Why I could've told you, Pick-and-Shovel, you'd never get anywhere impressing these people by being tricky. They *know* Shorties can be sneaky as all get out. The Tricky Teacher proved that. What they want to see is what you can do in the muscle-and-guts department. What you've got to do is just what you're set up to do—and that's tangle with Bone Breaker. Lay him out! *Then* these people will back you against the outlaws."

"I'll get started right away on that blade and buckler, Pick-and-Shovel," put in Flat Fingers. "Let's see if I can find something around here that's particularly good blade material."

"Guts-and-muscles department . . ." muttered Bill thoughtfully, echoing the Bluffer's words. That was certainly the department in which everyone seemed to be eager to have him operate—including whoever or whatever was responsible for his being in this place and situation in the first place.

It was hardly to be considered that Mula-*ay* had been telling the truth, this morning in the woods, when he had claimed Bill had been deliberately put on the spot by human authorities simply to save face in the case of the Muddy Nose Project. On the other hand, some of the things the Hemnoid had said had chimed uncomfortably well with some of the things Anita had said when he spoke to her in Outlaw Valley.

Either Anita had been as badly misled about the true situation here as Bill had, or. . . . It occurred to Bill that the cards might be stacked more heavily against him than he had thought, even when he had sat thinking in front of the communications console after his unsuccessful attempt to contact Greentree or anyone else off-planet. There seemed to

118

be no way out of his duel with Bone Breaker unless he could figure out who or what had put him in this situation, and what the true aims and motives of everyone concerned were.

In any case, Anita was going to have to provide him with some answers. That meant he must talk to her again, which meant another penetration of Outlaw Valley, which could hardly be done in the broad light of day. . . .

"Muscle-and-guts department?" he repeated again, looking up at the Bluffer. "I suppose it would take a little muscle—and guts too—to get in and out of that Outlaw Valley after it's been shut up for the night?"

The Bluffer stared back at him in astonishment. Sweet Thing and More Jam also stared. Some little distance away the blacksmith raised his head in astonishment.

"Are you crazy, Pick-and-Shovel?" demanded Flat Fingers. "The gate to that valley is locked and barred the minute the sun goes down and there are two armed men on guard until it's opened up at dawn. *Nobody* goes in and out of that valley after the sun's gone down!"

"I do," said Bill grimly. "I think I'll just drop in there tonight; and I'll bring back that piece of metal outside the outlaw's dining hall they use as a gong, to prove I've been there!"

Chapter 15

"Will we get there before dark?" Bill asked.

"Before dark?" The Bluffer, striding beneath Bill, squinted through the trees at the descending sun now, gleaming redly through black-looking trunks and branches, close to setting.

"Well, it'll be dark down in the valley. But up on top of the cliffs there'll be some daylight, still. And it's the north cliff-top you want, isn't it?"

"That's right," said Bill. "If it's still light there, that's all I'll need."

"All you need, is it?" muttered the Bluffer. "Mind telling a man how you're going to get into that valley, anyway?"

"I'll show you when we get there," said Bill.

In fact, while he was fairly confident that he would make it, one way or another, Bill himself would not know for sure until he actually got to the top of the cliff and made some measurements. There was a hundred feet of soft, quarter-inch climbing rope wound around his waist under his shirt, and with the help of the programed lathe he had produced some homemade pitons, snap rings, and a light metal hammer with an opposed pick end. These latter items were in a knapsack on his back.

As the postman had predicted, when they reached the north wall overlooking Outlaw Valley, the sunset was only falling on the buildings of the valley floor below them. The Bluffer stopped and let Bill down, but with a strong air of skepticism.

"What're you going to do, Pick-and-Shovel," the Postman asked. "*Fly* down into that valley?"

"Not exactly," said Bill. He had produced a jackknife from his pocket and opened it. Now, while the Bluffer watched with unconcealed curiosity, Bill found and cut off a couple of small tree branches with y-shaped ends. The branching ends he trimmed down to vee's; and stuck the long end of the branches in the ground, one in front of the other, with the vee's in line, pointing out across the valley.

Bill then found and cut another straight stick, long enough to lie in the two vee's, so that it lay like an arrow pointing across at the top of the opposite valley wall. Digging into his knapsack, he came up with one of his homemade pitons, looking like a heavy nail with one end sharpened and the opposite end bent into a loop. He tied one end of a length of string to the loop and the other end to the center of the stick resting in the forks of the two stakes he had driven into the earth. Then he adjusted the stakes until the piton hung straight up and down and in line with the two stakes, over a point midway between them.

"What is it?" demanded the Bluffer, unable to conceal his interest.

"Another of our Shorty gadgets," said Bill. There was, in fact, no Dilbian word for what he had just built—which was a sort of crude surveyor's transit. The dangling piton acted like a plumb bob which allowed him to check whether his line of sight—which was along the straight stick in the two forks of the stakes—was level. Now assured that it was, Bill knelt at the back end of the stake, so that he could sight along its length at the top of the valley wall opposite. It seemed to be almost directly in line. That should mean that the two valley walls were roughly of the same height.

From his pocket he took out a protractor he had located back at the Residency, and with this held against the end of the straight stick in the stake forks he rotated it through its angles of declination, making an attempt to get a rough approximation of the angle subtended by the height of the opposite cliff from its valley bottom to its tree-clad top.

He got the angle, and abandoned the transit for a pencil and a notebook. In the notebook, he jotted down the angle he had just observed. Then, using his eye, he made an attempt to judge the distance of the opposite cliff from where he stood.

Since both cliffs were more or less vertical, the gap between the point where he stood and the top of the cliff directly opposite should be roughly the same as the width of the valley floor at that point. His memory of the outlaws' eating hall down below enabled him to estimate its overall length now about eighty feet. Just about twelve such eating halls placed end-to-end would be required to stretch from this cliff to the other one. Twelve times eighty was nine hundred and sixty—call it a thousand feet roughly between the cliffs.

He sat back, with his notebook and his pencil, and—closely observed by the Hill Bluffer who had hunkered down nearby—performed the simple geometric calculation that gave him an approximate measurement of the opposite cliff as being some sixty feet in vertical height. If the other cliff was sixty feet high, it could hardly be much more than that from where he sat right now to the valley below. He had brought with him a hundred feet of rope, so he had more than enough to let himself down into the valley once darkness fell.

"Well, I suppose I might as well tell you," Bill said. "What I plan to do is climb down this cliff here into the valley, and climb back up after I've gotten hold of the gong I said I'd bring back."

The Bluffer stared at him. For a moment, it seemed that even the Dilbian postman was finally at a loss for words. Then he found his voice.

"*Down* the cliff!" he echoed.

He got to his feet; and, screened by the bushes that grew thickly along the lip of the cliff, and by the trees surrounding he moved to where he could peer over the edge of the cliff as Bill had earlier done. He peered for a long moment and then came back shaking his head sadly.

"Pick-and-Shovel," he said, "you're either plumb crazy, or better than any man or Shorty I've ever seen."

Bill had expected just this reaction. The cliff was a vertical face but not a smooth one. The dark granitic rock of which it was composed was roughened and broken by outcroppings and fissures large enough to supply adequate hand-holds for someone like Bill who had had rock-climbing experience. With a couple of other experienced climbers to help him and proper equipment, Bill would have felt quite confident about tackling it without any further aid. However, what were adequate hand- and foot-holds for someone with mountaineering experience were not necessarily sufficient to make climbable such a route for another human, without mountaineering experience—let alone a Dilbian, with his much greater weight and clumsiness. Consequently, it was not surprising that the Bluffer found the notion ridiculous—as undoubtedly would the outlaws themselves, or any of the other Dilbians resident in the neighborhood.

To tell the truth, Bill found it a little ridiculous himself. Not the idea of scaling it in full daylight with a team and proper equipment—but the idea of doing it by himself, with his few homemade devices, alone and in the dark. However, he had the rope up his sleeve—or rather, around his waist—which he now decided to keep secret even from the Bluffer.

"It's dark down in the valley now," he said as casually as possible. "Let's walk along the cliff until we find a good place for me to start down."

They started out together, the Dilbian postman shaking his head, with a renewed air of skepticism. A little farther along the edge of the cliff, in the rapidly gathering gloom, they came to a place where part of the rock had fallen away, leaving a notch about eight feet wide going down, narrowing as it went into the dimness below.

"Here's a good spot," said Bill with a cheerfulness that he did not completely feel. "Suppose you come back for me here about sunrise. I'll be waiting for you."

"It's your neck," said the Bluffer, with philosophy. "I'll be here. I hope you are."

"Don't worry about me," said Bill. As the Bluffer watched curiously, he began to climb cautiously backward down into the cleft—the notch in the edge of the cliff.

Setting himself securely, with his feet braced and his left hand firmly locked around a projection of the rock, with his right hand he unbuttoned his shirt and began to unwrap the rope from around his waist. It took a matter of some few minutes for him to get it all unwound. He was left at last with the rope lying in coils upon and between his feet and with one end in his grasp. He searched around him for some strong point of anchor.

He found it in a projecting, somewhat upward-thrusting boss of rock about half a foot to his right, just outside the cleft itself. He wrapped his end of rope several times securely around the boss and tied it there. Then, cautiously, bit by bit, he put his weight on the anchored rope until all of his weight was upon it.

The rope held firm around the boss. Gingerly, with his breath quickening in spite of all of his determination and experience, Bill abandoned the security of the cliff for the open rock-face with the rope as his only support.

For a moment, he swung pendulumlike, giddily upon the rope. Then his feet, catching the cliff face, stopped his movement. Slowly, carefully, he began to let himself down the vertical wall of rock, his hands holding firmly to the rope, and his feet walking backward down the vertical surface.

Both the valley floor and all its walls were in deep darkness now. The sun had been set for some minutes, and, so far, no moon had risen. In the obscurity, Bill lowered himself cautiously down the rope, stopping only now and then, when he encountered secure footholds, to rest his arms— which alone took the weight of his body upon the rope. By this procedure, slowly and with a number of pauses, Bill went down into darkness.

He had made knots in the rope at ten-foot intervals. He had counted off more than seven of these—which would make the distance from himself to the bottom of the cliff alone higher than he had figured the cliff face to be. He was wondering with the first, fine, small teeth of panic nibbling at his nerves whether his calculations might not have been badly in error and there was more cliff than he had rope, when, stepping down, his foot jarred suddenly upon a flat and solid surface.

Peering about, he saw that he had reached the valley floor.

Bill stepped down with his other foot and let go of the rope. With a sigh of relief, he turned about and stood supported by his own two legs alone. Now that he was on level ground, he could barely make out the black-against-black of bushes and trees nearby. Cautiously, he began to feel his way among them—not without a scratched face and scratched hands from the spidery limbs and branches he encountered.

Pausing, he turned and looked back up the cliff down which he had come. By the moonlight, he was able to make out the notch at the top of the cliff where he had started his climb down into the valley. It stood out clearly, now that the moon was risen, and he marked it in his mind—for he would have to find his rope again in order to get back out of the valley.

Having located himself, Bill turned about and peered through the open dimness of the valley floor, still in shadow from the rising moon. Some five hundred yards away, and barely discernible, chunks of heavier darkness, with here and there a little crack of yellow light showing about their walls where light from within escaped through the gaps of a high curtain, he made out the buildings of the outlaw settlement.

He went toward them.

As he got closer, it was easy for him to distinguish the large eating hall from the others. It was still occupied, for not only was light showing here and there through its curtains, but the sounds of cheerful, if argumentative, Dilbian male voices came clearly to his ear. Giving the building a wide berth, Bill circled to his left and began, one by one, to examine the smaller buildings as he encountered them.

Peering through a crack in one set of curtains where yellow light showed, Bill discovered what appeared to be nothing less than a regiment of young Dilbians evidently engaged in something between a pillow fight and a general game of Red Rover, for which purpose they had divided into two teams, one at each end of the building—from which they raced at intervals to the other end, roaring at the top of their lungs and batting out furiously at any other runner who came within reach.

Fascinated—for Bill had not seen any of the younger generation of Dilbia's natives until this moment—he stood staring through a gap in the curtain until the sound of a door opening at the far end of the room and the appearance of an

125

adult Dilbian not only brought the game to a close but reminded him that he was an intruder here. He turned back to his searching.

He had investigated all of the buildings but two, when distantly—but unmistakably—the sounds of a human voice fell on his ear. Turning about, he followed it to one of the buildings not yet investigated, found a window, and peered in through an opening—actually a tear—in the hide curtain.

He had found Anita. But, unfortunately, she was not alone. She was seated in a circle with at least a dozen powerful and competent-looking Dilbian females, working on what looked like a large net.

Dominating the group was a heavy-bodied, older female who looked like a small, distaff edition of More Jam. The group had all the cozy appearance of a ladies' sewing circle back on Earth. Bill could hardly stick his head in the door and ask Anita to step outside and talk to him. On the other hand, every minute he stood about out in the open in Outlaw Valley increased the chance of some local inhabitant stumbling over him.

And the rapidly rising moon would be shining full on the valley floor very shortly.

Chapter 16

As he continued to watch through the tear in the curtain, undecided as to what he should do, Bill's hypnoed information came to mind with the advice that this was a net of the sort used by Dilbians to capture the wild, musk-oxlike herbivores that roamed the Dilbian forest. Anita apparently had

126

been entertaining the others with some kind of a story. For, as Bill put his eye to the rent in the curtain, all the rest burst into laughter hardly less rough and boisterous than Bill had heard from their male counterparts at the eating hall.

"—Of course," said Anita when the laughter died down, apparently referring back to the story she had just been telling, "I wouldn't want Bone Breaker to lose his temper, and string *me* up by the heels."

"He'd better not try," said the fat matriarch meaningfully, looking around the circle. "Not while we're around. Eh, girls?"

There was a chorus of assent, grim-voiced enough to send a shiver down the back of Bill, watching at the window.

"*My* father—Bone Breaker's great-grandfather—" went on the speaker, looking triumphantly around the circle, "was a Grandfather of the Hunters Clan near Wildwood Peak," went on Bone Breaker's great-aunt. "And *his* father, before him was a Grandfather."

"What about Bone Breaker's own grandfather?" queried the smallest of the female Dilbians, sitting almost directly opposite Anita, who was at the left of Bone Breaker's great-aunt in the circle. "Was he a Grandfather too?"

"He was not, Noggle Head," replied Bone Breaker's great-aunt majestically. "He was a tanner. But a very excellent tanner, one of the toughest men who ever walked on two legs and a good deal sneakier than most, if I say so myself who was his blood sister."

"Indeed, No Rest," spoke up another comfortably uphol-stered female a quarter of the way around the circle from Anita, "we all know how you lean over backward, if any-thing, where your relatives are concerned."

Mutters of agreement, which Bill could not be sure were either real or feigned, arose from the rest of the group.

"But to get back to little Dirty Teeth here," said No Rest, turning to Anita. "The last thing we'd want to do is be without you and these interesting little tales you tell us about you Shorty females." The circle muttered agreement. "Some

127

of the funniest things I've ever heard, and so—*educational*."

The last word was uttered with a particular emphasis that brought a hum of approval from the other females.

"Oh, well," said Anita modestly, her hands, like the hands of the females about her, busy at tying knots in the net as she spoke, "of course, as you know, under our Shorty agreement with the Fatties, I'm not supposed to mention anything that they wouldn't mention. But I don't see any harm in telling you these little stories—which, for all you know, I'm just making up out of thin air as I go."

"Oh, yes," said Word-and-a-Half, with a wink and a nod at the others. "Making them up! Of course you are!"

"Well," said Anita, "there was this time my grandmother wanted a certain piece of furniture—" Anita broke off. "A sort of a chair—we call it an *overstuffed* chair. It's like a grandfather's chair, like a bench with a backrest to it. Only besides that, it's padded so it's soft, not only on the seat but on the backrest where you lean back against it."

A buzz of interest and astonishment convulsed the group.

"A grandfather chair! And soft?" said Word-and-a-Half in a pleased, but shocked tone of voice. "How did she dare—!"

"Oh, we Shorty females have gotten all sorts of things," said Anita thoughtfully. "And, after all, why shouldn't a female have a grandfatherlike chair? Doesn't she get tired, too?"

"Of course she does!" said No Rest sternly.

"Doesn't a female get old and wise, just like a grandfather?" said Anita.

"Absolutely!" trumpeted No Rest. The circle burst into a mutter of agreement.

"Go on, Dirty Teeth," urged No Rest, quieting the circle with a glance.

"Well, as I say," said Dirty Teeth, carefully watching the knot she was making as she spoke, "my grandmother wanted this chair, but she knew there wasn't much use in asking her man to make it for her. She knew he'd just give some reason for not making it. So what do you suppose she did?"

"Hit him on the head?" suggested Noggle Head hopefully.

"Of course not," said Anita. There was a chorus of sneers and sniffs from the rest. Noggle Head shrank back into silence. "She realized immediately this was an occasion that called for being sneaky. So one day when her husband was sitting dozing just after lunch, he heard chopping sounds out back. Well, the only ax around the house was his; so he got up and went out to see what was going on. And he saw my grandmother chopping up some lengths of wood.

" 'What're you doing with an ax?' shouted my grandfather. 'Women aren't supposed to use axes! That's *my* ax!'

" 'I know,' answered my grandmother meekly, putting the ax down, 'but I didn't want to bother you. There was this thing I wanted to build. So I just thought I'd try building it myself—'

" '*You* build it!' roared my grandfather. 'You don't know how to use an ax! How would you know how to build anything?'

" 'Well, I went and asked how to do it,' my grandmother answered quietly. 'I didn't want to bother you, so I went down the road here to our next neighbor, and asked her husband—'

"At that my grandfather let out a bellow of rage.

" 'Him? You asked *him*? That lard-head couldn't build anything more complicated than tying one stick to another!' he shouted. 'How did he tell you how to build it? Just tell me—how did he say you ought to do it?'

" 'Well ...' began my grandmother; and she went on to describe the thing she wanted to build, with its backrest and its padding and all that. But before she was halfway through, my grandfather had grabbed the ax out of her hand and was busy telling her how wrong her neighbor's husband had been in his direction, and he'd started to build the chair himself to prove it."

Anita paused, and sighed and looked up and around at her audience.

"Well, that was it," she said. "Inside of a week my grandmother had the padded chair with the backrest just the way she wanted it."

There was first a titter, then a roar of laughter that gradually built up until some of the females dropped the net, and showed signs of literally rolling about on the floor in an excess of enjoyment.

"I thought you'd like hearing about that," said Anita meekly, working away at the net when they were all silent once more. "—But I ought to tell you that that was only the beginning."

"The beginning?" echoed Noggle Head in awe from across the circle. "You mean afterward he figured out what she'd done to him and—"

"Not likely!" sniffed No Rest. "A man figure out how he'd been made a fool of? He wouldn't want to figure it out. Even if he came close to figuring it out, he'd back away from it for fear he would find out something he wouldn't like!" She turned to Anita. "Wasn't that the way it was, Dirty Teeth?"

"You're right as usual, No Rest," said Anita. "What I meant was, it was just the beginning of what my grandmother had set out to do. You see, this one chair was just the beginning. She wanted a whole house full of furniture like that."

Gasps and grunts of sincere astonishment arose from her audience. Even No Rest seemed a little shaken.

"A whole houseful, Dirty Teeth?" said the outlaw matriarch. "Wasn't that maybe going a litle bit too far?"

"My grandmother didn't think so," replied Anita seriously. "After all, a man gets anything he wants, doesn't he? All a woman has is her house and her children, isn't that right? And the children grow up and leave fast enough, don't they?"

"How true," said No Rest, shaking her head sadly. "Yes, every word of it's true. Go on, Dirty Teeth, how did your grandmother get her whole house full of furniture?"

"You'll never guess," said Anita.

"She hit him on the head—" Noggle Head was beginning

130

hopefully, when she was sneered into silence almost automatically by the rest of the audience.

"No," said Anita. "What my grandmother did was to take off one day and go down and visit her neighbor—the same one whose husband she had asked about building the piece of furniture she wanted—because she *had* really asked him, you see."

"Ah," said No Rest meaningfully, nodding her head as if she had known it all the time.

"And," went on Anita, "she quite naturally invited her neighbor up to her house for a bite to eat and to look at her new chair that her husband had built. Well, the neighbor came up and admired the chair very much, and went home again. And what do you think happened before a week was out?"

"That neighbor had her husband make her a chair just like it!" said Word-and-a-Half emphatically. "She told him about the chair, and he went up and saw it and got all fired up, and he came back down and built one just like it!"

"That's exactly right," said Anita quietly but approvingly. "And of course the neighbor invited my grandmother down to see *her* chair. So my grandmother went down and admired it very much."

"So they both had chairs," said Noggle Head. "That was the end, then?"

"No," said Anita. "That was still just the beginning. Because the next day my grandfather came in and saw that the chair he'd built my grandmother wasn't out in the center of the room where it used to be; it was tucked back in a corner where it was dark and pretty well hidden. Well, of course he asked why it was put someplace else. And my grandmother told him about the neighbor's chair. Which made him furious!"

"Why?" asked Noggle Head, blundering in where her older and wiser sisters hesitated to play the role of interlocutor.

"Why," said Anita sweetly, "you see my grandmother was such a modest, kindly, unassuming sort of a Shorty female that she wouldn't for any reason try to hold her head higher than her neighbor. So that when she told my grandfather about the chair her neighbor's husband had built for her neighbor, somehow the way she told it made the chair the neighbor had built seem a lot bigger and grander and softer and higher polished than the one my grandfather had built for my grandmother—almost as if the neighbor's husband had built a better chair than my grandfather had, just to spite my grandfather. So, as I say, my grandfather became furious and what do you suppose he did then?"

"Hit her on the head?" queried Noggle Head, but faintly and with a note of hope that was almost dead, in her voice.

"You think too much of hitting on the head, my girl!" snapped No Rest, in a tone of stern authority. "Only the most helpless sort of a woman tries to handle a husband that way. Little good ever comes of it. Most women don't hit their husbands hard enough, anyway, and it doesn't do anything but make the husbands mad!"

Noggle Head shrank up over her work again, once more properly crushed. No Rest turned back to Anita.

"Well, Dirty Teeth," said Bone Breaker's great-aunt, "go on. Tell us what happened next!"

"Nothing much," said Anita mildly. "Although, by the time it was ended, my grandmother had the best houseful of furniture you have ever seen. But the point is—she continued to put her good sneaky talents to work the rest of her married life with my grandfather. And by the time of his death, he had become one of the richest and best known male Shorties around."

The group considered this conclusion for a long moment in satisfied silence. Then No Rest sighed and placed her seal of approval upon the anecdote.

"There's always a woman behind a man who amounts to anything," she observed sagely.

Outside the window at which he was listening, Bill suddenly jerked his attention away from the aperture in the hide curtains, and strove suddenly with his light-dazzled eyes to pierce the night darkness surrounding him. There was no more time to waste. He had to get Anita outside and away from her net-weaving social circle before the rising moon exposed him to capture. He turned and peered in at the window again. Dilbians, he remembered, because of a difference from humans in jaw structure and lip muscles, could not whistle. Bill took a breath and whistled the first two lines of *"When Johnny Comes Marching Home."*

The results were far greater than anything he had expected. Anita's hands froze suddenly in their movement of making a tie in the net, and her face suddenly went pale in the lamplight. But the effect upon Anita was nothing compared to the effect that the sound of Bill's whistle had on the rest of the Dilbian social circle.

All the Dilbian females in the room checked in mid-motion and apparently stopped breathing. They sat like a tableau, listening. For a long moment the silence seemed to ring in Bill's ears. Then Noggle Head began to shiver violently.

"W-what k-kind of a critter's that . . . ?" she whimpered.

"Hush!" ordered No Rest in a harsh whisper, but one so full of terror that Bill himself chilled at the sound of it. "No critter—no bird—no wind in the trees ever made *that* sound!"

Noggle Head's shivers grew until she trembled uncontrollably. Others of the Dilbian females were beginning to cower and shake.

"A Cobbly!" hissed No Rest—and outside the building, Bill stiffened. For a Cobbly was a supernatural creature out of Dilbian legend—a sort of malicious but very powerful elf. "A *Cobbly*," repeated No Rest now. "And it's come for one of us women, here!"

The eyes of all the Dilbian females turned slowly and grimly upon Noggle Head.

"You—and your talk about hitting husbands over the head!" whispered No Rest savagely. "You know what Cobblies do to undutiful females! Now one of them's heard you!"

Noggle Head was shivering so hard she was making the floor creak beneath her.

"What'll we do?" whispered one of the other females.

"There's just one chance!" ordered No Rest, still in a whisper. "Maybe we can still frighten the Cobbly off. I'll give the word, girls, and we'll all scream for help. We'll have men with torches running out of all the buildings before you can wink. I'll count *one, two,* three—and then we'll all yell. All right? Ready now; and take a deep breath!"

Chapter 17

"Wait!" interrupted Anita's voice.

Bill, who had just been about to take to his heels at the prospect of a chorus of powerful female Dilbian lungs shouting for help, checked himself just in time.

"Don't shout," Anita's voice went on, hastily. "You don't want to get the men all roused up and over here, and then find out that the Cobbly's gone before they get here, and there's no way of proving it was here at all. Cobblies don't bother us Shorties. Let me go outside and see if I can get a look at it."

There was no immediate response to Anita's suggestion. Bill turned back to glance in through the tear in the curtain. The assembled Dilbian females were sitting and staring at her. If she had proposed that she try to walk up the wall, across the ceiling, and down the other wall of the room, or casually suggested flying to the top of the cliffs that surrounded the valley they could not have looked more upset. The thought of anyone—let alone a female, whether native or

Shorty—facing a Cobbly was evidently so enormous that it had rendered even No Rest speechless. But then that matriarch found her voice.

"Don't bother you?" she echoed, forgetting in her astonishment, to whisper. "But whatever—whatever—" words failed her in an attempt to state the concept of any kind of female world undeviled by Cobblies.

"Oh, we used to have something like Cobblies on our Shorty world," Anita said into the silence. "We had a different name for them, of course. But Cobblies and things like them don't like places where there's been a lot of building and making of things—you know that. You know they like the woods better than the villages and places like here, particularly in the daytime."

There were a few scared, hesitant nods around the circle.

"So our Cobblies sort of faded away," said Anita. "Just the way maybe yours will someday. Anyway, why don't I go outside and look?"

There was another long pause. But then No Rest visibly took a firm hold on herself. She sat up straight and spoke in a decisive voice.

"Very well, Dirty Teeth," she said sternly. "If you're not afraid to go out and look for the Cobbly, we'd all appreciate it very much."

"I'll look all around," said Anita, hastily getting to her feet. "But if I'm not back at the end of fifteen or twenty minutes, then you can always go ahead and shout for the men and torches, the way you were planning to."

She slipped quickly to the door, opened it, and went out. To Bill, transferring his gaze to the outside, she appeared like a black shadow, slipping through the suddenly lighted opening, which was immediately darkened behind her as the door quickly shut again. The sound of a bar being dropped across it from the inside followed closely upon its closing.

Bill went toward her dark silhouette. She had come down the three steps onto the grass and was standing still—probably trying to adjust her eyes to the darkness outside.

Bill came noiselessly up behind her and tapped her on the shoulder.

She gave a sudden gasp—like a choked-off scream—and spun about so abruptly and violently that he backed off a step.

"W-who's there?" she whispered, in English. "Is that you, Pick-and—I mean, Mr. Waltham?"

"*Bill,* blast it! Call me Bill!" whispered Bill fiercely in return. "Come on, let's get away from here to someplace where we can talk."

Without a further word, she turned and began to move off along the building and through several patches of shadow until they came up against the wall of a long, narrow, almost windowless building that was completely dark within.

"This is a storage place—sort of a warehouse," said Anita in a low voice and turning to face him as they stopped. "There won't be anyone around here to hear us. What on earth are you doing in the valley here? Didn't you know any better than to come back here—especially at night?"

"Never mind that!" snapped Bill. He was surprised to find a good deal of honest anger suddenly bubbling up inside him. Here he had risked his neck to find her, and she was adopting the same irritating, authoritative tone she had taken with him on his first visit to the valley. It was the final straw upon the heavy load of frustrations and harrowing experiences which had been loaded upon him ever since he had set foot on Dilbian soil. "I'm here to get some straight answers, and you're going to supply them!"

"Answers?" she replied, almost blankly.

"That's right!" Bill snapped. "Since I saw you last, I've spent an educational fifteen minutes with our Hemnoid friend—with me tied to a tree during the conversation ..." and he told her about his kidnapping and rescue of the day before.

"But you don't believe him!" exclaimed Anita, when he was finished. "Mula-*ay*'s a *Hemnoid*! The authorities wouldn't

136

send you here to get killed, just to get themselves out of a tough spot! You *know* that!"

"Do I?" said Bill, between his teeth. "How about the fact that I've been sent here to a job I never trained for? How about the fact the communicator wasn't working when I got here—oh, I found out what was wrong and fixed it . . ." he told her about finding the power lead disconnected. "But who knows how to use a power wrench? No Dilbian, for sure. That leaves you or Lafe Greentree as the only ones who could have disconnected it!"

"How about Mula-*ay?*" she demanded.

"Mula-*ay* doesn't control our relay stations and hospital ship computers. When I got it connected, all I could get was the hospital ship Greentree's supposed to have gone to, and the computer there wouldn't connect me with any live person, or give me anything but a bulletin on his health." Bill told her about his conversation over the communications equipment.

"But—" Anita's voice was unhappy, almost a wail, "it still doesn't prove anything! And the authorities *don't* want to close this project down! Don't you know what the name of the project itself stands for—"

"I know all right!" broke in Bill. "They told me at the reassignment center. 'Spacepaw—*Helping Paw from the Stars*,' in Dilbian translation, because according to the Dilbians they're the only ones who have hands, and we Shorties have 'paws.' " Bill laughed shortly. "Let's try another interpretation, shall we? Project Catspaw—with me as the 'catspaw' that bails our Alien Relations people out of a jam on this world!"

"Bill, you *know* better!" said Anita desperately. "Oh, if you only knew how hard Lafe's worked here, you'd know he'd never have agreed to anything to close this project, let alone helping in making you the catspaw, as you say. It's all coincidence, my being here, and his breaking his leg—"

"Were you there when he broke it?" interrupted Bill.

"Well, I . . . no," admitted Anita grudgingly. "I was away

137

from the Residency. When I got back, he hadn't waited for me. He'd already got a cast on it and called in, asking for transportation to a hospital ship—"

"Then you don't know for sure if he ever did fall and break it," said Bill grimly. "All right, maybe you can tell me what kind of a trick was used when this Half-Pint-Posted I keep hearing about beat up that mountain Dilbian with his bare hands."

"But there wasn't any trick! Honestly—" said Anita fervently. "Or rather, the only trick was that he used his belt. The Half-Pint—I mean, John Tardy—was a former Olympic decathalon champion. He got the Dilbian in the water with him, managed to get behind him and put his belt around the Streamside Terror's neck, and choked him. Outside of using the belt and the fact that he was able to maneuver in the water better than the Streamside Terror, it was a fair fight."

"Well, I'm no Olympic decathalon champion!" said Bill in heartfelt tones. "And if I was, how could I get a duel with swords and shield fought underwater? But I was set up for this duel with Bone Breaker in practically everybody's mind—Human, Dilbian, Hemnoid, and all—before I even got here—"

"But you weren't!" Anita was wringing her verbal hands. "Believe me, Bill—"

"Believe you? Ha!" said Bill bitterly. "You seem to be fitting in right with the rest of the scheme. Here you're supposed to be an agricultural trainee-assistant, but first you get the village females like Sweet Thing and Thing-or-Two all stirred up on opposite sides. Now I find you here stirring up the outlaw females. Why should I believe you any more than I would Greenleaf, or any of the rest who were part of getting me into this mess."

She made an odd, small, choked sound, and he saw the dark shape of her whirl and walk away from him for several paces before she stopped. He stared after her in some astonishment. He was not quite sure what reaction he had expected to his words—but it certainly had not been this. After a moment, when she still did not turn back or say anything, he walked after her and stopped behind her.

"Look—" he began.

"I suppose you think I like it!" she interrupted him without turning about, low-voiced and furious. "I suppose you think I'm doing it all just for my own amusement?"

He stared at the dark back of her head.

"Why, then?" he demanded.

With that, she did swing around to face him. He saw the pale oval of her face, gray in the dimness, without being able to read its expression. But the tone of her voice was readable enough.

"For a lot of reasons you don't even begin to understand!" she said. "But I'll try and make you understand part of it, anyway. Do you know anything about anthropology?"

"No," he said stiffly. "My field's engineering—you know that. Why, what do you know about it? Your field's agriculture, isn't it?"

"I also happen to have an associate's degree in cultural anthropology!" Anita snapped.

"Associate degree " he peered at her. "But aren't you an agricultural trainee-assistant?" He strove to see her face, through the darkness. He felt bewildered. He would have been ready to swear that she was no older than he was.

"Of course. But—" she checked herself. "I mean, I am. But I've also been under special tutoring and an accelerated study course since I left primary school. For example, I've also got an assistant's certificate in pharmacy, and a provisional research certificate in xeno-biology—"

"Grk!" said Bill involuntarily, staring at her through the darkness. She evidently was, he suddenly realized, one of those super-brains customarily referred to as Hothouse Types back in college-preparatory school. Those students with so much on the ball that they were allowed to load up on half a dozen extra lines of study. Well, that was nice. That was all it took in addition to everything else that was making him feel like everybody's prize fool in this Dilbian situation.

"—What?" Anita was asking him puzzledly.

"Nothing. Go on," he growled.

"Well, I'm trying to explain something to you," she went on. "Did you ever hear of the Yaghan—a nearly extinct Indian tribe that used to occupy the south coast of Tierra del Fuego and the islands of Cape Horn at the tip of South America?"

"Why should I?" grumped Bill sourly. "And what's that got to do with the situation, anyway? What I want to know—"

"Just listen!" Anita said fiercely. "The Yaghan were a very primitive tribe, but they were studied by, among other people, a German anthropologist named Gusinde who wrote a monograph on them in 1937. Gusinde found out that the laws or the social rules of existence of the Yaghan were not enforced by any particular specific authority but by what he called the *Allgemeinheit*, meaning the 'group as a whole.' But there had to be some individuals who spoke for this 'group as a whole'; and these speakers were men called *tiamuna* by the Yaghan—and Gusinde describes the *tiamuna* this way—'*men who because of their old age, spotless character, long experience and mental superiority gained such an extent of moral influence that it is equal to a peculiar domination.*'"

Anita stopped speaking. Bill stared through the darkness at her. What relation this lecture had to the subject at hand he had no idea. After a moment he said as much.

"Well, haven't you heard the Dilbians talk about Grandfathers?" demanded Anita. "These Grandfathers are the *tiamuna*-equivalents among the Dilbians. The whole Dilbian culture is a strongly individualistic one—even more individualistic than our human culture. But it keeps itself stable through a very rigid system of unofficial checks and balances. It *looks* as if it'd be easy to introduce new ideas to the Dilbian culture. But the trouble is, introducing any new idea threatens to disrupt the existing cultural system of these checks and balances, and so the new idea gets rejected. There's only one way a new idea can be introduced and that's by getting a *tiamuna*—a Grandfather—to agree that maybe it's a good thing for Dilbians in general. In other words if you want to introduce any element of progress among the Dilbians, you've got to get a Grandfather to back it. And of course, the Grandfathers, because they're old and thoroughly entrenched in the existing system, are highly conservative and not about to give their approval to some change. But that makes no difference—if you want change you've got to find a *tiamuna* to speak up for it!"

"But there aren't any Grandfathers around here," Bill said. "At least there aren't any in the village, or in the outlaw camp, here."

"That's just it!" said Anita urgently. "Nearly all of the Dilbians live up in the mountains, where there *are* Grandfathers, and the Grandfathers *do* control everything. It's only down here in the Lowlands, where old tribal customs have started to relax their hold in the face of the different necessities of an agricultural community that there aren't any Grandfathers to deal with."

"But you said—" fumbled Bill, "that you had to get a Grandfather to accept your new idea before you could get the other Dilbians to accept it. If there aren't any Grandfathers around here—"

"There aren't any *Grandfathers* here," said Anita. "But there *are* *tiamuna*-equivalent individuals. Male Dilbians, who under the proper conditions up in the mountains, or at the proper age, would be Grandfathers."

"You mean," said Bill, his befuddled wits finally breaking through into a glimmer of the light of understanding, "someone like More Jam—or Bone Breaker?"

"Not More Jam, of course!" she said. "Bone Breaker is right, enough. But in the village, the closest thing they have to a *tiamuna*-equivalent is Flat Fingers. That's why I told you to get him on your side."

"But More Jam—" began Bill.

"More Jam, nonsense!" Anita said energetically. "I know all the villagers have a soft spot for him, and he carries some

141

weight as the local innkeeper, to say nothing of his former glory as Lowland champion wrestler—Dilbians are very loyal. But him and that enormous stomach of his that he pretends can't stand anything but the daintiest of food—he's a standing joke for miles around. Remember, a leader can never be a figure of fun—"

"Are you sure?" asked Bill doubtfully.

But she was going on without listening to him. Bill's head was whirling. Just as he had seemed to hear a note of something incorrect in what Mula-*ay* had said the day before about Bill's not being likely to feel an empathy with someone like Bone Breaker, now he had just heard the same note again, accompanying Anita's statement about More Jam.

Chapter 18

"... I would no more consider you a subject of *sana* on the basis of our casual acquaintance here, *than you would be likely to emphathize with—say—Bone Breaker, or any of the Dilbians* ..."

"... *More Jam, nonsense!* ... *He's a standing joke for miles around. Remember a leader can never be a figure of fun*—"

There was something wrong, thought Bill strongly, about both statements. If he could only connect that wrongness with his strange situation here on Dilbia, he had a feeling he might be on the track of handling that situation. Clearly there were some human machinations at work or else he would not be here at all. Clearly Anita knew nothing about them. Also, clearly, the Hemnoids in the person of Mula-*ay* were attempting to exploit the situation. But what none of these individuals and groups seemed to have stopped to consider was that possibly the Dilbians concerned might be grinding some axes of their own in the tangle where all this was going on.

The Dilbians—even the Hill Bluffer, in some obscure way Bill's mind could not at the moment pin down—seemed to have a stake in Bill's situation, of which Hemnoids and humans alike—even Anita, with her anthropological knowledge—seemed to be ignorant.

Without being able to prove all this in any way, Bill still felt it—as he had felt the incorrectness of Dilbian-understanding, first in Mula-*ay* and now in Anita. He felt it in his bones. Anita was still talking. Bill's attention jerked abruptly back to her.

". . . so forget about More Jam and concentrate on the two important figures of Bone Breaker and Flat Fingers," she was saying. "They're the ones that have to be moved, and I'm trying, just as much as you are, to move them. That's why I've been working with the Dilbian women—in the village as well as here in the valley—the way I have. I suppose you don't understand that, even yet?"

"Ah—no," confessed Bill uncomfortably.

"Then let me tell you," said Anita. "It's because the one person that a *tiamuna* can listen to in the way of advice, without losing face, is his wife! That's because he can talk things over with her privately, and then announce the results in public as if they were his own idea, and she's not going to contradict him. And, of course, because of his physical and social superiority over the other male Dilbians, none of them are going to suggest it isn't his own idea, either."

"Oh," said Bill.

"So you see," Anita wound up, "I know what I'm doing. You don't—and that's why you ought to listen to me when I tell you what to do. And one of the things you shouldn't have done was come into this valley at night, to find me and talk to me. Maybe there *is* something strange about the way

143

you've been left alone to face things. But Lafe didn't have anything to do with it—you can believe me!"

Bill said nothing. Anita, evidently willing to carry the point by default, paused a minute and then went on to other subjects.

"So what you do," she said, "is get back to the village as quickly as you can and *stay there*! Bone Breaker won't come into the village after you—that'd be going too far, even for the Muddy Nosers. And even if Bone Breaker brought all his fighting men with him, there'd still be more villagers than they could handle. So as long as you stay in the village, you're safe. Now do it, and cultivate Flat Fingers as I told you. Now I've got to be getting back to No Rest and the others, before they think the Cobblies have eaten me up! You aren't going to waste any time getting out of the valley now, are you?" A thought seemed to strike her suddenly. "By the way, how did you get in here?"

"Rope," answered Bill absently, still caught up in his new understanding, "down one of the cliffs."

"Well, you get back to that rope and get up it as fast as you can!" said Anita. "Can I trust you to do that?"

"—What?" said Bill, coming abruptly back out of the thoughts that had been occupying him. "Oh, of course. Certainly."

"Well, that's good," said Anita. He voice softened, unexpectedly. She put her hand on his arm, and he was abruptly conscious of the light touch of it there. "*Please* be careful, now."

She took her hand away with that, turned about, and disappeared into the shadow. For a moment he stood staring into the darkness where she had been, strangely still feeling the touch of her hand even through the thickness of the shirt on his arm. It seemed to him that a little warmth seemed to linger where she had touched him.

Then he shook himself back to awareness. Of course, he was going to head back out of the valley as quickly as he could—but there was still something yet for him to do.

He turned and searched for the large building-shape of the mess hall. He found it and went toward it, keeping in the shadows. Five minutes later he glided up close to the front steps and paused. Here and there a gleam of light still showed between the hide curtains that covered the windows on the inside. But there were no guards standing on either side of the steps leading to the big doors—which were now closed. And the outlaw signal gong hung unguarded.

Bill came up to it and touched it. It was nothing more than a strip of bar iron, hung by a rope from one of the projecting rafter ends that supported the eaves above him. But he suddenly realized that he had made a serious mistake in boasting to the villagers that he would bring this back. For it was at least five feet long and two inches thick. It would be both too awkward and too heavy for him to carry while climbing back up the cliff by means of the rope.

He paused, baffled. If he was right about the Dilbians having their own axes to grind in the present situation, the fact that Bill should be able to produce evidence of having been in the valley this night loomed more importantly than ever. But if he could not carry the gong away with him, as he had promised, what could he do?

An inspiration struck him. He turned to the mess hall wall of peeled and weathered logs just behind the gong. His fingers, searching over its surface, found what he wanted, and unhooked it from the peg that held it by a thong through a hole in one of its ends. He brought it away from the wall, out a little toward the moonlight, so he could examine it. It, like the gong, was simply a length of bar iron. But it was no more than a foot and a half long, with a hole in one end where the thong attached, and below the thong that end was wrapped with cloths to provide a grip for an outsized Dilbian hand. It was, in short, the hammer with which the gong was habitually struck, and something Bill could easily tuck in his belt and take with him back up the cliff to the village.

Tucking his prize through his belt, where the rag-wound end kept it from slipping through, Bill turned and headed back toward the now-visible notch in the moonlit cliff from which his cord, invisible at this distance, was dangling.

The moon was round and full over the valley by this time, but an intermittent cloudiness hid its face from time to time, so that light became dark. This seemed like a good omen—offering a chance for him to cross the relatively open area between the last of the buildings and the fringe of brush and trees at the base of the cliff, without any chance observer from the outlaw buildings happening to glance out and see him moving. Accordingly, when he reached the edge of the shadow of the final building, he hesitated until a cloud hid the moon, and then made a dash for the nearest place of concealment, a small hollow in the valley floor perhaps fifty yards away.

He made it, and dropped flat, just as the moon came out from behind its cloud. But as he lay hugging the earth, he stiffened suddenly in apprehension.

He was lying face downward, with his head turned to one side and his ear pressed against the still-warm earth beneath the short grass. To that ear there had come the momentary sound of thudding feet—before it abruptly ceased and silence took its place.

The cloud that was just beginning to cover the moon with its fleecy, thin, outer edge was a dark and long one. It looked fully long enough to allow Bill to make it the rest of the hundred yards to the cliff and the cover of the undergrowth at the base of the cliff. He held his breath as the dark part of the cloud began to cover the moon. The light faded abruptly—and all at once it was dark.

At once, Bill was on his feet and running for the cliff. But his ears were alert now, and as he ran he was almost certain that he could hear, in time to his own pounding feet, the thud of heavier ones behind him. Winded and panting, but still under the safe cover of darkness, he saw the deeper shadow of the brush and trees at the foot of the cliff, looming up before him. A second later, he was among them. Ducking off to his right, heedless of the branches that lashed at his face and body, he ran off from the main line of his flight for about thirty feet or so, and stopped, as still as the shadows from the moonlight about him, striving to control the panting of his oxygen-exhausted lungs.

Darkness still held the valley. But now there was no doubt about it. Now that he was stopped, Bill heard plainly the heavy sound of his running pursuer come up to and crash into the undergrowth at the base of the cliff—then stop in his turn.

Suddenly there was silence all around. Bill stood, holding his breath—and, somewhere hidden in the darkness less than twenty or thirty feet away, whoever had been following him was standing, holding *his* breath.

Bill was abruptly conscious of the hard length of the hammer to the valley gong beneath his belt. He backed away along the base of the cliff and looked about, trying to find his rope, or at least the cleft in the top edge of the cliff from which it hung.

However, from this angle of vision—right underneath the cliff, with the bushes and the trees close about him in the now once more brilliant moonlight, the rope seemed nowhere in sight. He hesitated, trying to decide which way he would move to look for it and then, at that moment, he heard a sound that checked him in mid-movement.

It was the sound of a bush rustling less than twenty feet from him.

His pursuer had been closer than he thought. Bill turned desperately to the cliff beside him. It was pitted enough by cracks and holes so that it was just possible he might be able to climb it. He turned to the cliff-face and began to climb.

He went up as noiselessly as he could. For the first eight or ten feet, he made swift and quiet progress. But then, he reached upward with his right leg for a foothold upon a small projection from the cliff-face—and it broke beneath his boot sole.

With a sound that seemed to Bill's tense ears to be like the roar of an avalanche, the broken piece of rock and a few

147

shards of cliff-face it had carried away with it, went cascading down to the bushes below.—And with that, everything began to happen very swiftly.

He scrabbled frantically with his unsupported foot for a new resting place. But, as he did so, there was a tearing, rushing sound through the bushes below him, and something that sounded like a snarl of animal triumph. At the same time, the strain of his body weight upon his two hands and remaining foot proved too much for their precarious grasp upon the cliff-face.

The support beneath his other foot gave way suddenly, and he fell, spread-eagled backward, outward into darkness and downward toward the ground, fifteen or twenty feet below.

Chapter 19

As he fell backward through the darkness, Bill instinctively tried to roll himself about in midair as he had learned in Survival School, and land on his feet. But the distance was too short. Even as he tried to relax in expectation of a bone-shattering concussion against the hard ground at the foot of the cliff, his fall was interrupted.

He found himself, unexpectedly, caught in midair—by what appeared to be two very large and capable hands.

"So it's you, Pick-and-Shovel!" the voice of Bone Breaker rumbled above him. "I thought it was you. Didn't I get your promise you wouldn't come back here, except in daylight?"

He set Bill on his feet, as the moonlight broke finally free of all clouds and they saw each other clearly. Bill looked up at the towering, coal-black Dilbian form. His mind was racing. He had never thought faster in his life.

"Well," he said, "I wanted to talk to you privately—"

"Privately? That's a Shorty for you!" said Bone Breaker. "Don't you know that if anybody found out we've been talking together privately, anything might happen? Why, people would be likely to start guessing all sorts of things! But here you show up—"

He broke off abruptly, staring down at Bill.

"By the way," he asked in a tone of puzzlement, "just how did you get here, anyhow? The guards in the gates didn't let you in. And there's no way you could get over the stockade fence in the dark."

Bill took a deep breath and gambled that the truth would serve him better at this point than anything short of subterfuge. He pointed up the wall of the cliff alongside them.

"I climbed down there," he said.

Bone Breaker continued to stare at him for a long moment. Then the Dilbian outlaw chief's eyes moved slowly away from him and lifted, traveling up the sheer face of the cliff.

"You—" the words came out of him slowly with long, incredulous pauses in between, "came down that?"

"Why, certainly!" said Bill determinedly and cheerfully, "we Shorties can climb almost anything. Why, back on my own world once, I—"

"Never mind that," rumbled Bone Breaker. His eyes came back down to focus on Bill's face. "If you came down it, I suppose you can get back up it, again?"

"Well . . . yes," said Bill, a little reluctantly, his fall of a moment before fresh in his mind. "I can climb it, all right."

"Then you better get going," said Bone Breaker—not so much angrily as emphatically. "You don't know how lucky you are it was me who spotted you sneaking around the buildings, back there, instead of it being one of our regular watchmen. It's just a happy chance for you that I like to take a stroll around myself every evening before I turn in, just to

149

see that everything's all right. Why, you could've spoiled everything!"

"Everything?" echoed Bill frowning.

"Why, certainly," rumbled Bone Breaker reprovingly. "Why would anybody think you'd be here, except to have that duel with me? And what's the point of having a duel at this time of night, with no real light to see by and hardly anybody around? No, no, Pick-and-Shovel. You've got to get this sort of thing straight in your Shorty head. Something like our duel has to be held in broad daylight. With everybody looking on, too. I want everybody up in the valley, and watching. And as many villagers as can get here, as well." His voice took on, strange as it seemed, almost a wistful note. "It's just too bad we can't send runners out with the word so that anyone in the district could drop by. But, I suppose that'd be overdoing it."

"Er—yes," agreed Bill.

"Well, anyway," said Bone Breaker, his voice becoming suddenly brisk, "you'd better get started. Up that cliff with you and out of sight—and remember! Whatever you do, Pick-and-Shovel, make sure it's daylight when you come back again. Full daylight!"

"I will," promised Bill. He turned to the cliff-face without any further hesitation and carefully began to climb. Some ten feet above the ground, he paused to look down. The moon was out from behind its clouds, and by its light he saw the outlaw chief staring up at him. As he watched, Bone Breaker shook his head a little, as if in amazement, and then turned and went off toward the buildings, just as the moon slid once more behind a cloud, and darkness covered the scene.

As soon as the face of the cliff was cloaked in shadow, Bill ceased climbing. Cautiously, feeling his way with hands and feet in the gloom with his heart thudding, Bill climbed back down slowly onto solid ground. When at last he stood firmly upright upon it, he found his face was wet with perspiration. A single misstep on the way down could have set him falling, the way he had done once already. And this time, there would have been no Bone Breaker to catch him.

However, now that he was safely on his feet again, he began to work his way along the base of the cliff until he reached a spot where he was completely hidden by the undergrowth. Here he waited until the moon once more emerged from its cloud, and, looking up, he was able to make out the notch at the top of the cliff from which his rope decended.

It was still a little farther to his right. He continued on and came at last to the rope itself, nearly invisible in the moonlight against the light-colored rock of the cliff-face.

The climb required a number of stops to rest along the way. Whenever he found a spot where he could lean or crouch against the cliff-face to rest those muscles of his arms and legs which had been bearing his weight during the climb, he did so. In spite of this, by the time he could look up and see the bottom of the notch only ten or twelve feet above him, Bill was as exhausted as he could remember being.

He had no idea, as he paused for a final rest upon a ledge of rock outcropping from the vertical face, how long the upward climb had taken. It seemed to have taken hours. However, no alarm had so far been raised that would indicate anyone had caught sight of him. After resting on the rock ledge as long as he dared, without risking the stiffening of his weary muscles, Bill geared up his courage and his remaining energy for the last stretch to the bottom of the notch. Then he began to climb.

It was hard work. With each foot gained upward, he felt the already shallow reserves of his strength ebbing away. Eventually, the bottom of the notch came within view, but still more than an arm's reach away. Bill locked his feet in the rope and started to let go with his right hand in order to reach upward.

—And his exhaustion-weakened left hand almost let go.

Clutching desperately at the rope with both hands, Bill clung to his position. There seemed to be no strength left in him. For a second, a giddy picture of his grip finally loosening on the rope as he hung here, and his plunge to certain death at the foot of the cliff swam through his mind.

—And then he moved.

He moved upward. He and the rope together lifted a good four feet until the notch was almost level with his eyes. Before he could grasp what had happened, the rope lifted again, carrying him with it. Someone above was hauling it upward, pulling him to the safety of the cliff-top.

Wildly and unexpectedly it came to him that possibly the Bluffer had returned, although he was not due until dawn—or had stayed in position above the cliff, and was now bringing him up to safe and level ground. Bill looked upward, expecting to see the dark, furry mass of the Dilbian postman staring down at him. But it was not the Bluffer he saw.

He stared instead into the moonlit, Buddha-like countenance of Mula-*ay*. The hands of the Hemnoid had hold of the rope. The great, heavy-gravity muscles of the alien were bringing it easily in, and there was a smile of pure, gentle joy on Mula-*ay*'s face. Like a hooked fish, Bill was being drawn helplessly upward into the hands of his enemy.

If the shock and dismay that Bill felt were strong, they were overridden just at that moment by the prospect of getting off the cliff-face and onto the level top of the cliff, no matter with whose help. He clung desperately to the rope and let himself be pulled in, until at last he was hauled over the edge of the notch and collapsed weakly upon the soft ground above the vertical rock-face.

For a moment, he simply lay there, almost too weak to move, his arms and legs trembling from the strain they had just endured. Then, painfully, he let go of the rope and struggled to his feet.

Directly in front of him, and less than six feet away, with his arms now folded across his chest within the voluminous sleeves of his yellow robe, Mula-*ay* continued to smile contentedly at him in the moonlight.

"Well, well, my young friend," said Mula-*ay*, with a heavy, liquid chuckle. "And what are you doing here at this time of night?"

Bill had had a chance to collect his wits. As it had in the

moment at the foot of the cliff when he first found himself facing Bone Breaker, his mind was racing swiftly, turning up conclusions rapidly as it went.

"Why, I was just out," said Bill, panting slightly in spite of his attempts to appear calm, "for a little sport rock-climbing. Suppose you tell me what you're doing here,"

Mula-*ay* laughed again.

"Why, of course I could tell an untruth just like you, my young friend," replied the Hemnoid, "and say I just happened to be out for a moonlight stroll. But people like myself are always truthful—particularly when the truth hurts—and I'll tell you the truth. I was out here looking for you, and, behold, I have found you."

"Looking for me?" queried Bill. "What made you think you might find me here? Particularly, what made you think you might find me here at this time of night?"

"I thought it likely you would want to visit your female confederate down there in the valley before long," chuckled Mula-*ay* thickly. "And I was right."

Bill looked into the round moon-face narrowly. What Mula-*ay* said made sense—but only up to a certain point. His galloping mind seized upon the hole in the Hemnoid's statement.

"You might've been expecting me to try to get in to the valley and see Miss Lyme," said Bill bluntly, "but how would you know that I would try to get in by climbing down the cliffs—and how would you know just where on the cliffs I'd choose to climb down?" His gaze narrowed further. "You've got a robot warning system set up around this valley, haven't you? And that's in violation of the Human-Hemnoid agreement."

He pointed a finger at Mula-*ay*.

"The minute I report this," he snapped, "your superiors will have to pull you from your post here on Dilbia!"

"*If* you tell them, don't you mean, my young friend?" murmured Mula-*ay* comfortably. "I seem to remember something about your not being able to reach your superiors off-planet. And if you did, it would simply be your word against mine."

"I don't think so," retorted Bill grimly. "Any efficient warning system would require power expenditure, and good detection equipment would be able to find traces of power expenditure in the area, once they knew where to look—which they would, as soon as I told them how you had been warned by my entering the valley down the cliff. You must have a sensory ring set up all around the valley."

"And if I have?" Mula-*ay* shrugged. "And if detection equipment actually could find traces? There's still the question of your telling them about it."

These last words were said in the same light and careless tone in which Mula-*ay* had been conversing from the beginning. But something about them sent a sudden chill through Bill. He was abruptly aware of the position in which he stood.

This isolated spot at the cliff's edge, closely and thickly hemmed in by bushes, was now proving to work its former advantages to his present disadvantage. Directly before him, the gross and inconceivably powerful heavy-gravity form of the Hemnoid blocked Bill's only direct route of escape into the nighttime woods. Behind him was the cliff, where one step backward would send him plunging down through emptiness. To right and left the thickly grown bushes formed flanking walls, through which a Dilbian or a Hemnoid might be able to push by brute force, but which would slow down a human like himself, so that he could easily be caught by someone like Mula-*ay*.

These bushes grew almost to the very lift of the cliff. Only perhaps half a foot of crumbling, overhanging turf separated the last of them from the vertical drop. Bill was as neatly enclosed as a steer in a slaughter pen at a meat-packing company. Only his reflexes, which would be faster than the heavy-gravity being facing him—just as they were faster than the Dilbians'—because of his smaller size, remained in his favor. And he did not at the moment see how faster reflexes could help him here.

"You aren't—" he began and hesitated, "you aren't such a fool as to think of actually doing something to me yourself? There'd be bound to be an investigation, and the investigation would be bound to turn up the fact that you were responsible."

Mula-*ay* shook his head.

"I?" he said, and his smile broadened. "Who'd bother to push the investigation in my direction, when it will be plain that your Dilbian postman left you off here for the express purpose of climbing down the cliff? And when your body is found at the very foot of the rope down which you climbed, with every indication that your grip upon it failed so that you fell to your death?"

Mula-*ay* chuckled, and, withdrawing his hands from their sleeves, flexed their thick, wide fingers.

"Oh?" demanded Bill, on what he hoped was a convincing note of scorn, "if that's really what you mean to do, why haven't you just done it, instead of standing around talking to me about it?"

Mula-*ay* chuckled again, continuing to flex his fingers.

"Aren't you forgetting," he replied cheerfully, "that we Hemnoids enjoy the suffering of our victims?" He chuckled. "And mental suffering is so much more delicately satisfying than gross physical discomfort. I wanted to thank you— before pushing you over the cliff, for being so obliging as to put yourself in this exposed and compromising position after you were so lucky as to be rescued from the little execution I arranged for you at the hands of Grandpa Squeaky—"

"All right, Hill Bluffer," interrupted Bill swiftly, looking over Mula-*ay*'s right shoulder. "He's admitted what I wanted him to say. You can grab him now."

Mula-*ay* chuckled again.

"You didn't think you could fool me by saying something like that—" he began. But as he did so, his eyes flickered for a second backward over his right shoulder. And in that second, Bill acted.

Spinning on his heel, he dashed off to his left along the narrow strip between the end of the bushes and the cliff edge. He felt the ground giving under his feet as his weight came upon it—but then he was past, veering into the darkness of the forest beyond and the solid footing farther back. Behind him, he heard Mula-*ay*'s muffled shout, followed by the crashing of the bushes as the tremendously powerful, heavy-gravity body of the other bulldozed through them in pursuit. But without pausing, Bill ran on, taking advantage of every open spot and break in the undergrowth that he could find.

He covered perhaps seventy-five or a hundred yards this way. Then, winded, he stopped. Listening, he heard—quite some distance behind him now—the sound of the Hemnoid blundering and tearing his way through the undergrowth. Panting, and with sweat running off him in rivulets, Bill stood still and kept quiet.

After a few seconds, the sound of the Hemnoid's pursuit also stopped abruptly. Bill could imagine Mula-*ay* standing, listening, waiting for some sound to tell him in which way Bill was trying to escape. But Bill knew better than to give him that clue. Bill continued to stand still, and for the long, drawn-out space of perhaps two and a half minutes nothing but night silence held the cliff-top forest.

At the end of that time, Mula-*ay* moved again. He was evidently trying to move quietly, but sound of his passage, of leaves rustling and branches being swept aside by his passage, came clearly and unmistakably to Bill's ears. After perhaps half a minute of this, it must have become obvious to Mula-*ay* as well that he could not move anywhere near as quietly as Bill—nor could he find Bill in the darkened forest this way as long as Bill chose to hide. Amazingly and unexpectedly, the almost ghostly chuckle of the Hemnoid floated through the moonlit undergrowth and trees to Bill's ear. And the voice of Mula-*ay* came quite distinctly, although muted by distance.

"Very good. Very good indeed, my young friend . . ." The ghostly chuckle came again. "But there will be other opportunities and other ways. Good-bye for now—and pleasant dreams."

With the last word, there came the sound of the Hemnoid unmistakably moving off. The rustling and crashing sounds of his departure moved straight away from the edge of the cliff until they were lost in the distance. Bill sat down on a fallen log to catch his breath.

The fact that the Hemnoid had been willing to risk open violence against a representative of the human race here on this neutral world went far to confirm the sudden understanding that had burst upon Bill while he was talking to Anita Lyme in the valley below. There was no doubt now that there was a great deal more at stake between humans and Hemnoids, a great deal more wavering in the balance between them here on Dilbia in this situation than appeared on the surface. Why Bill himself had not been informed of this remained a puzzle.

Bill shook himself abruptly and stood up. A complete silence held the forest. He turned, and moving with a silence that was the result of his long practice and competitions, he found his way back to the cliff edge and followed it around to the valley's entrance. There, working along by moonlight, he measured the angle of the drop from the turn in the trail leading to the stockade gates some fifty yards away and then paced off the distance from the turn to the gates, in order to measure it exactly. Having done this he returned up around the cliff edge to the top of the notch, where Bone Breaker had left him. Hauling up his rope and once more rewinding it around his waist under his shirt, he scooped out with his hands a small depression in the lea of a large boulder at the cliff top, built a rough bower of branches around it, and then curled up inside the primitive shelter he had so created. It was no worse and a good deal better than many of the same

157

shelters he had created in Survival School, back on Earth. Curled up within it, his own body heat, reflected from the rock behind him and trapped by the enclosing branches, soon made him comfortable . . . and he slept.

Chapter 20

Bill woke to the confused impression that he was flying through the air. The jolt with which he landed brought him fully awake. He found himself being carried. For a moment he hung there, trying to puzzle things out as the mists of sleep evaporated.

Then it came to him. Evidently the Bluffer, coming and finding him asleep, had simply picked him up and plunked him in the saddle without further notice. This was entirely in line with the Dilbian way of doing things. There was even a sort of horrible humor to the situation. Bill opened his mouth and laughed—only the laugh came out more like a croak.

"Alive up there, are you?" queried the Bluffer, without turning his head, or slowing his pace. "You were really sleeping it up, when I found you back there. Have a good night?"

For answer, Bill let go of the Bluffer's straps with his right hand, fumbled under his belt, and brought out the hammer to the outlaw gong, which he held out in front of the Bluffer's eyes.

"Well, well!" said the Bluffer cheerfully. "Thought you were going to bring the gong itself, though?"

"This was easier to carry," said Bill, as indifferently as he

158

could manage. "I suppose it'll do as well as the gong, to prove that I was down in the valley last night?"

"Why, I guess it would," replied the Bluffer judiciously. "You couldn't get either one without going in and out."

The Bluffer's tone of approval it seemed to Bill, however, left something to be desired.

"Why?" asked Bill. "Something wrong with getting into Outlaw Valley by climbing down the cliffs and climbing back up them to get out again?"

"Wrong? No, I wouldn't say so," replied the Bluffer thoughtfully, "but it's just another thing that a Shorty might be able to do that a man couldn't do—not because the Shorty wasn't being better than a man at doing it, but because the Shorty was so small that it was easier for him to do it. Like crawling into a little hole in the ground, one that'd be too small for a real man to crawl into."

"Oh," said Bill, suddenly deflated. He himself knew how hard it had been to get up and down that cliff. It had never occurred to him that the difficulties and dangers involved would mean nothing to a Dilbian—simply because a Dilbian would have no means of duplicating them himself. That took climbing a sheer cliff out of the heroic class and put it into the class of magic to Dilbians. No one expected a human, back on Earth, to swim as well as a fish. After all, he wasn't a fish.

"You see," said the Bluffer, after a moment. "I just thought I'd let you know how things stand, Pick-and-Shovel. It's all very well doing tricks—everybody knows you Shorties have got all kinds of tricks up your sleeves. But what kind of good is it going to do us real men and women and children? *That's* what we want to know! So if you'll go around and climb up on my back again, we'll get going toward the village."

Bill did as the Bluffer suggested, in silence. And that same thoughtful silence he maintained until they entered the main street of the village itself. Nor did the Bluffer seem disposed to interrupt him.

However, when they came in sight of the Residency, and

the Bluffer seemed headed past that building on toward the blacksmith shop, Bill roused himself to protest.

"Hey!" he said, leaning forward toward the Bluffer's right ear. "Let me down here. I've got some things to do before I start talking to people—and one of them is getting something in the way of breakfast. I suppose you didn't think of the fact I haven't had anything to eat yet today?"

"You know," said the Bluffer in a tone of wonder, "it did slip my mind at that. Well, I suppose it's natural. If a man's had breakfast himself, he naturally assumes everybody else has too."

"I'll see you in about half an hour, up at the forge," said Bill, heading in toward the Residency.

There were some things he desperately needed to learn before he faced any assemblage of villagers. That was his main reason for stopping—but it was nonetheless true that he did need breakfast. He went first to the kitchen therefore, and it was not until he had surrounded a meal that was almost Dilbian in its proportion that he turned to his search for the information he wanted.

He found it easily enough in the information computer—a complete account of the nursery tale of the Three Little Pigs, and a concise account of methods and tactics in medieval warfare. Having absorbed this information, he put the gong handle through his belt—from which he had removed it for the sake of comfort, while eating breakfast—and went out of the Residency and up the street toward the blacksmithy.

He found not only the blacksmith there with the Hill Bluffer but a fair sprinkling of other citizens of the village, and others began to come out of their various houses and follow him up as he approached the blacksmith shop, until he had quite a crowd surrounding him as he stepped in under the roof of the open shed to greet the Bluffer and Flat Fingers.

"Morning, Pick-and-Shovel," the blacksmith replied, his eyes fastened on the object tucked under Bill's belt. "I've got your blade and buckler ready. Want to try them out?"

"In a minute," replied Bill, with elaborate casualness. "You don't have a nail and a hammer you could lend me, do you?"

"Why, I guess so," replied the blacksmith. He turned to one of the tables nearby, searched among the litter that covered it, and came up with something rather like a short sledgehammer and one of the nails he had made himself from the native iron.

The sledgehammer was difficult to handle with one hand, while holding the nail. The nail itself was some eight inches in length, a triangular sliver of gray native iron, with a bulge at one end for a head and a rather blunt point at the other. Nonetheless, Bill managed to knock it partway into one of the upright posts supporting the shed roof. Then he returned the sledgehammer to the blacksmith, took the gong hammer from his belt, and hung it by the hole in one end of its handle from the nail he had just driven into the pole.

A pleased mutter of deep-voiced and admiring comment went through the crowd that now surrounded the blacksmith shed closely. The blacksmith squinted at the gong hammer.

"Yes," he said, after a minute. "I remember cutting that piece of iron for Bone Breaker, myself. That must have been eight–ten years ago. Before that they were sounding their gong with just a chunk of wood."

He turned to face Bill. Behind and above the singed fur of the blacksmith's broad right shoulder, Bill saw the face of the Hill Bluffer looking at him expectantly.

"So I guess you really were down in outlaw territory last night, were you, Pick-and-Shovel?" said the blacksmith. "How did you do it?"

"Well, I'll tell you," said Bill. The crowd around the shed had quieted down, and Bill realized that something more than an ordinary relating of the night's activities was expected. This was not a time for modesty. Modesty, in fact, was not considered highly among the Dilbians—except as a cloak for secretive boasting. The Dilbians were like good fishermen, who made it a rule always to exaggerate the size, weight, and number of their catch.

"Well, I'll tell you," he said. "You all know how that valley is. High cliffs all the way around it, the only entrance blocked up by the stockade. And the gates in the middle of the stockade barred shut at sundown. You wouldn't think a fly could get into that valley. But I did. But I'm not boasting about it. You know why?"

He waited for somebody to ask him why. The blacksmith obliged.

"Why, Pick-and-Shovel?" asked Flat Fingers.

"Because it was easy for a Shorty like me," Bill said, keeping in mind the reaction to his climb shown by the Hill Bluffer on the way back to the village. "Even if it would be hard for a real man, the fact that it was easy for me makes it something that I don't need to feel particularly proud about. You asked me how I got into the valley? I'll tell you in just two or three words how I got into that valley. I climbed down one of the cliffs until I was on the valley floor. And when I was ready to leave again, I climbed back up that cliff!"

There was a moment's absolute silence and then a gratifying mutter of incredulity from the audience. Bill interrupted it with an upheld hand.

"No, no—" he said. "As I say, I'm not particularly proud of it. Well, then, you may say—I could be a little puffed up over having walked into that outlaw camp all alone, with nobody to help me in case I was discovered. How many of you would like to do that, especially after dark?"

Bill paused for an answer. But no volunteers from the audience spoke up to say that they would have enjoyed such an excursion.

"But again," went on Bill, after a moment, "I can't take any credit for that either."

There was a hum of amazement at this new statement that abruptly suggested to Bill the rather ludicrous picture of the base droning of a swarm of enormous bumblebees. He waited for it to die down before he continued.

"No, I can't feel very proud about that," he said. "Because

I really wasn't worried about going in among those outlaws all by myself to get this gong handle you see hanging there. You see, I knew that if I ran into any of them, I could handle him with no trouble at all."

"What if you ran into a whole bunch of them?" demanded a voice from the crowd. "How about that, Pick-and-Shovel?"

"That didn't bother me either," replied Bill. "I could've handled any number I might've run into." There was a slight stir in the ranks of the crowd directly before him, and he saw the incredibly rotund form of More Jam unobtrusively squeezing into the front rank. "We Shorties know these things. That's why I'm not afraid to face Bone Breaker in a duel. That's why, in spite of the fact that we're so much smaller than real men and Fatties, we Shorties don't have to take a back seat to anybody. It's because of what we know. And it was because of what I knew that it didn't bother me to go into that valley and bring that gong handle out."

Bill stopped. The crowd around the shed, he could now see from his superior position on top of the barrel, was as large or larger than it had been the day before when he had lifted weights with the blacksmith. They were all staring at him in fascinated interest. He let them stare, waiting for the question that one of them must ask if he was to go on. Finally, it was More Jam in the front rank who put it to him.

"That sounds mighty interesting, Pick-and-Shovel," said More Jam mildly. "Maybe you wouldn't mind telling us what it is you Shorties know that makes so much difference in handling outlaws? Because," went on More Jam, looking back over his shoulder briefly at his fellow villagers for a moment, and then turning back to Bill, "I don't 'spose most of the real active men around here would like to admit it, but an old fat, decrepit man like myself doesn't mind letting it out. We haven't been able to handle those outlaws, when you get right down to it. They come in a gang all at once upon some single farmer, and there's not much one man can do against a crowd. We never know when they're coming, and by the time we get together to go after them,

163

they're back safe in their valley. So we've just about given up trying to handle them. But you say, Pick-and-Shovel, that there is a way? Maybe you'd like to tell us what that way is?"

"Well," answered Bill, "as you know, we Shorties have an agreement with the Fatties not to go talking out of turn about things back on our home world. If the Fatties don't talk out of turn we don't—and vice versa. So that kind of stops me from telling you plain out what I know."

"You mean, Pick-and-Shovel," More Jam's voice held a strangely silky note that rang a sharp warning bell in the back of Bill's head, "you know something that would help us, here in this village, and you're refusing to tell us what it is?"

"Sorry," said Bill. A low mutter of annoyance began in the crowd, and deepened toward anger. Bill hurried hastily on. "I've given my word not to—just like all the Shorties and Fatties that come here to know you people. But"—Bill paused, took a deep breath, mentally kicked the Human-Hemnoid Non-Interference Treaty out of the window, and borrowed a page from Anita's book, as he had observed her in Outlaw Valley through the crack in the hide curtain—"let me tell you all a story about my grandfather."

Chapter 21

"It all began because of a story there used to be among us Shorties—" Bill had barely gotten his first words out, when he was interrupted.

"I'll just bet it did!" cried someone in the front of the crowd—and looking down, Bill saw several females standing in a group there, together. He recognized the speaker as Thing-or-Two, flanked by the tall form of Perfectly Delightful. "And it's another story you're going to be telling us all now, we can bet on that too. It's a shame, that's what it is—an absolute shame, the way the men of this village stand around and let the wool be pulled over their eyes by Shorties like you, with no regard for customs and manners and traditions! Why don't some of you speak up and tell this Shorty what he can do with his stories?"

"You shut up!" snapped a new female voice. Looking, Bill saw that Sweet Thing had appeared beside More Jam and was now looking around his enormous stomach at the older Dilbian female, like a rat terrier growling around the edge of a half-opened door at an intruder. "You just can't wait to get me out of the Inn, so you and Tin Ear can move in on Daddy. Well, I'm not leaving! You let Pick-and-Shovel talk—"

"Did you hear her!" shrieked Thing-or-Two, turning to the crowd. "Did you hear what she said to me—*me*, a woman old enough to be her mother! This is what things have come to! It's a good thing I'm not her mother, I'd—"

"You'd what?" demanded Sweet Thing belligerently, starting around her father toward the older woman. More Jam interposed a heavy arm.

"Now, now, daughter," he rumbled peaceably. "Manners, manners . . ."

Still growling, but complying, Sweet Thing allowed herself to be pushed back to the opposite side of More Jam.

"At the same time," went on More Jam, lifting his voice over that of Thing-or-Two, as she began to speak again, "as I remember it, Pick-and-Shovel was about to tell us something. And I guess I'm probably speaking for most of us when I say that, since he did something pretty interesting in going down into Outlaw Valley to get that gong handle, we ought to at least listen to what he has to say now. Besides, it sounds kind of interesting."

"Well," Bill began, "as I was starting to say, this whole thing came about because of a story we Shorties have. It concerns a sort of Cobbly we Shorties used to have—they've nearly all disappeared nowadays, back where I come from, but we used to have them. The story's about this Cobbly and three brothers."

The crowd had stilled amazingly. Bill was suddenly conscious of all eyes being fixed on him with the particular type of open, fascinated gaze he had occasionally seen in children hearing a story or watching a play.

"This Cobbly—" he stopped to clear his throat, then went on, "had one real powerful habit. He was able to blow rocks—even big boulders—right out of his way. He could even puff hard enough to blow a tree down, the way a storm might do. Well, these three brothers started out to set up their own home. None of them was married yet, so they headed off into the woods, and each one of them picked himself a place to build a house."

Bill paused for a moment to see if he still had the rapt attention of his audience. Gazing down at them, he decided that if anything it was more rapt than ever. He went on.

"You see, they all knew about the Cobbly who lived in this wood, and could blow down trees and things like that, so they were all particularly concerned to build a Cobbly-proof house."

Bill took a breath.

"Well, the first brother was the laziest of the bunch. He thought it would be good enough if he just took a lot of twigs and small branches, wove them together, and made himself a house that way. So he went to work and ran himself up a house in about a day and a half. The only thing he did that didn't call for light branches was to put a stout bar on the inside of the front door—a bar anchored to two doorposts that were set deep in the earth.

" 'Let's see that Cobbly break through that bar!' he said, and rolled himself up for the night.

" 'Meanwhile, the other two brothers, not having finished their building, had gone back to the nearest village where they'd be safe. Well, the moon came up, and the Cobbly came out and prowled around the woods, and pretty soon he smelled the brother in his house and he chuckled to himself—*because our type of Cobblies used to like to eat people alive, taking their time at it.*"

Bill uttered this last sentence in the most impressive and blood-curdling tone that he could manage. He was gratified to receive in answer a sort of low moan of suspense and terror, particularly from the females in the crowd.

"Yes," went on Bill, in an even firmer and more impressive tone of voice, "this Cobbly was just as hungry as a Cobbly had ever been. So he went up to the door of the house made of woven branches and he tried to open the door—"

Another, somewhat louder, low moan of suspense and anguish from the crowd before him.

"But the door held—" said Bill.

There was a grunt, almost of disappointment, from the crowd this time.

"But the Cobbly," said Bill, fixing his audience with his best glittering eye, "wasn't stopped by that. He knocked at the door—" Bill reached up and sounded his knuckles against a log rafter overhead. The crowd of village Dilbians shivered.

"He knocked again. And again," said Bill. "Finally the sound of his knocking woke the brother who was inside the house.

" 'Who's that, knocking?' asked the brother.

" 'It's just a late traveler, asking if you can't put me up for the night,' answered the Cobbly—"

There was a new moan of excitement from the crowd at the duplicity of this answer. Bill continued.

" 'You can't fool me,' answered the brother. 'I know you're the Cobbly that lives in these woods, and that you'd like to get in so that you could eat me up. But I've put too stout a bar on my door, and you can't get through it. And I'm not going to let you in, either. So go about your business, and let me sleep.'

" 'Let me in, I tell you!' shouted the Cobbly at that. 'Let

me in—or I'll huff, and I'll puff, and I'll blow your house over!'

"At that, the first brother was very much afraid, and he covered his head with his blanket. But the Cobbly outside began to huff and puff—and before you could wink, he'd blown the house over, snatched up the first brother and eaten him!"

The crowd groaned.

"Well," went on Bill. "The Cobbly, full after the meal he'd just had, went home to sleep until the next night. That next night he went hunting again. The third brother had not yet finished building and he'd gone back into town. But the second brother had finished building his house. And he'd built a pretty good house of logs. So when the Cobbly came up and tested that door, he knew by the feel of it that there was no point even in trying to break in that way. So he called out to the second brother, just as he'd called out to the first, saying he was a traveler who'd like to be put up for the night.

" 'You can't fool me!' shouted the second brother. 'I know you're the Cobbly who lives in this woods and who's already eaten one of my brothers. But you can't get in at my front door.'

" 'In that case,' answered the Cobbly, 'I'll just have to huff and puff until I blow your house down, too.'

" 'You can't blow down a house made of logs!' cried the second brother—but in spite of his brave words, he was afraid, and he covered up his head with his blanket just like the first brother had done.

"Meanwhile the Cobbly took a big lung full of air and began to huff, and puff, and huff, and puff—until at last, bang—a log flew out of the wall in front of him, and then another, and then another—and the next thing you knew he'd blown to pieces the house made of logs, and he got in and gobbled up the second brother!"

The groan that arose from the crowd at this point in the

168

story was the deepest and most sincere tribute that tale had received so far.

"The next night," said Bill, and paused dramatically, "the Cobbly went hunting again. He hunted and he hunted, and though he was sure the third brother was there in the forest, he couldn't seem to find where his house had been built. At last, a little ray of light shining out through the darkness led him to it. It was no wonder the Cobbly hadn't been able to recognize it as a house. He had passed it two or three times already. Because this house was made—" Bill paused again and his audience held its breath, "of stone!"

For a long moment the villagers continued to hold their breath in automatic anticipation. But then, slowly, expressions of puzzlement grew on their faces. They began to breath again. Many of them were casting sidelong glances at each other, and a muttering began which spread through the whole group. Finally, from the rear somebody spoke up.

"Did you say of *stone*, Pick-and-Shovel?"

"That's right," said Bill.

"You mean, of pieces of rock?" asked More Jam from the front ranks.

"That's exactly right," replied Bill. "The third brother made his walls by starting with large boulders at the bottom, and working up to smaller and smaller rocks, fitting them together as he went and packing them tight with wet clay that dried hard after a little while. He bedded his rafters in the stone walls at each end and then built a roof of heavy timbers sloping down from a rooftree mounted on four posts lined up and sunk in the earth inside."

As far as Bill knew, no Dilbian had ever thought of making a house with walls of stone. Apparently, he noted now as he watched and listened from the top of his barrel, the idea was equally as novel to the villagers. It took some little time for the buzzings of incredulity and amazement to die down. But at last, they all quieted like interested children, and he saw their eyes were back on him once again.

"Go on, Pick-and-Shovel," said More Jam. "Here the third

brother was inside his house made of stone, and there was a Cobbly outside knowing he was in there. What happened next?"

"Well, I suppose you can guess," said Bill, "that Cobbly just didn't turn around and go away and leave the third brother alone."

The villagers hummed their understanding and hearty agreement. It would be no sort of Cobbly at all, they obviously thought, who having gobbled up two of three brothers should leave the third brother in peace.

"The Cobbly knocked at the door—it was a wooden door but three bars held it securely on the inside—" began Bill, but this time he was interrupted from the front rank of the audience.

"*Soheknockedonthedoorandsaidhewasatravelerandaskedifhe couldcomeinandthebrothersaidno—*" exploded Perfectly Delightful, plainly unable to stand the suspense any longer.

"That's right," said Bill quickly, before the rest of the audience could jump on the excited Perfectly Delightful for interrupting. "And, of course, the Cobbly replied the same way he had to the first two brothers, saying he'd huff and he'd puff and he'd blow the house over. And do you know what the third brother said?"

Shaking their heads, his audience replied almost as one Dilbian that they did not—not without some hard glances thrown in Perfectly Delightful's direction, although she was insisting on her ignorance as loudly as the rest of them.

"The third brother said," said Bill, " 'You may huff and puff as long as you want, Cobbly, but you won't be able to blow this house over!' And with that, he turned back to his work, which was putting some final clay around the fireplace he had built into one wall of his house."

"Well," went on Bill, "the Cobbly huffed, and he puffed, and he Huffed and he Puffed! And he HUFFED! But he wasn't able to move that house of stone at all."

Spontaneous cheers rose from the inhabitants of Muddy Nose Village at this information.

"But that Cobbly wasn't giving up—" said Bill when the cheering had died down somewhat. Instantly, a new, complete hush prevailed. He felt the Dilbian eyes hard upon him.

"The Cobbly looked at the door and knew he could never get in there," said Bill. "But then the Cobbly looked up at the roof—and what did he see up there? It was the chimney of a fireplace that the third brother had just built. And in the top of it, was an opening leading right down to the inside of the house. So he jumped up on the roof—"

The audience groaned in new dismay.

"He crept up the logs of the roof until he was at the base of the chimney. He climbed up the chimney. He saw the hole was there. And, without stopping to look, he dived right down it!"

The villagers gasped. Bill stood where he was, in silence, letting the image of the Cobbly's springing down the chimney on a defenseless third brother build itself in their minds. Then he spoke again very slowly.

"But—" he said, and paused again, "the third brother had expected something like this. He had already had some twigs and wood ready in the fireplace underneath his cooking pot, and he had the cooking pot, which was a very large one, full of water. When he heard the Cobbly sneaking around the roof and beginning to investigate the chimney, he had lit the fire under the cooking pot. When the Cobbly dived down the chimney, he dived right into the cooking pot, right into the water and drowned. And the third brother cooked him and had him for dinner, instead!"

It must have been doubtful whether Muddy Nose Village in the Lowlands of Dilbia had ever witnessed such a reaction over the happy ending of a story as took place then. Even Bill himself, half-deafened on top of his barrel, where he deemed it prudent to remain—could hardly believe in his own success a storyteller.

"There's just one thing, Pick-and-Shovel," said More Jam, when order was restored. "Didn't you say something about all this having something to do with your grandfather? How does your grandfather come into it?"

"Actually," said Bill, "he was my grandfather several times removed. And he actually didn't come into it until quite a few years later. You see, after the story of the three brothers got around, a lot of us Shorties started building houses out of stone. It was back at a time called the 'Middle Ages,' back where I come from. They built some stone houses that were as big as this village, and you just couldn't get into them."

There was a momentary mutter of puzzlement from the crowd at this unfamiliar name, but it quieted quickly. Bill found that their attention was still with him.

"Some Shorties," said Bill, with a heavy emphasis "some," "began to take advantage of these big stone houses of theirs that nobody could get into—sort of the way the outlaws and Bone Breaker take advantage of that valley of theirs. So ways had to be found to get into those stone houses, somehow. So my grandfather came up with an idea. You couldn't walk up too close to one of the walls of the stone houses because they'd throw big rocks and things like that down on you from windows high up in them. There were even some houses that had extra walls around them with platforms inside so that people could throw things down on anyone trying to get over the wall from the outside—"

"That's what those outlaws do," muttered a voice from the crowd.

"But you say your grandfather figured a way around that sort of thing?" put in More Jam mildly. The crowd quieted down, waiting for Bill's answer.

"As a matter of fact, he did," said Bill. "He got to thinking, why not make a sort of big shield you could push ahead of you to keep the rocks off and push it up close to the wall, and then start digging inside the shield and dig down and underneath both the shield and the wall and come up on the inside!"

Bill ended on a bright, emphatic note. Then he waited. But there was no reaction from the villagers. They merely stood, staring at him as the seconds slid away into silence. Bill saw More Jam stir and sneak glances to his right and left, but the fat Dilbian held his silence. It was Flat Fingers, who finally broke it.

"Well, I'll be chopped!" exclaimed the blacksmith. "Why didn't we think of that!"

Flat Fingers' words suddenly released the tongues of the individuals in the staring audience—it was as if a plug had suddenly been pulled out of a full barrel—comment and exclamation gushed forth. Suddenly, all the villagers were talking at once—more than this, they were breaking up into small groups to argue and discuss the matter among themselves.

A crowd of villagers surrounded Flat Fingers, who was hoarsely giving directions and expounding upon the practical steps that could be taken to build such a shield.

Bill felt a sudden punch on his elbow that staggered him. He turned swiftly and found himself facing Sweet Thing, who was apparently trying to get his attention.

"Pick-and-Shovel, listen!" said Sweet Thing urgently. "I came up here to tell you but you were talking to everybody at the time, so I had to wait until you were through!"

"Tell me what?" asked Bill.

"What I saw, of course!" said Sweet Thing. "What do you think?"

Bill took a strong grip on his patience.

"What did you see, then," he inquired in as calm a tone as possible.

"Him, of course!" said Sweet Thing exasperatedly. "Aren't I telling you? And he was sneaking out of the Residency. Well, I knew he wasn't supposed to be in there when you weren't in there, so I came right up here to tell you about it. But you were so busy talking I had to wait. So I'm telling you now. That Fatty was up to something, as sure as I'm More Jam's daughter!"

"Fatty?" echoed Bill jolted. "You saw Mula—I mean Barrel Belly coming out of the Residency just now?"

"Just a little while ago, while you were talking. Probably just after you started talking."

Bill felt a sudden, grim uneasiness clutch at him just under his breastbone.

"I'd better go take a look—" he said, and began to head out through the crowd and down the hill. He discovered that Sweet Thing was coming along with him, and thought briefly of telling her to let him investigate alone. Then it occurred to him that it might be handy to have her along in case there was more information about the sighting of Mula-*ay* at the Residency, which she had not yet managed to get out.

At any rate, she stayed beside him as they reached the Residency, and went in through the front door. Nothing semed amiss in the reception room, so Bill proceeded to go through the rest of the building. Room after room, he found nothing wrong, no evidence of any reason that would explain a visit by the Hemnoid to the human Residency.

It was not until they got clear back into the warehouse and the workshop corner where the program lathe and other tools were racked and hung on the walls that Bill got his first feeling that something was wrong. He stopped, facing the workshop corner, and slowly ran his eyes over it. What was different about what he was seeing now from what he had seen when he was last here? For a long moment he was unable to identify that difference. Then suddenly an empty space on one of the tool-hung walls seemed to leap at him.

Where the empty space was, the hand-laser welding torch had hung. It hung there no longer.

"What's the matter, Pick-and-Shovel?" demanded Sweet Thing, almost crossly, in his right ear. "What are you just standing there like that for?"

He hardly heard her. Understanding had leaped upon him like a wolf from the underbrush. Mula-*ay* knew that Bill had gone down into the valley the night before. He also knew that now all the village Dilbians also knew it, and shortly the whole countryside would know it. The connection between that knowledge and the missing laser torch flashed suddenly white and clear upon Bill's mind. That torch could kill, its murderous beam slicing through the bone and muscle of a Dilbian back to a Dilbian heart, from as much as fifteen feet away. With that torch, this coming night, back in the valley, Mula-*ay* could find a moment when Bone Breaker was out between the houses, alone in the darkness. He could torch the outlaw chief from behind, and leave him there with the obviously Shorty-made weapon beside him. After that no one could blame the Dilbians for believing that Bill had once more reentered the valley and avoided a duel by killing his opponent in the most cowardly and treaty-breaking way possible.

Bill jerked suddenly out of his thoughts and spun on one heel. He had to catch Mula-*ay* before Mula-*ay* could get back into the outlaw valley.

Then his shoulders sagged, and his spirits with them. He remembered now how long he had gone on talking after first spotting Sweet Thing in the crowd, standing beside More Jam. Mula-*ay* would have too much of a head start. There was no hope of Bill catching him before he was safe back behind the gates and the stockade of Outlaw Valley. And the villagers would never be able to finish making their shield, get it up against the outlaw wall, and dig in to the valley under the stockade wall before night would put a halt to that operation.

Mula-*ay* would be left safely behind that stockade wall in Outlaw Valley as night came down. And a word from him to Bone Breaker would be enough to set sentinels on watch, so that Bill could not safely climb down the cliffs a second time to warn the outlaw chief.

Chapter 22

Sweet Thing was still demanding to know what was wrong with him. Bill collected his wits. He pointed at the empty space on the wall.

"There's a thing gone," he said to her. "A sort of a Shorty thing, but if Mula-*ay* uses it, he could hurt somebody. And he's already got a head start toward the valley so that we couldn't catch up with him and get it back from him."

"But what'll we do now?" said Sweet Thing.

"Why don't you tell your father to wander out and into the outlaw camp," suggested Bill. "He can keep an eye on Mula-*ay* without letting anyone know what's up, and if Mula-*ay* tries to do anything with the thing, he can set up an alarm."

"Set up an alarm, huh!" said Sweet Thing scornfully. "If Barrel Belly tries anything with that thing, whatever it is, my dad would just jump him—from behind, of course, so as not to get hurt by the thing—and squash him!"

"Ah—yes," agreed Bill warily. Personally, he had little faith that any Dilbian, even Bone Breaker himself, would come close to being a match with the massive, heavy-gravity muscles of the Hemnoid. More Jam may have been something of a terror in his youth, but he was old now, and he was fat—there was no gainsaying those two points. Bill did not share Sweet Thing's daughterly confidence in More Jam's physical abilities. But on the other hand, More Jam was as wily as anyone among the Dilbians, and not likely to let himself be trapped into a match with somebody who could easily overpower him.

"I'll go right away," said Sweet Thing, and not wasting any time about it, she turned and barreled out of the room. Well, he thought, that was that. But it was not much. The situation called for move active measures than simply sending More Jam to keep an eye on Mula-*ay*.

It was still only midmorning, but there was no hope of getting the villagers up to and under the stockade barring the entrance to the valley before night fell. And once night had fallen, it was an odds-on chance that Mula-*ay* would be able to evade More Jam long enough to kill Bone Breaker.

Something must be done—and it must be done before sundown. Bill thought about the plan of attack on which he had sold the villagers, running over it in his mind to see if there was not some way by which it might be speeded up so that they could take the valley this same day, while daylight lasted. But it was just not possible.

Suddenly he jumped to his feet with an almost Dilbian-like snort of triumph. It was true the mantelet and sapping operation . . . which was the technical, military term for the tactic he had explained to the villagers—would not breach the Outlaw Valley's defenses before nightfall. But he had forgotten entirely that the Middle Ages had had other, even simpler ways of taking castles by storm. He had forgotten, in fact, the most obvious one of them all.

He turned and hurried out of the Residency, and back up the road to the blacksmith shop, which was now a-swarm with male Dilbians from the village and the farms around, most of them with weapons of some sort—ranging from actual swords down to axes, or heavy-handled native scythes. The Bluffer was looking on interestedly as Flat Fingers supervised the construction of the mantelet, or shield, which Bill had described. Bill slowed his headlong pace and sauntered up to the group. As usual, it was a few seconds before the Dilbians looked down and noticed him standing there.

"Oh, there you are, Pick-and-Shovel," said the blacksmith. "What do you think—shouldn't the skids be longer, there, under the back of the shield?"

Bill examined the structure. It looked to his human eye to be nearly as tall, wide, and heavy as the actual stockade fence of the outlaws themselves. Only the brute muscles of the Dilbians could entertain the thought of using such a thing, let alone transporting it through the several miles of woods that separated the village from the valley entrance. It was evidently designed to be moved on three pointed logs which served as its base and would operate as skids or runners on which the weight of the shield would bear, as it would push toward the wall. The shield was set just behind the points of these logs, sloping backward, and was heavily braced, towering to perhaps fifteen feet above the logs at its upper edge. Bill smiled agreeably at the sight of it, and nodded his head vigorously.

"That's just fine, Flat Fingers," he said. "The men pushing it certainly ought to be safe behind that, as they go up to the wall. Yes, it'll be good protection, that shield. There's nothing like being *safe,* when you attack a bunch like those outlaws."

"Well, it'll get us in close all right," said the blacksmith, though he frowned a little at Bill's second repetition on the word "safe." "Then once we're close, we'll dig under and tear into them."

"That's the spirit!" said Bill enthusiastically. "Guard yourself as much as possible until you get inside, and then tear into them. Don't be disappointed if it takes a little while to dig under the wall. Better to be safe than sorry, I always say."

By this time the rest of the Dilbians working on the shield had abandoned their jobs and clustered around. Like Flat Fingers, they were all frowning now.

"Oh, we won't be disappointed, Pick-and-Shovel," rumbled Flat Fingers grimly. "We've been waiting to tangle with those outlaws too long to cool down, just because we have to do a little digging to get at them."

"Good, good!" said Bill strongly. "I know you are. But it doesn't do any harm to play safe, does it?"

"What do you mean *'play safe'*?" exploded the village

178

blacksmith. "What's all this about, 'playing safe' you keep talking about. We're going in there to tangle with those outlaws, the sooner the better!"

"Of course you are!" replied Bill hastily. He saw the Bluffer's face approach and peer interestedly down at him over the left shoulder of the blacksmith. Bill went on. "There's just no point in getting any more men hurt than have to be. That's why I suggested this way of getting into the valley. After all, it's the safest way, even if it does take a longer time than some other ways."

"What other ways?" roared Flat Fingers. "You mean to say there's other ways—quicker ways? Ways you didn't tell us about because you thought we were worried about keeping *safe*?"

"There's lots of other ways, of course," said Bill. "But after all, as I understand it, man for man those outlaws are a lot tougher than you are—"

"Who says so?" roared one of the Dilbians who had been working on the shield. He was holding an ax which he flourished in Bill's direction in a way that made Bill's throat go dry. Suddenly there was bedlam, all of the village males shouting at Bill. Flat Fingers bellowed them all back into silence, then turned ominously back to face Bill.

"Now, you listen to me, Pick-and-Shovel!" said Flat Fingers. "We're all Muddy Nosers, here—the sort of men here who'd tear that wall down with our bare hands, if we thought it could be done that way! Are you trying to start trouble—or something?"

"Why, no—of course not!" said Bill hastily. "Why, I'll be glad to tell you of quicker ways to get in through the gates in that stockade. As I say, there's lots of them—"

"What's the quickest?" demanded Flat Fingers.

"The quickest?" echoed Bill. "Well, the quickest would be to use a tree trunk."

The assemblage of Dilbians stared at him blankly. It was hard for Bill to believe that their minds did not spring immediately from his suggestion of using a tree trunk to the idea of using it as a battering ram against the gates. The concept was so obvious to him that it was hard to see how it could not be obvious to these Dilbians.

"You take a log," explained Bill. "You trim off all the branches, except for a few that you leave along its length for handholds. Then you get as many men to pick up the log all as the same time as you can. Then, holding the log, they ran at the gates in the stockade end-on."

To his surprise, the Dilbians continued to stare at Bill, after he had stopped speaking, with blank or puzzled looks.

"And what'll that do, Pick-and-Shovel?" asked Flat Fingers finally.

"Stop and think," answered Bill, "and you can imagine it for yourself. Suppose we had a bunch of men pick up one of those logs over there"—he pointed to the pile of loose logs on which he had climbed the day before to hang the block and pulley from the rafter—"and ran that log at you, end-on, as hard as they could. What do you think the end of that log would do to you—or to anything else that it hit?"

For a long moment, it seemed that Flat Fingers still did not understand. Then, very slowly, his expression began to change. His eyes opened wide, his jaw dropped, his nostrils spread—and without warning he let out a war whoop that seemed to split Bill's eardrums—and leave him slightly deaf for several seconds.

At that, it was probably just as well that he did not have the full sense of his hearing in the moments that followed. Because, in a second Flat Fingers was explaining it to the rest of the villagers, and inside of two minutes the area was bedlam again. Villagers whooped, hollered, roared with laughter, and pounded each other on the back as they described the principle behind the use of a tree trunk as a battering ram.

"Let's go!" trumpeted Flat Fingers, making himself heard over the rest of the din. "We don't need to take a log to them. We can chop one down when we get there!"

Take off, they did. Bill, staring after them in a sort of

deafened wonder, was in danger of being left behind as they streamed off from the village into the woods at a pace that his shorter human legs could not match. But, abruptly, he felt himself snatched up and sailed through the air to land with a thud in the saddle on the Hill Bluffer's back.

"Hang on, Pick-and-Shovel!" the postman shouted, infected himself by the general excitement. "We'll be up with the ones in the lead in two minutes."

Chapter 23

Having said this, the Bluffer proceeded to increase Bill's steadily growing respect for him by proving himself almost as good as his word. In his ride on the Bluffer before, Bill had somehow come to assume that the pace at which they traveled was pretty close to the practical limit for the Dilbian beneath him, considering the burden he was bearing on his back. In short, Bill had not experienced the Hill Bluffer's running before. But now the postman set out to stretch his legs—and the result from Bill's point of view was awesome. The landscape whizzed by at something between twenty-five and thirty-five miles an hour. And the jolting threatened to shake Bill out of the saddle within the first fifty yards.

Luckily for him, however, once the Bluffer had caught up with the leaders of the group, he dropped back to a rapid walking pace, which was a good deal easier on his rider.

Bill unlocked his legs and arms from the straps and sat up. He looked back over his shoulder. The whole village seemed to be streaming after them. The citizens of Muddy Nose were on the march at last against the outlaws.

In the front strode the biggest and best males of the community, literally tramping out a path through the brush, and chopping down small trees that impeded their way. They detoured only around the larger trunks. Behind them came the younger members of the community and the village women, flanked on both sides and followed by a rear guard of lesser and older Dilbian males. Then Flat Fingers began to sing, and the others took it up until the whole party was joining in.

The subject matter of the song—or chant—was nothing remarkable. It seemed to deal with an individual who had a perfect mania for throwing other individuals and things down his well. But it seemed to please its singers vastly.

> *Souse-Nose's wife's old uncle*
> *He liked his grub real well.*
> *One day he came to visit,*
> *And said, "I'll stay a spell."*
> *"Oh, no you won't!" said Souse-Nose*
> *And he threw him down the well!*
>
> *—Threw him down the well!*
> *Now wasn't that a sight?*
> *He threw him down the well so far*
> *That he was out of sight!*
>
> *Souse-Nose's wife saw him do this*
> *And she let out a yell.*
> *"What do you mean by doing that?*
> *I love my uncle well!"*
> *"Then go with him!" said Souse-Nose*
> *And he threw her down the well!*
>
> *—Threw her down the well ... etc.*

After disposing of his wife's uncle and his wife, Souse-Nose rapidly threw down the well, according to the song, a number of other relatives, some neighbors he didn't like, a hammer that had dropped on his toe the week before, the family cooking pot (because it was empty)—and then proceeded to start throwing down the well various individuals among the marching villagers themselves, as the singers began to pick on each other.

It was all apparently hilariously funny to the Dilbians—but at the same time, Bill felt a slight shiver run down his back. The song was a humorous song, but it was also a grimly humorous one, and the tone in which it was sung was very nearly more grim than it was humorous. In fact, for all the comedy in the words, Bill realized that what he was listening to was the Dilbian equivalent of a war song. The villagers were working themselves up emotionally for combat with the outlaws. For the first time, Bill began to feel some misgivings about the forces he had set in motion. Leaning forward, he spoke into the Hill Bluffer's right ear.

"Bluffer—" he said. "Bluffer, listen to me for a moment, will you. I'd like to ask you something—"

But he might as well have been speaking to some ten foot-high boulder tumbling at the head of an avalanche. The Bluffer was roaring out the song about Souse-Nose with the rest, completely carried away by it.

Bill sat back in the saddle, abruptly prey to a new fear. If the Bluffer was beyond his control—how about Flat Fingers and the rest of the villagers? The rolling chant of the voices around him was hypnotic—even Bill himself felt his breath coming quicker and the blood pounding in his ears.

He was still fighting for self-control, when the Bluffer beneath him, with the other leaders of the village party, rounded the turn into the narrow ravine that led down to the entrance to the valley, and stopped.

Before them, the gates in the stockade were already shut and barred, and the heads of outlaws, as well as the upper rims of shields were showing over the points at the upper end of the upright logs which made up the stockade. There was nothing surprising in finding the valley prepared in this way.

Singing and marching as they had been, the villagers undoubtedly had been heard a good half-mile or more off. Now, a few furry arms swung in the air above the stockade, and a few good-sized stones sailed toward the front rank of the villagers—but fell short. In reply, the villagers crowded into the narrow entrance of the valley and began to sing about outlaws being thrown down the well. The outlaws shouted back insults and challenges, but the solid chorus of the villagers overwhelmed them.

> ... *Throw you down the well so far,*
> *That you are out of sight* ...

—chanted the villagers.

Meanwhile, Flat Fingers had ceased singing and was rapidly issuing orders. A team of axmen had already headed off into the woods nearby, and the sound of chopping could occasionally be heard in the moments of relative silence between the singing of the villagers and the insults hurled by the outlaws. Shortly, there was the crash of falling timber—followed by a male-voiced cheer that drowned out even the singing.

Then the sound of chopping began again. Shortly, the team returned, carrying at least thirty feet of tree trunk two feet in diameter. Here and there along the trunk, they had left the stubs of branches for handholds. But most of those carrying the logs simply had one large hairy arm wrapped around it, as they grinned savagely at each other and at the outlaws.

The Bluffer squatted down and let Bill slip off his back. Bill started to approach Flat Fingers—but at this moment there was a sudden crashing sound from the forest behind them, as if a second tree falling and everybody turned around. A moment later, a second party came trotting up, carrying a second trunk stripped down to little stubs of branches for handholds.

"No you don't!" roared Flat Fingers, waving them back.

"One at a time! Here, lay that other pole up against the side of the cut, and give us some room."

The blacksmith's huge finger indicated the vertical rock wall that formed one side of the narrow entrance to the valley. Reluctantly, the second batch of Dilbians leaned their log up against this and fell back.

"All right, the rest of you!" shouted the Bluffer to the rest of them standing around. "Here we go! Ready with those rocks!"

Bill had noticed these others arming themselves with rocks—and in some cases, the very ones that had been thrown at them from behind the stockade. Now, looking again, he saw that almost everyone who was not on the battering-ram crew had at least two or three of these missiles in his or her hands.

"Shields, here!" bellowed Flat Fingers. Those of the battering-ram crew who already had shields swung them up into position overhead. The rest hastily borrowed shields from friends or relatives standing around and did likewise.

"All right, then!" cried the blacksmith, taking his place at the head of the battering-ram crew. "Here we go-o-o . . ."

The last word ended in a long, drawn-out howl, as the battering-ram crew started off at full speed toward the gate of the stockade. In a black furred wave behind them, surged the rest of the Dilbians—but they surged only to within throwing distance of the stockade wall, and began to loose a literal barrage of rocks.

The heads of the outlaws to be seen above the points of the stockade ducked hastily down out of sight as the first flight of stones reached them. They stayed down. Meanwhile, the battering-ram crew was carrying on full tilt for the gate in the very center of the stockade. For a moment, they seemed to be galloping away and making no progress. But a moment later, they loomed over the gate, and a second later, they struck it. The results were all but unbelievable.

The gate split from top to bottom with a sound like a crack of thunder. But this was the least spectacular of the results of the impact. The battering-ram crew, shaken loose

185

by the impact, piled up against the gate and the walls of the stockade themselves, like so many Dilbian-furred missiles. As a result, not merely the gate but the whole stockade wall quivered and shook like a fence of saplings.

There were glimpses of hairy arms thrown in the air briefly above the stockade's points, as the outlaws on the catwalk inside were shaken loose and dumped backward. Evidently, not one of them up there had been able to retain his grip, for although the stones had stopped flying from the crowd of Muddy Nosers, not one head made its reappearance above the stockade wall.

"All right—up and at it!" Flat Fingers was shouting, down by the gate, as he scrambled himself to his feet. *"On your feet and let's hit it again!"*

The battering-ram crew recollected itself, picked up its log, and began to swing its front end rhythmically against the cracked gate. With each blow, the entrance to the valley resounded, and gate and wall shivered together. Slowly the crack widened, and another crack split the door into three pieces. Around Bill, back at a stone's throw distance from the gate, the rest of the villagers were going wild with triumph, and the din was deafening.

A cold feeling clutched suddenly at Bill's chest. He had not fully imagined the violence and excitement that surrounded him now. He had not planned to get outlaws and villagers killed or maimed—

The sudden, hard poke by something rigid behind him, sent him stumbling forward half a step. He spun about, swiftly and angrily, to find himself confronting Sweet Thing. She was carrying a rectangular shield and a sword slung in its supporting strap, both of which were too small for any Dilbian's use.

"Well, put them on!" hissed Sweet Thing, almost in his ear. "Flat Fingers left them behind, but I went back and got them. They're yours, Pick-and-Shovel! Put them on, will you? You can't fight Bone Breaker without them, and you're the only one who can stop the war by fighting him!"

She thrust shield and sword at Bill. Bill found himself numbly taking them and strapping the sword around him. The shield, fitted with an elbow loop and a hand grip and made of inch-thick wood covered with half-inch hide, dragged his left arm groundward when he tried to hold it up in proper fashion.

He—? Stop the war—? His head whirling, he stared about him at the shouting, leaping villagers as they cheered on the battering ram crew down at the gates.

Of course! Suddenly the whole Dilbian picture fell into place. Suddenly he understood everything, including why he had been assigned here and then apparently abandoned by Greenleaf and his other superiors! He turned and looked about him. The second battering ram still leaned against the rock wall of the valley entrance, a little ways off.

"Here, hold this," Bill grunted, shoving the sword and shield back into Sweet Thing's hands. He turned and ran for the tree trunk leaning against the cliff, and went quickly up it, using the handholds almost as the rungs on a ladder. Twenty feet above the heads of the Dilbians below he stared down and over the top of the stockade into the valley beyond.

He saw that there were no outlaws inside the gate now. The tall, coal-black figure of Bone Breaker was in the center of a line that was drawn up perhaps halfway between the gate and the outlaw buildings. They were all armed and ready. The noon sun glinted on six-foot swords, and the shiny metal of an occasional piece of body armor or protective cap. Behind the line, back by the buildings themselves, was a small knot of outlaw women, and close to them was a round figure in a yellow robe whom Bill had no difficulty in recognizing as Mula-ay. As he watched, Mula-ay lifted something to his face that winked in the sunlight in Bill's direction. A second later, the Hemnoid's hands lifted and flicked outward in a human, military-type of salute. It was the kind of gesture only a human being would be able to recognize for what it was. Mula-ay was thumbing his nose at Bill from the distance, and, having done so, Mula-*ay* turned about and disappeared around the corner of the eating hall.

In spite of his new understanding, the coldness in Bill's chest tightened into a hard, unmeltable lump. Bluff and bluster made up a large part of the Dilbian nature, but only up to a point. Now, neither the villagers nor the outlaws were bluffing—or at least, only half-bluffing.

Mula-*ay* had caught Bill neatly in a trap. He had known that taking the laser-welding gun might stampede Bill into inciting the villagers to just such an attack as this. An attack in which both outlaws and villagers would be killed or hurt. It was not necessary for the Hemnoid to risk killing Bone Breaker himself in order to get rid of Bill and discredit humans on Dilbia. All he had to do was wait for the attacking villagers to come to grips with the outlaws—and this Mula-*ay* must have planned from the very moment in which he decided to take the laser-welding gun.

There was only one solution to the situation now. The hard way out that had been available to Bill from the beginning. Only at the beginning he had not understood the way Dilbian minds worked. Now he was sure he did, and it was that extra knowledge that gave him his advantage over the Hemnoid, who not only did not understand, but was racially incapable of understanding.

Bill skidded hastily down the tree trunk. He ran back to Sweet Thing and snatched the shield from her. It was quite true, what she had said. Only he could stop the war.

"Where's the Hill Bluffer?" he demanded urgently. "Help me find him!"

"There he is!" she shouted, and started for him. Bill ran after her.

The lanky postman was standing a little apart from the group, his eyes fixed and all his attention riveted on the battering-ram crew, which had now widened the original split in the gate to the point where only the bars beyond it were holding its planks together. Sweet Thing punched the Bluffer unceremoniously in the ribs, and he twisted about, angrily.

"Pick-and-Shovel!" said Sweet Thing economically, jerking her thumb back at Bill as he came pounding up.

"Bluffer," panted Bill, "I've got to get down into the valley before anybody else does, so I can reach Bone Breaker first. Can you get me to him?"

For a moment the Hill Bluffer stared as if he did not understand. Then, with a sudden whoop of joy and excitement, he reached out, picked up Bill and all but tossed him over a furry shoulder into the saddle. Bill grabbed for the straps, as the Bluffer pivoted on one heel and ran down toward the gate, which was beginning to disintegrate under the impact of the battering-ram crew.

It did, in fact disintegrate, falling apart in a shower of broken wood, just as the Bluffer reached the crew. Without pausing, the Bluffer hurdled the nearest member of the crew, who had collapsed, out of breath, wheezing on the grass, and ran directly toward the center of the armed and ready outlaw line, where the massive, black-furred figure of Bone Breaker towered, waiting with shield and sword.

Bill glanced over his shoulder, waited until they were midway between the gate and the outlaw line, and then shouted to the Bluffer to halt. As the postman did so, Bill jumped from the saddle and landed clanking with shield on the turf. Turning so that he could face first left toward the outlaws and then right toward the villagers who were now beginning to pour through the broken doorway, Bill shouted to them all—and a second later the powerful Dilbian lungs of the Hill Bluffer took up his shout and repeated it, so that it was plainly to be heard in the silence that had fallen over both attackers and defenders.

"Stop the war!" he shouted. "None of you are going to tangle on either side until I've first had my own personal crack at Bone Breaker!"

Chapter 24

It was only then that Bill realized he did not have his sword.

He had left it back in the hands of Sweet Thing. However, it seemed that the apparent ridiculousness of one unarmed small Shorty standing between opposing lines of armed giants and calling on them to give over the idea of fighting, apparently did not strike home to the Dilbians. Even as Bill looked, the outlaws on either side of Bone Breaker were relaxing, sheathing their swords and ambling forward. Looking in the other direction, he saw the villagers pouring through the broken gate, but also without signs of hostility. Two groups met and mingled around Bill as with the Hill Bluffer he went forward toward Bone Breaker, who stood still, waiting.

When Bill and the Bluffer reached him, the outlaw chief turned abruptly on his heel.

"Come on!" he said to Bill, and strode off toward the buildings. Bill, the Bluffer, and everybody else followed.

Bone Breaker stopped at last beside a long, narrow building, with only one or two windows, and a door at each end. Bill recognized it as the storehouse into the shadow of which Anita had led him that night when he had climbed down the cliff to see her. It was here that they had talked. Now Bone Breaker had brought him back here for their duel. Close up, now, he loomed over Bill like a mountain.

"Here's your sword—" muttered Sweet Thing's voice abruptly in his ear, and he half-turned to receive the hilt of his sword thrust into his palm. The leather-wrapped hilt was

190

cold to his grasp and the weight of the sword seemed to drag down at his arm, even though it was less than half the length of Bone Breaker's great blade. In spite of his certainty that he had now figured matters out, it was a calculated gamble he was taking here; and the fact that it was calculated did not lessen the fact that it was a gamble.

"All right, Bone Breaker," he said, speaking as loudly and scornfully as he could, "how do you want it?"

"I'll tell you how I want it," retorted Bone Breaker. He pointed at the warehouse beside them. "I had the windows in there blocked off yesterday. The place is full of stuff, but there's room to get from one end to the other. I'll go in at this end—you go in at that. And the first one out the other end on his two feet wins. Right?"

"Right!" said Bill, glancing at the storehouse with a queasy feeling. He heard the crowd behind him making guesses as to the outcome of the duel. Although there was a small minority that seemed to feel that you should never sell a Shorty short, most of them seemed firmly convinced that Bone Breaker would have no trouble at all encountering Bill in the gloom of the darkened building, and chopping him into small pieces.

Meanwhile, there was no hanging back. Bone Breaker had already headed off toward one end of the building. Bill turned, with the Bluffer beside him, and headed for the other. The crowd made way for him as he went. They came to the end of the building and rounded it to find three wooden steps leading up to a heavy door. With a tight throat, which his inner confidence did not seem to help, Bill mounted the steps.

"Good luck—" he heard the Bluffer say. Then he had opened the door and was through it, stepping into a darkness heavy with a mixed odor of leather, wood, root vegetables, and other dusty smells.

The door banged shut behind him.

He stood. The sword was in his hand now, and now its handle felt slippery in his grasp. He waited for his eyes to adjust somewhat to the darkness, but for a couple of long minutes it seemed that even with their pupils at full dilation he would not be able to make out any of his surroundings. Then, slowly, vague shapes of darker black began to emerge out of the general gloom. He made out finally that he stood in a little cleared space, facing what seemed to be a corridor between ten- to fifteen-foot piles of assorted, unidentifiable objects.

The rattle of something displaced and rolling across a wooden floor sounded distantly, without warning, from the far end of the building. Bill froze. For a moment he was conscious only of the heavy pounding of his heart, and the heavy weight of the sword and shield on his arms. Then he began to breathe again.

That sound, unintentional or not, was adequate announcement that Bone Breaker was coming in his direction. Bill could not simply stay here and wait for him. It was necessary to go and meet the outlaw chief.

Cautiously, Bill began to inch his way forward down the corridor between the high piled contents of the storehouse.

The corridor was nothing but a lane connecting a series of spaces between stored goods. Occasionally the lane widened out into areas that were certainly big enough to give room for a sword fight between a Dilbian and a human. Again, it narrowed down so that a Dilbian, at least, would have had to go sideways to make his way through. But there was never any more than the one path among the things piled up. There was to be no chance, apparently, for Bill to sneak past his larger opponent without meeting him face to face.

Bill heard no more sounds from the far end of the building to inform him of Bone Breaker's progress toward him. But under Bill's own feet, the boards of the building's flooring occasionally creaked, and once or twice he stumbled over something lying in the path, with some little noise.

Each time he did so, he stopped still, sweating and listening. But there was nothing to be heard from the far end of the building to let him know whether Bone Breaker had heard him, or not.

By this time, Bill had covered some little distance. He found himself wishing that he had measured the building with his eye before going in, and then counted his steps once he was in, so that he would have an approximate idea of how far along its length he had traveled. It seemed to him that he must have reached the middle of the building by this time. But he had not yet encountered Bone Breaker, and certainly the outlaw chief would meet him at least halfway?

Bill went on, making his way, sword extended point first, before him along the narrow aisle of darkness. Still—there was no sign of the outlaw chief. By now, Bill was sure that he had covered at least half the length of the building. The only possible conclusion was that somewhere up ahead of him the huge Dilbian was waiting at some convenient place of his own choosing. And still, in the face of that conclusion, there remained nothing for Bill to do but to keep moving forward.

Surprisingly, however, this new conclusion of Bill's did not increase his tension or his emotion. In fact, a good deal of the downright fear and uncertainty he had felt on stepping into the dark building was beginning to slip away from him now. The handle of the sword no longer felt slippery with perspiration in his grip. His heart had slowed and calmed its beating. There was even beginning to kindle in him now a sort of warm grimness of purpose—a readiness, foolish as it seemed —to be ready to fight back, if Bone Breaker should, after all, suddenly spring upon him out of the further shadows.

The Dilbian was huge—but that very hugeness, thought Bill, out of this new grim warmth inside him, made the outlaw chief clumsy in comparison with a human. If Bill could manage to dodge the first devastating blow of that man-long sword in Bone Breaker's grasp, it might be that he could get in under the other's guard and do something with his own small sword before his opponent could recover. If it came to that, it would probably be wise to throw away his shield the minute they came together, thought Bill. A shield was of some use to a Dilbian who could use it to deflect a blow from another's sword blade, but for a human to even be brushed by such a Dilbian weapon would be disaster. Bill would do a better job of running and dodging without the shield on his arm. Inspiration struck him suddenly—as long as he had to throw it, he would throw it at Bone Breaker. There might be a way of gaining some small advantage out of the surprise element of such a maneuver. What were the terms of the duel, as Bone Breaker had said before they went in the building?

"The *first* one out of the building on his feet . . ."

If it were possible for Bill to dodge the first assault of Bone Breaker, trip the big Dilbian up somehow, and get past him; a quick rush could carry Bill to the door at the end of the building and out—

Less than fifteen feet in front of Bill, there was a sudden rattle of something set rolling by the movement of an incautious foot.

Bill checked, suddenly taut in nerves and muscles. Directly in front of him, the corridor was narrow, but a little beyond—Bill screened his eyes against the dimness—it seemed as if the corridor might open up again into one of its wide spaces. If that were true, it was from that wide space that the sound Bill had heard had just now come. It was there that Bone Breaker was waiting for him.

Bill reached out with the back of his sword hand to explore by touch both sides of the aisle, without letting go of his weapon. To his left were sacks full of some hard, lumpy objects, too heavy to lift, and stacked clear to the ceiling—he had had some thought of climbing up on them and approaching the open space across their top. To his right, was a stack of logs, their farther ends reaching off ahead of him into darkness. These were not stacked more than halfway to the ceiling, barely above Bill's head—their top would be shoulder-high on Bone Breaker. Bill took hold of one of them, testing it by putting his weight on it—and it shifted slightly.

Hastily, he let go. A log rolling from under him, as he attempted to creep along it, would not only destroy the surprise approach he planned, but possibly leave him helpless at Bone Breaker's feet. There was nothing forward but to continue creeping along the aisle as quietly as possible and hope to steal upon the waiting Dilbian, before Bone Breaker knew he was close.

Accordingly, Bill inched forward, setting his feet down lightly and only gradually shifting his weight upon them. He was lucky—no boards creaked as that weight came on them. Slowly, in this manner, he stole forward until he reached the point where the aisle widened.

Unexpectedly, the foot he reached forward stubbed its toe against something hard above floor level. Bill stopped, trying to hover in mid-air and bent forward to inspect by touch what he had encountered. It was the end of a log, evidently fallen off the pile and angling up ahead into the darkness. Cautiously, Bill began to circle around it, holding his breath.

Where was Bone Breaker? The wide space in which Bill stood now, was more open than any he had encountered so far. To his left the sacks of hard lumpy objects had completely disappeared. It was evidently clear to the far wall of the narrow building. To his right the logs appeared to have changed their orderly piling for a dim tangle, from which several of them had rolled out onto the floor. Bill began carefully to pick his way among them.

Suddenly, he stopped. His foot had come down on something yielding. He snatched it up again and stood on one leg, like a crane.

But nothing happened. After a moment he reached down with the back of his sword hand toward the object on which he had stepped.

For a moment he felt nothing, then the skin on the back of his hand came in contact with the coarse curly fur of a Dilbian. It was motionless to his touch. Shock raced through him. Hastily he shifted his sword to his shield hand, and reached down to feel what he had touched.

It was a large, motionless, Dilbian foot pointing up at the ceiling and attached to a leg stretched out upon the floor.

"What—" began Bill, incautiously speaking out loud. Then, abruptly, everything happened at once.

With an ear-splitting roar and a rumble, the murky tangle of logs at his right suddenly seemed to disintegrate, falling and rolling about with great noise. Bill leaped away from the pile, but, curiously, none of the logs rolled in his direction. After what seemed like several minutes, but was only probably a second or two, the sound and motion ceased. But now the darkness was reinforced by a thick cloud of dust raised by the falling logs. Bill sneezed loudly.

It was a moment before he got his wits back. When he did, he stepped back and searched about for the Dilbian foot and leg with which he had been in contact just before the logs fell. After some groping he found it, lying just as motionless as before. He groped his way up along it, and eventually made out that what he was touching was Bone Breaker, lying silent and apparently unconscious underneath a log.

Bill stood up quickly. He had no intention of looking a gift horse in the mouth. Taking his sword in his right hand, he turned and raced toward the farther entrance of the building, that one through which the outlaw chief had entered. That door, with the line of light around it, dimly illuminating that end of the building to Bill's now darkness-adjusted eyes, loomed in a little open space of its own, not more than twenty feet away. Bill made that opening in three running strides—and burst out from the mouth of the narrow aisle just in time to catch sight, out of the corner of his right eye, of the glint of whirling steel descending upon him.

He jumped away, throwing up his own sword instinctively. In the same instant it was hammered from his grasp, as if that grasp had been the grip of a child, and sent flying against the wall behind him. Something terrifically hard crashed against the side of his head, and he staggered back until the wall itself stopped him from falling.

Blood was streaming down onto his face, half blinding him.

He grabbed his sword from the floor instinctively, and raised his head to face his attacker. The end of the building was swimming around him, but the sight that greeted his eyes from the leakage of daylight around the door, brought him to a halt.

Facing him, half-held in mid-air and with Bone Breaker's great sword just now dropping from his paralyzed grasp, was the yellow robed figure of Mula-*ay*. But he was neither attacking nor making a sound—and for very good reason.

Around his waist, pinning one arm to his side and enclosing the wrist of the other, sword-carrying arm in a crushing grip, was a black-furred forearm the size of a young water-main. Another black-furred arm encircled the Hemnoid's thick throat in a choke hold, and above that choke hold Mula-*ay*'s eyes were popping and his mouth was gasping for breath. Over the Hemnoid's shoulder grinned the ferociously cheerful, round features of More Jam.

For just a moment, Bill goggled at the sight. He would not have believed that any Dilbian on the planet could not only have overpowered Mula-*ay*, but lifted him right off his feet in the process. If More Jam was capable of something like this now, what indeed had he been like as a wrestler in the days of his youth?

But it was not a sight that Bill could stay to enjoy. The building was swaying around him now like a ship upon heavy seas, and his strength was beginning to desert him. At all costs he must make it out of the door of the building.

He turned and staggered toward the door. He had to drop his shield to get it open, but he hung onto his grip on his sword as he staggered down the steps, into the blinding, sudden sunlight. Into the center of a circle of black, furry faces that danced and wavered around him.

Barely, he heard the mounting cheer that went up from those faces. Suddenly, the whole earth and crowd and sunlit sky whirled about him; and he tumbled, sprawling forward into darkness.

At some indefinable time later, he swam up briefly from the darkness to find himself lying on a human-style bed, within the white walls of a room. The walls shimmered, advancing and retreating to his unsteady eyes. A face moved into his field of vision. It was the face of Anita and it seemed to Bill to be the most beautiful face he had ever seen. It too wavered in unreliable fashion.

There was a touch of something cold and wet against his forehead and the side of his head. Anita seemed to be sponging him off with something.

"Is this a hospital ship?" he croaked.

"Certainly not!" replied Anita, and her voice was strangely choked. "You're back at the Residency. You don't need a hospital ship. There's nothing wrong with you I can't fix. I've got a medical assistance certificate."

He looked at her wonderingly.

"Is there anything you haven't got?" he asked her.

To his surprise, she burst into tears.

"Oh shut up!" she said, threw the cloth, or whatever it was she had in her hand, into the basin where she had been dampening it, and ran out of the room.

Startled, baffled, dismayed, Bill tried to push himself up on his elbows to call after her. But as he lifted his head, a heavy weight seemed to swing from the inside front of his skull and smashed dizzyingly against the inside of the same skull at its back. Unconsciousness rose and sucked him down into it once more.

Chapter 25

"—Then you'll be going back to Earth with me for debriefing?" asked Bill, delighted.

"I will be traveling on the same ship, if that is what you mean," replied Anita, very coldly and distinctly.

She turned and marched off toward the courier ship lying lengthwise on the grass in the center of the meadow. It was a sleek, heavily built ninety-footer, capable of interstellar travel on its own; and its size, which was several times that of the usual shuttle boat, had attracted the attention of several Dilbians, who were now examining it curiously.

Bill gazed after the retreating shape of Anita wistfully. How could he talk to her if she would not talk to him? Recovering from the blow on the head he had gotten from Mula-*ay*, he had admitted to himself that he liked her. Liked her a good deal in fact. In short, the idea of parting company with her was suddenly very painful.

But even as he had come to realize this, his relationship with her had seemed to be getting worse and worse. It had started with that unfortunate question of his, about there being anything she didn't have, when he had just come to and she was sponging his head. He had tried to explain later that he had actually meant it as a compliment. He realized that she was a hothouse type and he was a pretty ordinary sort of individual. In fact, he had just sort of muddled through to a fortunate conclusion of the situation, while she was attacking it properly with all the unusual resources of her unusual mind and training. He wasn't trying to pretend he was anything like her equal, or anything like that.

But the more he had tried to explain, the more displeased Anita had become. It was as if every time he opened his mouth, he dug himself in that much deeper.

"Well, Pick-and-Shovel—" the voice of the Hill Bluffer interrupted his thoughts and Bill started guiltily. He had completely forgotten he had been talking to the postman when Anita had passed by, just now on her way to the ship. She was, he saw, being met in a very familiar way by a tall man who had just stepped out of the hatchway. The tall man was himself vaguely familiar. Bill peered at him somewhat grimly.

"—So I guess I'll be off, back to the mountains," the Bluffer's voice boomed on Bill's ear. "They'll all be wanting to hear up there if you turned out the way I said you would."

"They will?" Bill was startled. Then he remembered how he had speculated on the Hill Bluffer's having some stake of his own in the outcome of the situation in which Bill had been trapped. Bill looked sharply up at the lanky Dilbian.

"Why sure," said the Hill Bluffer comfortably. "They all remember the Half-Pint-Posted, but there was considerable discussion about whether you Shorties could do it twice in a row."

"Twice in a row?" echoed Bill. "Do what?"

"Come out one up on a Fatty, of course," replied the Bluffer. "You know, like him!"

He nodded over at the far side of the meadow, behind Bill. Bill turned and saw the yellow-robed figure of Mula-*ay* standing solitary in the shadow of the trees in his yellow robes. The heavy-gravity figure was not likely to slump in the Dilbian gravity, but there was something defeated about its isolation.

"Word is, a flying box like yours is coming in anytime now," said the Bluffer, "—only one run by Fatties—to take him out. That's probably the last we'll see of old Wasn't Drunk around these parts."

"Who?" Bill blinked at the distant figure. He had been sure that it was Mula-*ay*. In fact, he still was. "But that's Barrel Belly over there, isn't it?"

The Bluffer snorted with contemptuous good humor.

"Not any more. Got his name changed," he said. "You didn't hear—?"

"No," said Bill.

"Why, after your hassle with Bone Breaker was over, it turned out that More Jam had found old Wasn't Drunk passed out cold behind the eating hall, with half a barrel of beer spilled down his front. It was pretty plain for everyone to see that he'd figured the villagers swarming down on the valley would keep the outlaws so busy he could sneak a bellyful. So he'd poured most of a barrel of beer down himself on the sly and passed out." The Bluffer stopped to laugh uproariously. "Result was, he missed all the fun, just by getting drunk at the wrong time!"

"Fun?"

"Why, your duel with Bone Breaker. He missed all that!" said Hill Bluffer. "So, after More Jam found him and brought everybody to see, they poured some water over him to bring him to, and he sat up to find everyone laughing at him. After all his talk about how tough the Fatties were! Turned out he'd rather drink than fight!"

The Bluffer chortled again, at the memory.

"But," said Bill, "how did his name—"

"Oh, that!" interrupted the Bluffer. "That's the funniest part of all. When he sat up with all that water streaming off him and everybody started kidding him about getting drunk and missing the duel, he lost his head and tried to say it wasn't so. Why, if he'd only kept his mouth shut, or admitted it and laughed at himself—but he had to go and claim he wasn't drunk. *'But I'm not drunk!'* That's the very first words he used. Only when they asked him how come he was out cold, he didn't have any good answer. Tried to come up with some weak story about maybe tripping and hitting his head on the side of the building. Well, you know that's a lie, Pick-and-Shovel. No one's going to trip and hit his head on a log wall hard enough to knock himself out. So, naturally, he got his name changed."

"Naturally," echoed Bill automatically. He was aware enough of Dilbian attitudes now to realize that Wasn't Drunk was as much a liability of a name as Barrel Belly had been an advantage to Mula-*ay*. What it boiled down to was that the Hemnoid had become a figure of fun to the Dilbians and his usefulness to the Hemnoid purpose on Dilbia was at an end. No wonder he was being withdrawn. Bill could even find it in himself to feel a little sorry for Mula-*ay*, now that he had come to understand how the Dilbian mind worked.

Remembering the vagaries of Dilbian thought, he woke abruptly now to the fact that the Hill Bluffer, in the oblique Dilbian way, was trying to tell him something.

"But you were saying," said Bill hastily, "that the people up in the mountains were interested in how I worked things out down here? Why would they be interested?"

"Oh, lots of reasons, Pick-and-Shovel," said the Bluffer carelessly. "Some of them might've been wondering, of course, just how things might work out, with you helping these Muddy Nosers to grow all kinds of stuff. Of course, Lowland folk like this don't count for much in the minds of mountain people, but they're still real people down here, just the same, and a lot of Upland folk were kind of interested to see who the Muddy Nosers'd end up going along with—you or the Fatty. Just in case they ran into the same sort of situation themselves, some day."

"I see," said Bill. It was pretty much as he expected, he thought, interpreting what the postman was saying in the light of his newfound Dilbian knowledge. The Hill Bluffer had been more than a hired companion for Bill. He had been an unofficial—almost everything practical was unofficial among the Dilbians—observer for the Uplanders, with the duty of reporting back on the feasibility of accepting Shorty, rather than Hemnoid, help in agricultural and other matters. And the Bluffer was now delicately informing Bill of that fact.

"How do you suppose they'll feel at the way things turned out?" Bill asked the postman.

"Well," said the Bluffer judiciously, "I think there might be some people, maybe quite some people, who'll be kind of pleased things worked out the way they did. Guess I'm one of them myself." Abruptly, the tall Dilbian changed the subject. "By the way, I passed the word to Bone Breaker the way you told me. I said to him you'd like to see him before you leave."

"You did?" Bill looked hastily off in the direction of the village. He had seen no sign of the former outlaw chief, and has assumed that Bone Breaker had not got the message, or had refused to come—though that was unlikely. "He said he wouldn't come?"

"Oh no. He's coming," said the Bluffer. "He started out with me when I left Muddy Nose."

"Started out?" Bill, staring about, could still not see any sign of Bone Breaker. "What happened—"

"Oh, well, I sort of outwalked him, you know," said the Hill Bluffer comfortably. "He's slowed down a mite. Not that he ever could have kept up with me before either, if I'd been minded to leave him behind. There's no man living who could do that."

"I believe you," said Bill honestly. And he did.

"There he is now," said the Bluffer, nodding over Bill's head at the courier ship. "Must have circled around to look at that flying box of yours."

Bill turned. Sure enough, there was Bone Breaker, towering amidst the other Dilbians examining the ship. As Bill watched, the former outlaw chief turned and ambled in Bill's direction.

"Well," said the Bluffer's voice, "guess I'll be throwing my feet. See you again maybe, sometime, Pick-and-Shovel."

Bill turned back to the postman.

203

"I hope so," said Bill.

"Right. So long," replied the Hill Bluffer. He turned and went—his abrupt farewell being quite in accordance with Dilbian lack of ceremony over both meetings and partings. Bill stared after the tall, striding figure for a moment. Being human, himself, he would have liked to have made a little more out of the process of saying good-bye, particularly since he had come to have a strong feeling of friendship for the Bluffer. But the other was already dwindling in the distance and a moment later he disappeared among the trees not far from where the solitary figure of Mula-*ay* was standing.

"Well, Pick-and-Shovel!" said a different, deep, bass voice, and looking around, Bill saw that Bone Breaker was indeed upon him. "I heard you were asking around about me since you got back on your feet. So I told the wife I'd step over and see what you had on your mind before you took off."

"The wife?" echoed Bill. "Sweet Thing?"

"Who else?" replied Bone Breaker, patting his stomach gently in a manner vaguely resembling More Jam's favorite gesture. "Yes, I'm an innkeeper now, Pick-and-Shovel, and I guess the old gang in the valley's just about broken up. Most of them came to the village with me, and the rest lit out for parts unknown. But what were you asking for me, about?"

"Just a little idle curiosity about something," said Bill, approaching the subject obliquely in the best Dilbian manner. "So you gave up outlawing after all and settled down, did you?"

"What else could I do?" sighed Bone Breaker sadly, "after the way you licked me in fair fight the way you did, Pick-and-Shovel? Not that I miss the old days too much, though. There's been some compensations."

"There have?" asked Bill.

"Why, sure there have," said Bone Breaker. "There's that little wife of mine, for one—what a prize she is, Pick-and-Shovel." Bone Breaker lowered the volume of his kettle-drum bass voice confidentially, "Not only is she the best cook around, but she can lick any other two females, hands-down. She may not be the best-looking female in the region—"

"She isn't?" said Bill, considerably surprised. It was true Perfectly Delightful had called Sweet Thing stubby and little, but Bill had put this down more to jealousy than fact. His human eyes of course were no judge of Dilbian beauty, but he had taken it for granted that Bone Breaker, being the locality's most eligible bachelor, would naturally take an interest only in the better-looking of the available females.

"I wouldn't admit this to any other man," said Bone Breaker, still confidentially, "but you're a Shorty, so of course you don't count—my little wife isn't *exactly* the world's best-looking. No. But what's the good of getting someone with a figure like Perfectly Delightful's, for instance, if you've got to take the rest of her along with it? No, Sweet Thing's the wife for me, on all counts—to say nothing of getting a daddy-in-law like More Jam, thrown in. That old boy's *smart*, Pick-and-Shovel—"

Bone Breaker's nose twitched in the Dilbian equivalent of a wink.

"—As I guess you know," he went on. "Between him and me, I suppose we can get most of the people in Muddy Nose to agree to just about anything we want. So, you can see I'm pretty well off, in spite of the fact my outlawing days are over. I guess that was what you wanted to know, come to think of it, wasn't it, Pick-and-Shovel?"

"Why, I guess that was part of it, anyway," said Bill slowly.

He and Bone Breaker were eyeing each other like fencers. What Bone Breaker had said was, indeed, only part of what Bill wanted to get the ex-outlaw chief to say. In total, the admission Bill wanted was necessary ammunition for a certain private and entirely non-Dilbian hassle toward which he was eagerly pointing.

He was going to make someone pay for what had been done to him. To do that, he needed Bone Breaker to admit certain things. Bone Breaker knew that Bill knew that these things were true. But the big Dilbian was not necessarily going to admit them, just for that reason.

That was not the Dilbian way, Bill had learned. Even though, in a sense, Bone Breaker owed Bill the admissions and that was why he was here. The necessary words would be forthcoming only if Bill was clever enough to trap Bone Breaker into a position between them and an outright lie.

"Yes, I guess that was part of it," Bill went on, cautiously. "I did wonder how you were making out. After all, it's a pretty free and easy life, being an outlaw—going out and taking whatever you wanted when you wanted it. It must be pretty dull after that, just being an innkeeper."

"Well now, it is, at times," said Bone Breaker easily. "I won't try to deny it."

"Of course," said Bill thoughtfully. "More Jam managed to settle down to it, all right, in his time."

"That's true," said Bone Breaker, nodding. "I imagine he had a pretty high old life for a while there, when he was younger."

"I'd guess so," said Bill. "And that's what got me wondering—about More Jam, now that I stop to think of it. There must have come some sort of time when he made a decision. Somewhere along the way, he must have said to himself something like—*'Well, it's been fun and all that, but sooner or later I'll be getting along in years; and it'd be nice to quit while I was ahead.'*—Do you suppose he might have thought something like that?"

"Well, of course I don't know," said Bone Breaker, "but I'd guess he might well have, Pick-and-Shovel."

"I mean," said Bill, "he might have thought what it would be like if he just kept on going until he started to slow down and some young buck came along and took him some day in a regular, fair, man-to-man tussle out in the daylight where everybody could see. Then, all of a sudden, the fun and reputation would be gone and he wouldn't have anything to show for it."

"I guess he might," said Bone Breaker.

"He might even have thought," said Bill, "how smart it would be to settle down and get married to Sweet Thing's mother and become an innkeeper ahead of time. Only, of course it must have been a problem for him, because he couldn't quit just like that, without an excuse. People would have figured he'd lost his nerve. Luckily, about that time, his stomach must have started going delicate on him, and that solved the problem for him. He didn't have any choice but to marry Sweet Thing's mother to make sure he had her to cook for him—and of course that meant he had to take up innkeeping and give up wrestling, and all. Of course, I don't *know* it happened that way. It just seems to me it might have."

"Well, that's pretty surprising, Pick-and-Shovel," rumbled Bone Breaker, "as a matter of fact, that's just what did happen with More Jam."

"You don't say?" said Bill. "Now, that's interesting—my hitting the nail on the head just like that. But, of course, much of it isn't hard to figure out, because almost any man with a terrific reputation as a fighter would have trouble quitting. Wouldn't you say that?"

"Yes," said Bone Breaker, staring off across Bill's head at the distant courier ship, "I guess I'd have to say that. A man can't just give up being Lowland champion wrestler without some kind of good reason."

"Or," said Bill, "being outlaw chief."

"Well, that too," admitted Bone Breaker.

"Yes," said Bill thoughtfully, "I guess you might have had your problems too along that line if luck hadn't turned out the way it did. You had Sweet Thing on your side, and she knows a thing or two—"

"She," said Bone Breaker, "surely does."

"To say nothing of her old daddy, who's as tricky as they come; and who probably wouldn't have objected at all getting a real tough cat for a son-in-law to help him with the innkeeping business."

"Well, now that it's all over," said Bone Breaker, "I have

to admit More Jam's pretty much been on my side all along."

"But there wasn't much they could do directly to help you," said Bill. "So it was sort of handy—my coming along. You couldn't very well quit outlawing without being licked in a fair fight. And you couldn't very well let yourself get licked by any other real man, especially from around these parts, and still keep your reputation after you'd retired. But of course, if a Shorty like me won a fight with you, and I flew out of here a few days later, that'd still leave you top dog—locally, at least. Of course, you didn't *have* to quit outlawing just because a Shorty beat you. It wasn't as if I was a real man."

"No, but it was a sign to me—you winning like that," said Bone Breaker sadly. "I was getting slow and weak, Pick-and-Shovel, and it was only a matter of time until somebody else took me. I could tell that."

"Oh, you don't look all that old and weak yet," said Bill.

"Nice of you to say so, Pick-and-Shovel," said the Bone Breaker. "Oh, I might stand up to any other real man around here for a few years yet. But I sure can't stand up to a fire-eating Shorty like you."

"Well, it's particularly nice to hear you say that," pounced Bill. Bone Breaker's gaze centered on him remained calm and innocent. "Because this mixed-up memory of mine's been giving me all sorts of trouble about that fight."

"Memory?" queried Bone Breaker, with rumbling softness.

"That's right." Bill shook his head. "You remember you must have hit me quite a clip in that storehouse, even if I did get out of it on my feet, first. I was laid up for a few days afterward. And that knock on the head seems to have got my memory all mixed up. Would you believe it, I find myself thinking that I touched your leg, lying on the floor, *before* all those logs came tumbling down, and covered you up."

"My!" Bone Breaker shook his head slowly. "I really did clip you one, then, didn't I, Pick-and-Shovel? Now, what would I be doing lying down on the floor, waiting for some logs to roll down on me?"

"Well, I guess you'll laugh," said Bill. "But it just seems to stick in my head that you were not only lying there, but that you pulled those logs down on yourself, and it was that that made folks think I'd won. But anyone knows you wouldn't do that. After all, you were fighting for your old free way of life. The last thing you wanted was to get married and settle down to innkeeping. So I tell myself I shouldn't think that way. *Should I?*"

Bill shot the last two words hard at the big Dilbian. Bone Breaker breathed quietly for a second, his eyes half-closed, his expression thoughtful.

"Well, I'll tell you, Pick-and-Shovel," he said at last. "As long as it's just you, and you being a Shorty, I don't guess I mind your thinking that, if you want to. After all, your thinking it happened like that doesn't do *me* any harm as long as you're getting in that flying box there and going away. So, you go ahead and think that, if you like and I won't mind."

Bill let out a deep breath in defeat. Bone Breaker had managed to weasel out of it.

"But I'll tell you something," went on Bone Breaker, unexpectedly. "I'll tell you how I like to think of our fight."

"How's that?" asked Bill, suspiciously.

"Why, I like to think of how I was tiptoeing along in the darkness there—and suddenly you came at me like a wild tree-cat," said Bone Breaker. "Before I was half-ready, you were on me. Next thing I knew you'd knocked my sword spinning out of my fist and split my shield. Then you picked up a log and hit me. And then you hit me with another log and the whole pile came tumbling down as you threw me through the wall of the storehouse, jumped outside and threw me back in through another part of the wall, just as the rest of the logs came tumbling down and covered me."

He stopped speaking. Bill stared at him for a long moment before he could find his voice.

"Threw you through the wall, *twice?*" echoed Bill, his voice cracking. "How could I? There weren't any holes made in the storehouse walls!"

"There weren't!" said Bone Breaker, on a note of surprise, rearing back. "Why, now, that's true, Pick-and-Shovel! I must be wrong about that part. I'll have to remember to leave that part out when I tell about our fight. I certainly am obliged to you, Pick-and-Shovel, for pointing that out to me. I guess my memory must have gotten a little mixed-up—just like yours did."

"Er—yes," said Bill.

Suddenly, a great light burst upon Bill. Anything a Dilbian said had to be interpreted—and he had been looking for Bone Breaker to admit the truth about the duel in a different way. *This*, then, was the admission—in the shape of a story about Bill's prowess too wonderful to believe. So he had picked up this nine-hundred-pound hulk before him and thrown it through a wall of logs, not once, but twice, had he?

"But, after all," Bone Breaker was going on, easily, "there's no reason for us to go picking on each other's memories. Why don't I just remember the fight the way I remember it, and you remember it your way, and we'll let it go at that?"

Bill grinned. He could not help it. It was a violation of the rules of Dilbian verbal fencing, which called for a straight face at all times, but he hoped that his human face would be alien enough to Bone Breaker so that the Dilbian would not interpret the expression.

Whether this was the case or not, Bone Breaker did not seem to notice the grin.

"All right," said Bill. Bone Breaker nodded in satisfaction.

"Well, I guess I'll be rolling home for dinner, then," he said. "You know, Pick-and-Shovel, you're not bad for a Shorty. Something real manly about you. Pleased to have met you. So long!"

He turned and left—as abruptly as had the Hill Bluffer. Watching him go, Bill saw him stop to speak to another male

210

Dilbian who had been examining the courier ship, but who now hurried to intercept the ex-outlaw chief.

There was something undeniably respectful about the way the other Dilbian approached the big, black-furred figure. Whatever other changes had occurred in Bone Breaker's life as a result of his losing the fight to Bill and taking up innkeeping, it was plain to see that he had not lost anything of his local stature and authority in the process.

But just at that moment, out of the corner of his eye, Bill caught sight of the tall, lean man who had been talking to Anita by the open hatch of the ship, picking up what was evidently a suitcase and turning as if to head off through the woods.

"Hey!" shouted Bill, starting to run toward him. "No, you don't! Hold up, there! I've got some talking to do to you!"

Chapter 26

The man stopped and turned as Bill ran up to the ship. Anita, who had been just about to go in through the hatch, also stopped, turned, and waited—thereby presenting Bill with a small problem. He had wanted a clear ring for his encounter with the tall man.

"If . . . you don't mind," said Bill, stammering a little with breathlessness from his run, "this is a little private . . ."

"Oh, all right!" she exploded furiously. "Go on, make a perfect fool of yourself! See if I care!"

She turned and stamped up the steps, through the hatch and into the ship. Bill looked after her, unhappily. There was the sound of a chuckle behind him.

"I wouldn't worry about it," said the voice of the tall man. "She'll come around shortly."

Bill turned sharply. Facing him was the same lean, long-nosed figure he had first met as the reassignment officer who had changed his course from Deneb-Seventeen to Dilbia. The man was smiling with an altogether unjustified cheerfulness. Bill did not smile back.

"What makes you so sure?" Bill snapped.

"For one thing," answered the tall man, "the fact I know her better than you do. For another, I know some other facts you don't know. For one thing, it's a pretty fair guess she's in love with you."

"She—*what*?" said Bill, jerking himself up in mid-sentence. He goggled at the tall man.

"She can't help it," said the tall man, the smile spreading across his face under the long nose. "You see, at heart she's a Dilbian. And so are you."

"Dilbian?" Bill was completely adrift on a sea of bafflement.

"Oh, your body and mind are human enough," said the tall man. "But you're strongly Dilbian—especially you, Bill—in your personality characteristics. Both of you were carefully chosen for that. You've got roughly the personality of a Dilbian hero-type, as closely as a human can have it. And Anita has a complementary Dilbian heroine-personality. You can hardly help being attracted to each other—"

"Oh?" interrupted Bill, grimly cutting the other short and hauling the conversation back to the main topic he had in mind. "Let's forget that for the moment, shall we? You're Lafe Greentree, aren't you?"

"I'm afraid so," said the tall man, still smiling.

"You never were a reassignment officer? And you never really did break your leg, did you?"

"No, I'm afraid those were both bits of necessary misinformation we had to give you." Greentree laughed. "And it was worth it—what you've done here is breathtaking. You see, you were being used without your knowing it—"

"I figured that out, thanks," said Bill harshly. "In fact I

212

figured out a little more than you figured I would. I know what the real story was here, and I can guess from that what kind of a scheme you sold your superiors on, to get me assigned here. Mula-*ay* told me I was thrown in here, all untrained and unbriefed, deliberately to mess up the situation and give you a chance to close down a stalemated project without losing face. *That's* the idea you sold your superiors on. But what you had in mind was a little bit more than that, wasn't it?"

The smile faded into a puzzled look on Greentree's long face.

"More than that—" he began.

"That's right!" snapped Bill. "You didn't just want me to mess things up here; you wanted me *killed*!"

"*I* wanted you killed?" repeated Greentree, in a tone of astonishment. "But Mula-*ay* wouldn't try anything like that, unless—"

"I'm not talking about Mula-*ay* and you know it," snarled Bill. "I'm talking about Bone Breaker and the duel!"

"But we never thought you'd actually fight the duel!" protested Greentree. "All you had to do was hole up in the Residency. Bone Breaker and his outlaws wouldn't have come into the village after you. You'd have been quite safe—"

"Sure," said Bill, "that's what you told your superiors, wasn't it? Only you knew better. You knew that I'd have been gotten to that duel if Sweet Thing had to kidnap me herself and carry me to it!"

"Sweet Thing?" said Greentree. "What's Sweet Thing got to do with it?"

"Don't try to pretend you didn't know. Anita didn't know— I thought at first she did, but it was plain she didn't understand the male Dilbians at all. She thought More Jam was just a figure of fun, instead of being the leading male in the Village. And Mula-*ay* didn't know. But *you* must have figured it out some time before and realized that you'd been doing things exactly the wrong way around with the Dilbians.

213

Officially, the Alien Cultures Service couldn't fault you for not finding out sooner how the Dilbians worked—but unofficially, the way you'd been made a fool of would have been a joke from one end of the Service rankings to the other. And that joke could just about kill any hopes of promotion for you, later. So you set me up to be killed—so the project wouldn't merely be closed 'temporarily' but hushed up, and its records buried in the files; and that way no one would find out how you'd been fooled!"

"Wait a minute—" said Greentree bewilderedly. "As I said, you've been used here without your permission or knowledge. I admit that. But the rest of all this—I give you my word I'm no more a villain than Anita is, except that I knew why you were sent here and she didn't. Now, what's all this about Sweet Thing carrying you to that duel with Bone Breaker?"

"As if you don't know!" snapped Bill, getting hold of himself just in time as his voice threatened to scale upward to a shout that would be heard inside the courier ship. "Do you think you can talk me out of what I know? You set me up too beautifully for it to be an accident; and if you set me up, you had to have the Dilbians figured out; and if you'd figured them out, you couldn't help knowing just what Bone Breaker was after!"

"I don't—"

"Oh, cut it out!" said Bill. "You know it as well as I do. Bone Breaker wanted to quit outlawing and settle down before he began to lose his speed and strength. He wanted to quit and become a villager while he was still on top, but he couldn't just abdicate as outlaw leader without a good reason—unless he wanted to lose face, tremendously—and face is what the Dilbian community runs on. So he settled on marrying Sweet Thing; and More Jam, by way of dowry, cooked up a scheme to get him out of being outlaw chief without loss of face."

"What scheme?" Interest had begun to dawn on Greentree's face beneath the frown of bafflement.

214

"You know!" growled Bill. "All Dilbia knew that a Dilbian—the Streamside Terror—had once fought a human and lost, so, More Jam planned to get Bone Breaker in a duel with a human, so Bone Breaker could pretend to lose, too. Since it would be a human he'd be losing to, he'd still be top dog among his fellow Dilbians; but he could use the loss as an excuse to give up outlawing, and go to live in Muddy Nose. It was you More Jam planned on Bone Breaker fighting, but you saw the duel coming, so you ducked out and got me stuck with it instead. That was supposed to kill two birds with one stone—get the project closed up, and also get you off Dilbia before the duel took place. Because if you went through with the duel and survived, you'd have to explain to your superiors how you did it—and the whole business of your understanding the Dilbians and keeping the fact a secret would come out!"

Bill stopped. Greentree was staring at him strangely.

"Admit it!" demanded Bill. "I've got you cold and you know it!" But, though his words were angry as ever, a slight uneasiness was beginning to stir in Bill. It was incredible that Greentree could go on pretending to be innocent this way, in the face of what Bill had told him. Unless he really was innocent—but with what Bill knew, that was impossible.

"Maybe you'll tell me," said Greentree in an odd voice, "just what it was—this understanding of the Dilbians you say I have?"

"You know!" snarled Bill.

"Tell me anyway," urged Greentree.

"All right, if you want it spelled out, so you can be sure I've seen through the whole thing!" said Bill furiously. "What you found out was what I finally figured out—just in time to tip off Bone Breaker that I understood, by pushing the duel through after all. If he hadn't understood that I understood, he might have had to make a real fight out of it. Just to make sure I didn't tell the other Dilbians afterward that he'd deliberately lost to me. And that a real duel would have left me very dead indeed!"

"But," said Greentree, "you still haven't told me what this knowledge about the Dilbians was."

"Why, it's their different way of doing everything, of course!" burst out Bill, exasperated. "A Dilbian never lies, except in desperate circumstances—"

"We know that—" began Greentree. "It's a capital offence under the tribal laws in the mountains—"

"—But he never tells the exact, whole truth, either, if he can possibly twist it or distort it to give a different impression!" said Bill. "He admits nothing, and acknowledges nothing. He exaggerates in order to minimize, and minimizes in order to exaggerate. He blusters and brags when he wants to be modest, and he practically quivers with modesty and meekness when he's issuing his strongest warning to another Dilbian to back off or prepare for trouble. In short—the Dilbians do everything backward, inside out, and wrong-way-to, on principle!"

Greentree's face lit up.

"So that's how—" he broke off, sobering. "No, that can't be the answer. We concluded a long time back that the Dilbians had some kind of overall political system, or understanding, that they wouldn't admit to—they worked too well together as individuals and communities for them not to have something like that. But what you're talking about can't be the answer. No political system could exist—"

"What're you talking about?" said Bill harshly. "They've got a perfect political system. What they've got here on Dilbia is a one hundred percent, simon-pure, *classic* democracy. Nobody tells anybody else what to do among the Dilbians. Under cover of a set of apparently iron-clad visible rules like that one about not lying, there's a set of invisible, changeable rules that really govern their actions. Also, no matter what the circumstances, every Dilbian has an equal right to persuade any other Dilbian to agree with him. If he gets a majority to agree, the new invisible, unacknowledged rule that results is applied to all Dilbians. That's what makes More Jam and Bone Breaker top dogs in their community—

they're champion persuaders—in short, makers of invisible laws."

Greentree stared.

"That's hard to believe," he said, at last, slowly. "After all, as chief outlaw, Bone Breaker headed a strong-arm band—"

"Which only took from the villagers what the villagers could spare!" snapped Bill. "And if they took more, the villager complained to Bone Breaker, who made the outlaws who took it give it back."

"But obviously—"

"*Obviously!*" Bill snorted. "The whole point of the way the Dilbians do things is that whatever is obvious is a smoke screen for the real thing—" he broke off suddenly. "What're you doing here? Trying to make me sound as if I'm telling you all this? You know as well as I do the Dilbians were running a test case on you and Mula-*ay*, to see which of you would win out in the end—instead of you and he competing to sway the primitive natives to your side, as you thought at first—and that was the joke you wanted so badly to bury. Even if you had to get me killed to do it."

"A test case?" Greentree had stared at Bill before during this conversation, but not the way he stared now. "A *test case?*"

"You know that," said Bill, but with suddenly lessening conviction. Either, he began to think, Greentree was telling the truth—or he was the best actor ever born.

"Tell me," said Greentree in a hushed voice.

"Why . . . the whole idea of the agricultural project in updating Dilbian farming methods was a debatable question. The Dilbians wondered if the advantages you claimed for it were all true, or if there weren't hidden disadvantages. So they took sides—the way they always do. The villagers took your side, and those who took the other joined the outlaws and cosied up to Mula-*ay*. Then they all sat back to see which one—human or Hemnoid—would break the stalemate wide open in his own favor. Look," said Bill, almost pleading now. "You know this. You know all this!"

Greentree slowly shook his head.

"I swear to you," he said, slowly, "I give you my word—I didn't know it. No one in the Alien Cultures Service knew it!"

It was Bill's turn to stare now.

"But—" he said after a long moment, "if you didn't know, how could *I* find out—"

He checked, baffled. Looking again at Greentree, he saw the beginnings of a smile starting to dawn again beneath the long nose.

"I'll tell you—if you'll listen now," said Greentree.

"Go ahead," said Bill, cautiously.

"You found out—" began Greentree, and the smile was breaking out now like gleeful sunshine across the tall man's face, "because you're the most unique subject of the most important experiment in the duplication of alien psychologies that's ever been tried!"

Bill scowled suspiciously.

"It's the truth!" said Greentree energetically. "I was going to tell you all about it—but you started talking and now it turns out that you're even more of a success than we dreamed you'd be. You see, you *were* sent here to Dilbia to break up a stalemate between the project and Hemnoid opposition. And you've done that—but you've also given us a whole new understanding of Dilbian nature, and proved that we've got a tool in dealing with other alien races that the Hemnoids can't match!"

Bill scowled harder. It was all he could think of to do, in view of the tall man's words.

"*You* weren't just pitched into the Dilbian situation without consideration," Greentree said. "But somebody else once was. It was John Tardy, the one the Dilbians called the Half-Pint-Posted. It was sheer accident, and our lack of understanding of the Dilbians, that caused him to be caught in an impossible situation—faced with a fight against the Streamside Terror, and the Terror really wanted to win *his* fight."

"I don't get it, then," said Bill feebly.

"Well you see," said Greentree, "John Tardy managed—almost miraculously—to come out on top. He managed to win his battle with the Terror and solve the situation. It was something that by all the rules simply could not have happened. And figuring out how it could have happened became a Number One priority project that took several years. Finally, they came up with an answer—a sort of an answer."

"What?"

"The one thing that came out of all the investigation," said the tall man, with deep seriousness, "was the fact that John Tardy by accident happened to fit the Dilbian personality very closely with his own. The point was raised that he had perhaps been able to solve his situation on Dilbia because he was able to think more like Dilbians than the rest of us. In short, that perhaps he had been just exactly the right man in the right place at the right moment. And a new concept was born; a concept called the Unconscious Agent."

"Unconscious—" even the words sounded silly in Bill's mouth.

"That's right," said Greentree. "Unconscious Agent. A man who's had absolutely no briefing—and therefore has no visible ties to his superiors, but who so exactly fits the situation he meets and the personalities in that situation, that he's ideally fitted to improvise a solution to it. The difference between an Unconscious, and an ordinary, Agent is something like that between the old-fashioned sea-diver with his helmet and air hose tethering him to a pump on the surface, and a free-swimming scuba diver of the mid-twentieth century."

Bill shook his head again.

"The Unconscious Agent isn't only free to improvise," went on Greentree. "He's *forced* to improvise. And, being ideally suited to the situation and the characters in it, he can't fail—we hope—to come up with the ideal solution."

The last two words of this penetrated deeply into Bill.

"You hope—" he echoed bitterly. "So I was an Unconscious Agent, was I?"

"That's right," said Greentree. "The first one—of what will probably be many, now. Of course, we insured our bet on you by supplying you with a hypnoed storehouse of general Dilbian information and another complementary Dilbian-like human who was Anita. But the solution was all your own. And now I'm finding out you've also come up with an insight into the Dilbian character and culture we've never had before. But the best of it all is that you've proved the workability of something we have that the Hemnoid can't match."

Bill frowned.

"Why?" he asked. "You mean—they can't find and send in personality-matched Unconscious Agents of their own? Why?"

"Because of a lack in their own emotional structure!" Greentree's smile hardened a little. "Don't you know? The Hemnoid character has a cruel streak (as we would call it) that prohibits their having anything but the most rudimentary capacity for empathy. Empathy—the ability to put yourself in somebody else's shoes, emotionally. That's what we humans have, that they haven't. And that's why your likeness to the Dilbians paid off the way it did. Your being like them wouldn't have helped, if you hadn't instinctively tried to think the way they did, in order to figure out what they were doing!"

Of course, thought Bill, suddenly. All at once he remembered his first clue to the fact that perhaps there was more to Dilbian nature than even a trained Hemnoid agent like Mula-*ay* seemed to know. He remembered how Mula-*ay* had taken it for granted that Bill did *not* empathize with someone like Bone Breaker, and had even used that as an example in explaining his own, Hemnoid nature. But Greentree was still talking.

"—if you only knew," he was saying to Bill, "how many millions of individuals on Earth and even on the newly settled worlds were screened to find you, as the closest Dilbian-like human. And how much of our future dealings with alien races has been riding on your success or failure here. Did you know you can just about write your own ticket as far as future work or study goes, after this? Did you know at the moment you're currently the most valuable man off-Earth in the whole Alien Cultures area . . ."

He went on talking, and slowly Bill's spirits began to rise, in spite of himself, like a cork released in deep water and headed for the surface. Within himself—though he was far from admitting it to Greentree, yet—he had to face the fact that he was not the revengeful type, and if there had been a shadow of an excuse for what he had believed Greentree had done, he would probably never have pushed matters to the point of filing charges against the tall man, anyway. Particularly since, after all, Bill had come out of the situation on Dilbia without harm, and even with some benefits in the way of new knowledge and experience.

Certainly, therefore, now that it was turning out that there were strong extenuating circumstances, there was no reason why he shouldn't sit back and ride with the situation. Was that his Dilbian-like nature counseling him how to act? As he stopped to question himself, suddenly a new aspect of the situation burst upon him like sunlight through an unexpected break in a heavy cover of clouds.

If he was Dilbian-like and Anita was Dilbian female-like, he saw at once why she had been so intractable and upset these last few days. Of course! Here, when he was in charge of the situation, he had been going around pretending he had done nothing, and was nothing—at just the time when Anita had expected him to show his authority and strength.

Sweet Thing, now that he stopped to think of it, had provided him with considerable insight into the way Anita's mind might be working. He woke from his thoughts to find that Greentree was shaking his hand and saying good-bye.

". . . You'll understand in the long run, Bill, I know," the tall man was saying. "I've got to go now. Somebody's got to hold down the situation at the project here, for the moment. But I'll be following you and Anita to Earth shortly. We'll talk some more then. So long . . ."

"Good-bye," said Bill. He watched the tall man move off toward the woods where Barrel Belly—Wasn't Drunk, that is, Bill corrected himself—was still standing disconsolately. Poor old Mula-*ay*, thought Bill; he was the real loser—and the only real villain there had been in the whole situation. But then Bill shivered, suddenly, remembering the episode with Grandpa Squeaky; and, later on, the cliff-edge above Outlaw Valley, where only a light shove from the Hemnoid had been needed to send Bill plunging to his death. Mula-*ay* had been a real enough villain and enemy, at that. Bill shifted his gaze to another part of the meadow. The sun was moving into later afternoon position between the trees, and Bone Breaker, having finished his talk with the smaller Dilbian male, was finally headed off toward Muddy Nose and his dinner table. Bill stared after the big Dilbian, his attention suddenly caught.

"Bill!" It was Anita's voice calling exasperatedly from the open hatch of the courier ship behind him. "Come *on!* We're ready to go!"

"Just a minute!" he shouted back.

He squinted impatiently against the sunlight, striving to catch the tall figure of Bone Breaker in silhouette again. Yes, there it was. There was no doubt about it.

Marriage was apparently being good to the Bone Breaker. It was visible only when you caught him blackly outlined against the sun this way, but it was undeniably a fact, all the same.

Bone Breaker had begun to put on weight.

MORE BERKLEY SCIENCE FICTION

GALACTIC POT-HEALER   (N2569—95¢)
  Philip K. Dick

THE STARS MY DESTINATION   (Z2780—$1.25)
  Alfred Bester

THE SPACEJACKS   (N2847—95¢)
  Robert Wells

THE STARDUST VOYAGES   (Z2972—$1.25)
  Stephen Tall

I AM LEGEND   (N2937—95¢)
  Richard Matheson

THE COMPUTER CONNECTION   (D3039—$1.50)
  Alfred Bester

DUNE MESSIAH   (D2952—$1.50)
  Frank Herbert

THE FABULOUS RIVERBOAT   (Z2808—$1.25)
  Philip Jose Farmer

DESTINATION: UNIVERSE   (S1912—75¢)
  A.E. van Vogt

Send for a *free* list of all our books in print

These books are available at your local bookstore, or send price indicated plus 25¢ per copy to cover mailing costs to Berkley Publishing Corporation, 200 Madison Avenue, New York, N.Y. 10016.

SCIENCE FICTION FAVORITES
BY ROBERT A. HEINLEIN